lake como

Also by Anita Hughes

Monarch Beach

Market Street

lake como

ANITA HUGHES

St. Martin's Griffin ✖ New York

LAKE COMO. Copyright © 2013 by Anita Hughes.
All rights reserved. Printed in the United States of America.
For information, address St. Martin's Press,
175 Fifth Avenue, New York, N.Y. 10010.

www.stmartins.com

Library of Congress Cataloging-in-Publication Data

Hughes, Anita, 1963–
    Lake Como / Anita Hughes. — First edition.
        pages   cm
    ISBN 978-1-250-01773-4 (trade pbk.)
    ISBN 978-1-250-01772-7 (e-book)
    1. Single women—Fiction.   2. Man-woman relationships—Fiction.
3. Self-realization in women—Fiction.   4. Americans—Italy—Fiction.
5. Family secrets—Fiction.   I. Title.
    PS3608.U356755L35 2013
    813'.6—dc23

                                                            2013004024

St. Martin's Griffin books may be purchased for educational, business, or
promotional use. For information on bulk purchases, please contact
Macmillan Corporate and Premium Sales Department at 1-800-221-7945
extension 5442 or write specialmarkets@macmillan.com.

10   9   8   7   6   5   4   3   2

To my mother

lake como

chapter one

For Hallie Elliot, it was the summer of weddings. The first was a three-day affair at a private estate in Napa Valley. The pool was filled with calla lilies, the cake was decorated with pearls, and the dance floor was the tennis court covered in Carrara marble. Hallie and Peter drank Veuve Clicquot, ate shrimp cocktails, and marveled at the ice sculpture that was a bust of the bride and groom.

Every weekend in June and July, Hallie slipped into a silk Pucci dress or a Diane von Furstenberg wrap and strapped on Bottega Veneta sandals. Peter donned black tie for receptions at the Ritz and the Fairmont. He put on a sport coat to wear in tiny stone churches in Sonoma and ceremonies under the redwood trees in Muir Woods.

Hallie and Peter had stood under starry skies, admiring the bride and groom's first dance. They had listened to the best man tell stories that should have remained private. They drove home after the bouquet had been tossed and the rice had been thrown, running commentary like sports announcers post game.

"I loved their vows," Hallie mused, returning from a wedding at a private home in Los Altos. "Katy promised to respect Hank's career choices, and Hank vowed to always put his laundry in the washing machine."

"That's fine until Hank decides to throw in his partnership and buy a hot dog stand at AT&T Park," Peter said, grinning. "Then he'll find himself doing his own laundry."

"Her dress was gorgeous." Hallie sighed. "The train was longer than Kate Middleton's."

"Did you see the grounds?" Peter whistled. "There were three swimming pools, as if two swimming pools mated and had a baby."

"I would love to get my hands on their guest house." Hallie looked out the window at the approaching lights of San Francisco. "It should be done in blues and greens, with shag carpet and a saltwater aquarium."

"Did you give Katy your card?" Peter asked, putting the car in first gear as they climbed Russian Hill.

"That would be rude," Hallie said, frowning. "But I might send her a thank-you, and mention I'm working at Kendra Larsen's."

"You can use me as a reference." Peter grinned. "I got a beautifully designed apartment and a beautiful designer in one package."

"That was a one-time deal." Hallie giggled and saw Coit Tower appear at the crest of the hill. Hallie always thought it was like a lighthouse perched above the city, beckoning her home.

Peter was already in bed when Hallie slipped out of her dress, putting on one of Peter's old Stanford T-shirts and white boxer shorts. She loved their bed. It had a high suede headboard and cream satin sheets. When she sat against the pillows, she could see whitewashed houses cascading down to the bay. At night, the ships bleated in the dark like sheep finding their way home.

Hallie had lived in San Francisco her entire life, but moving in with Peter made the city seem brand new. Flowers bloomed in sidewalk cracks; trees burst with cherry blossoms. She had never noticed so many bistros with colored awnings and cramped round tables. Hallie and Peter ate focaccia with olive oil, sipped cold Chardonnay, and entwined their fingers over flickering candles.

"I wrote you something," Peter said as she slid under the comforter. "I promise to always make eggs sunny-side up, and never let the coffeepot grow cold."

"I thought you were working on an exposé of Frank Marshall." Hallie glanced at Peter's open laptop.

"I am." Peter closed the laptop and ran his fingers over Hallie's mouth. "But writing about a guy who sold his dad's *Playboy* collection on eBay to fund his company seems a little sleazy after eating chocolate mousse wedding cake."

"When exactly do you plan on making those promises?" Hallie looked at Peter. After every wedding, he dropped some sort of hint: he couldn't imagine making his groomsmen wear purple shirts under their tuxedos; he would never invite old girlfriends to his wedding. Hallie would feel her heart leap into her throat, wondering if his next words would be a proposal. But he always stroked her straight blond hair, kissed her lips, and turned the conversation to something else.

"Every day." Peter grinned, putting the laptop on the bedside table. He pulled Hallie down and covered her with his body. Peter was built like a runner: long legs, narrow hips, thin, angular shoulders. But when he made love he was like a wrestler, pinning her to the bed. She loved the feel of his chest rubbing against hers, his tongue exploring her mouth.

Hallie felt Peter's breath hot against her cheek. He opened her legs and slid deep inside her. She felt their bodies push and pull as if they were playing a child's game of tug-of-war. She came first, clinging to his back, his sweat sticking to her fingers.

Peter mumbled sleepily and draped his arm over her chest. Hallie closed her eyes and dreamed about weddings and sunny-side-up eggs and oval diamond rings.

Hallie glanced at the engraved invitation on the bedside table. Next weekend's wedding would be the most extravagant of the season. Four hundred people under the rotunda at City Hall. A carpet made of pink and red roses imported from Japan. Oysters served on the half shell and live fish as centerpieces.

The bride was Patsy Mane, one of Kendra's newest clients. Patsy had been popping into the store daily, fretting over linen swatches. Hallie listened to her moan and wondered if next summer she would be in her shoes.

Sometimes Hallie thought her friends were marking time until they walked down the aisle. They studied feng shui and Cordon Bleu cooking. They prowled the bridal registries at Gump's and Fenton's. They researched beach resorts for their honeymoon.

Hallie's friends thought Peter was perfect. He was bright and handsome and treated her like a princess. They admired his green eyes, the cleft on his chin, the way he caressed her hair in public. Hallie turned the invitation over, imagining her name entwined with Peter's in gold embossed letters.

Hallie met Peter when he entered the design store last summer. Kendra Larsen's usual clientele were women carrying Louis Vuitton bags and wearing Prada heels. Peter looked like a boy who had wandered into his mother's lingerie closet. He wore jeans and tennis shoes and carried a khaki backpack. He stood at an Edwardian rolltop desk and fingered a gold-tipped quill pen.

"William Shakespeare wrote all his plays with one of these," he said to Hallie. "Six hundred years later we've got laptops and tablets and writing software. No one has been able to produce a *Hamlet* or a *Romeo and Juliet*."

Hallie looked at Peter's short brown hair brushed to the side, his sharp cheekbones, and his Roman profile. She thought he looked familiar; maybe they had met at a cocktail party or at the bar at PlumpJack's. Then she realized she had seen his face on a poster in the window of Books Inc.

"You wrote *Paul Johns Unplugged*!" Hallie exclaimed.

Paul Johns had graduated from Stanford, studied in Tibet with the Dalai Lama, and developed an Internet site promising its subscribers the secrets to enlightenment. The book was Paul's unauthorized biography. It told stories of Paul's wild college days: jumping naked into the pool during water polo games, creating multiple Facebook profiles and dating several women at the same time.

Peter wrote that in Asia, Paul spent more time in brothels than meditating. He quoted Paul as saying the only things he had learned in Tibet was how to smoke a pipe and avoid contracting herpes. The book became a national bestseller and Peter was lauded on talk shows for exposing Paul as a charlatan.

"I did." Peter nodded. "And now I'm supposed to use some of the royalties to furnish my apartment like a grown-up."

"Is this your style?" Hallie frowned, glancing at the Oriental rugs, the French tapestries, the red lacquer Chinese armoires.

"Do you think I should be looking for leather sofas and shag rugs?" Peter grinned.

"Most of our clientele prefer Regency furniture and silk drapes," Hallie admitted. "I like shag carpeting. But don't tell Kendra, she'd fire me on the spot."

"Your secret is safe." Peter put his hand over his heart. "Maybe we could have lunch, and I can describe what I'm looking for."

Hallie hesitated. She didn't usually mix work and dating. But Peter looked sincere. And Hallie had an itch to do something besides furnish another Pacific Heights mansion with authentic Louis XIV chairs and Aubusson wool rugs.

They sat at a table at Café Nicoise. Peter drummed his fingers on the tablecloth and stabbed a Cobb salad with his fork. "I've never interviewed a designer before."

"I thought you interviewed people for a living," Hallie replied, drizzling raspberry dressing on a spinach salad.

"Internet mavericks with skeletons in their closets." Peter grinned. "Not blond socialites moonlighting as interior designers."

"My grandmother may live at the top of Pacific Heights, but I have a studio apartment in the Marina," Hallie protested. "The hallway reeks of garlic and meatballs—hardly San Francisco high society."

"According to my sources, your grandmother, Constance Playfair, is on more boards than any other female in the city," Peter replied.

"How do you know anything about me?" Hallie asked, suddenly wary.

"Kendra and I were in freshman seminar together at Stanford," Peter said, smiling. "I ran into her at PlumpJack's and she told me she just hired a brilliant new assistant. I did a quick search on the computer."

"You Googled me?" Hallie said, jumping up.

"I'm sorry." Peter grabbed her hand. "I have an empty flat on Russian Hill that's crying out for furniture. I can't help being curious about people; it's like a tic. Can we start over?"

Hallie sat down. She should have been angry. She should have grabbed her purse and run back to the store. But there was something endearing about the way Peter apologized. He was like a foreigner who didn't know the rules of the country.

"Most clients just ask for a list of references." She smiled faintly.

"I have complete trust in your abilities." Peter relaxed. "And I am prepared to live with shag carpet."

"What are your favorite colors?" Hallie toyed with her napkin. "Do you like to watch television in bed, and do you prefer satin or cotton sheets?"

Peter sat back in his chair and whistled. "Those are some pointed questions."

Hallie felt a slight shiver, as if someone had run a feather down her spine. "I need to know everything about a new client."

"I grew up in Atlanta and attended Stanford on a scholarship," Peter began. "I majored in journalism, was editor of the *Stanford Daily*, wrote an exposé of the vice chancellor that almost got me kicked out of school. After graduation, I bummed around for a couple of years, writing press releases for Internet start-ups. I ran into my old roommate Paul Johns when he launched VisionQuest.com. Paul's girlfriend had just broken up with him. I spent many nights drinking tequila shots and nursing him through a broken heart."

"Which you turned into a tell-all book that ruined him," Hallie broke in, interested despite herself.

"He had an original Rembrandt on his office wall—paid for by subscribers to his site." Peter shrugged. "I didn't want him buying a Van Gogh."

Hallie grinned. "Go on."

"I wrote the book, sold the rights to Hollywood, and plunged most of the money into my new baby."

"A yellow Lamborghini or a silver Bentley?"

"A new magazine called *Spilled*. I'm going to write about the human side of techno-celebrities. Sergey Brin's dark past and Mark Zuckerberg's relentless pursuit of excellence."

"Sounds interesting."

"It better be profitable." Peter pushed away his salad. "Between buying the apartment and starting the magazine, I'm almost broke."

"How can you afford me?" Hallie asked.

Peter leaned forward and touched her hand. "Beauty and art are priceless."

Hallie loved Peter's apartment the moment she stepped through the door. She walked through the foyer, past the living room, past the arch that led to the master bedroom and the study, and stood on the balcony. The whole city lay at her feet. Hallie could see boats bobbing in the bay and cable cars zigzagging to Fisherman's Wharf. She saw the sky meet the water in a thick blue line.

"This is what your apartment is about." She waved her arms like a conductor leading an orchestra. "Every piece of furniture, the rugs, the artwork, has to say: 'Look out here.'"

Peter stood at the railing, putting one arm on either side of her. He leaned close and whispered in her ear, "In the words of George Bernard Shaw, 'I think she's got it.'"

Hallie furnished the apartment with classic pieces mixed with art deco. A Queen Anne chair stood under a Picasso, a crystal chandelier hung over a teak dining table. The result was serious but whimsical.

"When your guests walk in, they'll be surprised at every turn." Hallie showed Peter around the rooms. Every corner was filled with color. Purple love seats formed a conversation pit. A bright orange vase stood on the glass coffee table. On the walls were framed covers of Peter's book and the first edition of *Spilled*.

Peter walked into the kitchen. Hallie had installed a granite counter and leather barstools. There was a silver espresso machine, a chrome toaster, and an iron waffle maker. "I'm having a house-warming party in two weeks."

"It's almost ready." Hallie nodded. "I just need a couple of more pieces for the bedroom."

"I'd like you to be there." Peter sat on a stool and swiveled around so he could see the bay.

"I'd love to come." Hallie ran her hand over the granite.

Peter had turned into a model client. He gave her free rein to make decisions, scribbling checks without blinking. Occasionally they shared a cup of coffee or a glass of wine while she waited for deliveries. They talked about Monet and Matisse. They discussed Ken Kesey and T. S. Eliot.

"I want you to be there permanently." Peter drummed his fingers on the counter.

"What do you mean?" Hallie asked.

"I want you to move in with me."

"We've never been on a date," Hallie protested.

"I know you love espresso but hate cappuccino. You're a fan of Tom Wolfe but think Jonathan Franzen is overrated. You admire Jackson Pollock and have a slight crush on Julian Schnabel. Have I missed anything?"

"I don't have a crush on Julian Schnabel," Hallie replied. "I like his work."

"I can read people." Peter looked at Hallie seriously. "It's a gift or a curse, but I can see right through them. I look at you and I see your soul. It's twenty-four-karat gold."

"We haven't even kissed," Hallie murmured.

Peter stood up and drew Hallie toward him. "We can fix that right now."

"Hallie!" Kendra waved from the top step of City Hall.

Hallie stopped and instinctively checked her skirt. Kendra was only a few years older than Hallie, but she made Hallie feel as if she was still wearing braces. Kendra dressed like a 1940s Hollywood siren: low-cut bodice, pencil-thin skirt, and heels like needles. Her chestnut hair was so silky it belonged on one of the dolls that still sat on Hallie's dresser.

No matter what Hallie wore, she felt it was somehow wrong. She should have put her blond hair in a bun instead of a ponytail. She wished she had worn a low heel instead of flats. She shouldn't have worn Stella McCartney to meet French clients, or Ralph Lauren when Kendra introduced her to the wife of the British consulate.

"Style doesn't end in the showroom," Kendra had explained. "Our clients put their trust in us. We have to look elegant, understated, classic. Exactly the way they see their homes."

"Where's Peter?" Kendra asked as Hallie climbed to the top step.

Kendra wore a midnight blue evening gown. Her hair was lifted off her shoulders and revealed diamond teardrop earrings. She wore a matching diamond choker and gold Manolo pumps.

"He's parking the car." Hallie touched her hair. She wore a pale pink chiffon dress that stopped below the knee. In front of the mirror, it had set off her blue eyes and creamy skin. But Hallie glanced at the other guests' long silk gowns and felt like a ballerina on top of a jewelry box.

"Stefan has a summer flu," Kendra replied. "I was hoping I could borrow Peter's other arm, and we could enter together. Arriving alone doesn't look good for business."

Stefan owned an art gallery on Post Street. He wore silk suits and handmade loafers and drove a silver Aston Martin. Stefan escorted Kendra to weddings and black-tie dinners, and they made an entrance like Brad Pitt and Angelina Jolie.

Kendra had a handful of men who texted her or lingered near the store to see if she was free for dinner. But she was determined to be the most sought-after designer in the city. She didn't want to be weighed down by a boyfriend.

"If I have to make some guy salmon every night, I couldn't devote myself to work," Kendra had said when Hallie announced she was moving in with Peter.

"Maybe you'll find someone who cooks for you," Hallie had replied. "Peter makes the most delicious eggs."

"Eggs have too much cholesterol." Kendra had shrugged. "Patrice's makes the best salmon. I order it and pick it up on the way home."

"Don't you miss having someone in your bed?" Hallie had asked, picturing the cream satin sheets she picked out for Peter.

Kendra had stopped arranging tulips in the store window and smiled. "I have plenty of men in my bed, I just ask them to leave before breakfast."

"Rumor has it Patsy's mother spent more on this wedding than on redecorating the house in Tahoe," Kendra continued, scanning the guests for familiar faces.

"I hope Patsy eats at the reception," Hallie replied. "The last time she was in the store she looked like a toothpick."

"She'll relax when she finds out her wedding present is her own Tahoe cabin," Kendra mused. "Her mother hired us to decorate it. It's a secret till after the wedding. I'm flying up on Saturday to draw some sketches."

"Hallie!" Peter called, weaving through the crowd. He wore a black tux with a crisp white shirt. His hair was slicked to one side and his shoes were black and shiny.

"You clean up nicely." Kendra nodded.

"We're not in college anymore." Peter reached the top step and put his arm around Hallie. "I don't attend formal events in jeans and a black T-shirt."

Kendra turned to Hallie. "Peter was the hit of every college party. Even in faded dungarees he looked like James Bond."

"Kendra wondered if you'd escort both of us into the ceremony," Hallie interrupted. "Stefan has a head cold."

Peter offered one arm to Hallie and one to Kendra. "How could I say no to having two beautiful women by my side?"

The reception seemed to drag on forever. The father of the bride gave a toast that detailed Patsy's accomplishments, from her first steps to the pilot's license she received at sixteen to her MBA from Harvard. Hallie was suddenly tired of caviar balls and cake pops. She thought if she heard one more band play "At Last" she might erase it from her iPod forever. She searched for Peter but he had disappeared, chasing the Apple programmer he had spotted at the bar.

"Hallie Elliot!" A tall girl in a yellow dress approached her table.

"Melinda." Hallie smiled, wondering why her old school friend would pick a dress that made her look like a giraffe.

"This is the fifth wedding I've seen you at this summer." Melinda held an empty champagne flute. "Are you training for your big day?"

Hallie blushed. "Peter and I are just living together."

"Which must make your grandmother turn over in her canopy bed." Melinda giggled. "Remember when we were at St. Ignatius and the teachers caught us kissing a Justin Timberlake poster in the bathroom? They made us say five Hail Marys."

"My grandmother likes Peter," Hallie replied. "There's no rush to get married."

"Everyone's getting married," Melinda countered. "You don't want to be the last couple at the altar."

"I love weddings." Hallie sighed. "But Patsy's is a bit over the top. There's a Fabergé egg at every place setting."

"They certainly didn't skimp on champagne." Melinda raised her glass. "Every time I lift my hand, a waiter fills my glass."

"Maybe that's why I have a headache." Hallie glanced at her crystal flute. "I'm going to find Peter and go home."

"When Peter proposes I want an invitation." Melinda smiled.

"I'm the only one who can tell stories about you in braces and kneesocks."

"In that case we'll elope." Hallie grabbed her purse.

"Now that would make Constance Playfair really happy." Melinda giggled again, raising her glass for the passing waiter.

Hallie walked over to the bar to find Peter. Kendra had melted into the crowd during the toasts. She had seen Beatrix Traina sitting with Jennifer Newsom and had whispered to Hallie that she was going to snag two new clients.

"The trick is to make Beatrix think Jennifer has already hired me," Kendra had whispered. "Then they'll fight over me and we'll get both jobs."

Hallie scanned the room. Gold pinpoint lighting lit the dance floor. Red velvet curtains draped the stage. Suddenly Hallie felt like the trumpets were blaring in her head. She could feel the drums beating in her chest. She weaved between the tables and ducked out a side door.

Hallie breathed in the cold night air. The fog had come in, lying on the tops of cars like a blanket. She walked to the side of the building and saw two figures leaning against a column. The woman had her arms wrapped around the man. The man was running his hands down her skirt. Hallie turned to leave and caught sight of the woman's shoe: a gold pump with a diamond bow.

Hallie moved closer and recognized Kendra's chestnut hair plastered against the column. She saw Kendra's gold Cartier pressed against the man's back, her other hand tearing at his tux jacket. She watched the man wriggle out of the jacket and Kendra plunge her hand under the man's shirt.

Hallie froze. The man had narrow shoulders and a slender chest. His hair was brown and cut short around his ears. Hallie saw the outline of his face and put her hand to her mouth.

"Peter!" she shouted.

"Hallie!" Peter pushed away from Kendra. He threw on his tux jacket as if he was naked. He buttoned his shirt and blinked under the floodlights.

"What are you doing?" Hallie demanded. Her cheeks were burning and she felt like her skin was on fire.

"Kendra's drunk," Peter explained. "I came out here to get her some air and she attacked me."

"You had your hands on her skirt," Hallie spluttered.

"She was taking it off," Peter insisted.

"Peter has lovely hands," Kendra slurred, hugging the column. "And he's a very good kisser."

"I didn't kiss her." Peter's face was white. He grabbed Hallie's arm and pulled her toward him.

"Leave me alone." Hallie shook free of his hands.

"I was doing the right thing," Peter implored. "Kendra would have passed out at the bar."

"It looked like you were enjoying yourself," Hallie said, her arms and legs trembling.

"You know me better than that," Peter insisted. "I'm not a cheater."

Kendra teetered toward Hallie. She put one hand on her lips and whispered in Hallie's ear, slurring, "I might be a teensy bit tipsy. I know he's yours, I was just borrowing him."

"Let's go home," Peter said gruffly.

Hallie felt the fog cut through her pink chiffon. She looked at Kendra's wrinkled gown and Peter's creased tux jacket.

"I'll take a cab." She ran down the steps and fled.

Hallie entered the apartment and tried to stop shaking. Her head throbbed and her body ached. She threw her purse on the floor and collapsed on the purple sofa in the conversation pit.

Peter had never been one of those guys who flirted at parties.

He took Hallie's hand when they crossed the street, holding it like a prize. He bought her chocolates and left books he wanted her to read on the bedside table.

"At Stanford I studied Byron and Keats," Peter had admitted when he filled the apartment with candles to celebrate their six-month anniversary. "I'm a closet romantic; it's a terrible flaw."

"I think it's wonderful." Hallie had watched the room glow like a garden lit by fireflies.

"I'm crazy to think a beautiful blonde with a pedigree would fall for a scrappy hack like me," he had replied, blowing out the candles one by one.

For Christmas, Peter gave Hallie a framed portrait of her standing in front of a Queen Anne chair. Her hair was piled in a chignon and she wore a Chanel suit and a strand of pearls.

"I don't own a Chanel suit," Hallie had said, baffled when he presented it to her.

"It's the artist's interpretation," Peter had explained. "I gave him your photo."

Hallie had studied the painting critically. "I look like my grandmother."

"According to *San Francisco* magazine, Constance Playfair is still one of the great lights of San Francisco society." Peter had smiled. "You have impressive genes."

"I thought you only read *Spilled*," Hallie had mused, admiring the way the artist made her blond hair look like a halo.

Hallie had never seen Kendra drunk. She glided around parties perfectly poised, her chestnut mane swinging back and forth like a pendulum. But at Patsy's wedding the waiters were more attentive than flight attendants in a first-class cabin. Maybe Kendra didn't notice how many times they filled her glass. She probably bumped into Peter at the bar. Maybe she made a scene, threatening to dance on a table.

Peter would have taken her arm and guided her outside. Hallie imagined Kendra stumbling in the dark. Kendra grabbed Peter to steady herself and pulled him toward her. She started taking off her skirt, tugging at Peter's jacket. Peter was trying to break free when she discovered them.

Hallie ran her fingers along the beveled glass coffee table. She remembered Peter's house-warming party. All the guests had complimented her, saying she had achieved a perfect union of classic and modern pieces. She had been so pleased, keeping her relationship with Peter a secret, held tight to her chest.

After the guests left, Peter led her out to the balcony. They stood under the stars, swaying to the Harry Connick, Jr., tune he hummed in her ear. Then they walked back into the living room, surveying the half-eaten plates of rice balls and asparagus tips.

"You turn me into someone who belongs in this apartment," Peter whispered, putting his arms around her. "Without you I'm just a guy with a laptop and a backpack."

Hallie got up and walked to the bedroom. Maybe what she saw had been perfectly innocent: Peter playing Lancelot to Kendra's maiden in distress. But she flashed on references Peter had made about Kendra: Stanford football games they attended together, a group ski vacation to Tahoe. Hallie always assumed they just ran in the same circles. Maybe she was wrong, maybe something had happened in the past and tonight it was rekindled.

Hallie hung her pink chiffon dress in the closet and climbed into bed. She put her head on the down pillow and closed her eyes. In the morning, everything would be clearer.

chapter two

Hallie woke up and smelled eggs and toast. She opened her eyes and saw a plate of sunny-side-up eggs, whole-wheat toast, and sliced melon. There were two cups of steaming coffee, a jug of cream, and a pot of strawberry jam.

"The lady awakens." Peter hovered over her, like the prince in a fairy tale.

"I didn't hear you come in last night," Hallie replied.

She sat up, looking at Peter. He wore black bicycling shorts and a white nylon shirt. He had hung his tux in the closet and thrown his shirt in the laundry. All traces of the evening were erased. The curtains were open and the bedroom was bathed in morning sun.

"You were already asleep." Peter handed her a cup of coffee.

"You didn't have to do this." Hallie nodded at the eggs and toast. Suddenly the memory of Peter's hands on Kendra's skirt jolted her like an earthquake.

Peter sat on the bed. "Hallie, look at me. Nothing happened last night."

"I saw you." Hallie drank the coffee, flinching as the hot liquid hit her tongue.

"You saw me trying to get away," Peter replied. "Kendra was an octopus."

"You took off your jacket," Hallie mumbled.

"I would have taken off my pants if it meant I could escape faster." Peter sighed. "She was like the Bionic Woman."

"Kendra is the Bionic Woman." Hallie giggled. "She's made of steel."

"Honestly, Hallie"—Peter held her hand—"I would never risk what we have."

Hallie looked into Peter's clear green eyes. He was like a Boy scout. If he found a stray cat, he knocked on every door to locate its owner. When an old woman in the building lost her keys, Peter combed the hallways to find them.

"You've known Kendra for years," she said slowly. "Maybe you were closer to her than I thought."

"Christ, Hallie. I would have told you!" Peter exclaimed. "We were just friends. Kendra is all hard edges; I would never date a woman like her."

Hallie nibbled her piece of toast. Peter had never lied to her, and Kendra never alluded to a relationship. Even in college she was too focused to waste much time on men.

"I believe you," she said finally.

Peter's shoulders relaxed and the light came back in his eyes.

"I can skip my bike ride and join you for lunch at Constance's." Peter kissed Hallie on the lips, scattering crumbs on the cream sheets.

"Aren't you riding with Frank Marshall?" Hallie asked. "You were going to pry secrets out of him while pedaling over the Marin Headlands."

"I could reschedule," Peter replied doubtfully.

"I'm a big girl." Hallie put the coffee cup on the bedside table. "I can handle Constance."

"I'll make it up to you." Peter put his hand under Hallie's T-shirt.

"You're going to get jam on the sheets," Hallie protested, feeling her nipples stiffen.

"I'll be careful," Peter whispered, pulling Hallie's shirt over her head.

Hallie sat back against the pillows. Her cheeks were flushed and her skin smelled like sex. She thought about calling her grandmother and begging off. She could spend the rest of the day reading *Architectural Digest* and *Vogue Home*.

Constance had a couple of small strokes six months ago. She no longer attended charity functions and opening galas while swathed in yards of Italian silk. She spent most days sitting at the grand piano playing Mozart and Chopin. Hallie knew Constance looked forward to Sunday lunch and planned the menu a week in advance.

Hallie wished her mother, Francesca, would spend more time with Constance. But there had always been friction between Constance and Francesca. Even when Hallie and her mother lived in one wing of the mansion on Broadway, Francesca and Constance hardly spoke. When Francesca finally made enough money to afford her own apartment, she whisked Hallie away to a cramped one-bedroom in Cow Hollow.

Hallie missed the ballroom where she pretended her dolls were dancing to an unseen orchestra. She missed Louisa, who smuggled hot chocolate and marshmallows into her room at night. But mostly she missed Constance, who moved around the house like a figure from a Victorian novel.

Constance didn't let Hallie wear makeup, even when she was old enough to own a bra. She interviewed every friend, boy or girl, who came over to play. But Constance listened to her like no one else did. She trained her sharp gray eyes on Hallie and let her pour out her dreams. Constance was a calm ocean liner in the choppy waters of Hallie's youth.

Hallie parked under a cherry blossom tree and climbed the steps to Constance's house. It stood between two neoclassical mansions with marble columns and slate roofs. The three houses occupied their own block, commanding dazzling views of the bay. Hallie could see freighters cruising under the Bay Bridge, and the distant green hills of Berkeley.

When Hallie was a girl, her grandmother used to walk her to school. They would set off, Hallie in her brown school uniform, Constance in a London Fog coat and boots, and walk four long blocks to the Burke School. Hallie thought everyone lived in a house with three stories and a garage that contained a fleet of cars. It wasn't until she was fourteen, and Francesca moved them to a one-bedroom walk-up apartment, that Hallie realized there was another way to live.

"Hallie." Constance opened the front door. "I'm so glad you're here. Where's Peter?"

Hallie shrugged off her cardigan and hung it in the hall closet. She followed her grandmother into the grand salon, admiring the arrangements of tiger lilies that filled the room.

"He had a cycling date he couldn't break." Hallie sat on a plush gold sofa, glancing around the salon. Heavy chandeliers dangled from the ceiling. The marble floors were buffed and polished. The windows were covered by velvet curtains that Hallie used to wrap around herself like an evening gown.

Hallie fell in love with the house at the age other children became fixated on puppies. When she was six she was left alone after school, and she would walk from room to room, admiring the silk sofas and mahogany tables. She knew in the first grade she wanted to be an interior designer. Her taste changed over the years: sometimes she thought a room should be filled with color, other times only beiges and browns appealed to her. Now when she needed inspiration, she sat in the grand salon, or the library, or the music room, and gazed at the ornate plastered ceilings and thick Oriental rugs.

"I asked your mother to join us, but she's delivering a wedding cake in Woodside." Constance poured a glass of Scotch from the decanter on the sideboard. "One would think after twenty years of baking wedding cakes, she could find a husband."

"Francesca doesn't want a husband." Hallie caught a whiff of the Scotch and her stomach flipped uneasily. "She said being married was like being in a convent, with stricter rules."

"That was thirty years ago." Constance sighed. "No one should get married at nineteen. I still blame myself; if I hadn't sent her to Europe she wouldn't have met Pliny. I'm so glad you found the right man. Will there be a wedding next summer?"

"You ask me that every Sunday," Hallie said, frowning. "Peter hasn't proposed yet, but he has been dropping hints."

"I would love to see one happy marriage in this family."

Constance wore a pink silk blouse and a gray pleated skirt. Her hands were the only thing that showed her age: her knuckles were gnarled, and the diamond and emerald rings squeezed her fingers.

"I promise you'll be sitting in the front row of the church," Hallie replied, placing her glass on the end table.

"Portia left her husband." Constance sat on the sofa facing Hallie. "He's been seeing an actress in Milan. She moved back into the villa with Sophia and Pliny. Poor Sophia, it's a terrible scandal."

"How could Riccardo cheat on Portia?" Hallie exclaimed. "She looks like Carla Bruni."

"Portia is almost thirty, that's ancient by Italian standards." Constance frowned. "The actress is twenty-two. Sophia is beside herself. Riccardo has disgraced Portia and the whole Tesoro family."

Hallie pictured Portia living under the strict Catholic roof of her father and grandmother. Portia had wild black hair and emerald green eyes. She wore multicolored Pucci dresses and five-inch Louboutin heels. The only sign that she came from a religious family was the gold cross she wore around her neck.

Hallie remembered the first summer Portia and her brother came to visit. Hallie was seven and Constance appeared in her bedroom. She had sat at the foot of the bed, stroked Hallie's bunny slippers, and turned the pages of a Beatrix Potter book.

"Your half brother and sister are coming to stay with us."

"What's a half sister?" Hallie had asked, hoping it was a doll that she could play hopscotch with.

"Your mother refused to go to college, so I sent her to Switzerland to finishing school." Constance had watched Hallie to make sure she was listening.

"Finishing school!" Hallie had exclaimed indignantly. "I thought I'm finished with school after the second grade."

"Finishing school is a place where young ladies learn to be good hostesses." Constance had smiled. "Your mother met an Italian prince named Pliny Tesoro on the ski slopes. They fell madly in love, got married, and moved into his mother's villa on Lake Como."

"My mother was married to a prince!" Hallie's eyes had danced with excitement. "Did she have ladies in waiting and a carriage like Cinderella?"

"It was a beautiful villa. You'll visit when you're older. Francesca and Pliny had two children: Marcus and Portia. But then Francesca became very unhappy and she wanted to come home to America."

"How can anyone not want to be a princess?" Hallie had frowned, sucking a blond pigtail.

"It's hard to explain," Constance had said tentatively. "But sometimes when you marry very young, you don't know the person you are marrying."

"Then I'll wait till I'm really old," Hallie had replied emphatically. "At least till I'm twenty."

"Francesca came home but her mother-in-law wouldn't let her take Marcus and Portia. Pliny's mother is a very fierce woman named Sophia. Everyone was scared of her; someday you'll meet her."

"Is she a wicked witch like in *Sleeping Beauty*? Did she make my mother eat a poisoned apple?"

"Francesca was very sad to leave her children," Constance had mused. "Luckily she met your father and had you."

"Is my father a prince?" Hallie had asked hopefully.

"No." Constance had paused. "I'm only telling you this because Sophia is finally allowing Portia and Marcus to come for the summer. You and Portia will share a room; you can teach her how to be American."

Portia and Marcus arrived the next day and the two girls circled each other like jungle cats. Portia was barely nine, but she carried herself with a European sophistication that thrilled and puzzled Hallie. Portia wore perfume. Portia wore a bra, though her chest was as flat as Hallie's. Portia's hair was wild and curly, but it didn't look messy like Hallie's when she woke up in the morning. Portia's hair looked like it belonged in a fashion magazine.

Marcus was ten and had no time for his American half sister. But Hallie and Portia quickly became inseparable. Portia was used to living in a mansion and invented new games to play.

They slid down the grand staircase. They pretended the ballroom was an ice-skating rink. They bought a family of black mice and a pumpkin and played Cinderella getting ready for the ball. At night they lay side by side, Portia in the twin bed that had been installed in Hallie's room, and described the men they were going to marry.

"My husband is going to have a speedboat," Portia declared. "He's going to take me out on the lake and feed me grapes and smelly cheese."

"I hate cheese." Hallie pinched her nose. She wore a pink nightgown and her hair lay in a thick braid down her back.

"All grown-ups eat smelly cheese," Portia replied knowingly. "Every Saturday night the villa is full of adults eating stinky cheese and drinking bottles of wine. One night I snuck into the courtyard and saw my father kiss a woman. She had black hair and her mouth was as big as a fish. If you both eat stinky cheese, it cancels each other out."

"My husband is going to buy me chocolate-chip ice cream," Hallie replied. She had never seen her mother kiss a man. Occasionally her mother went out to dinner but she came home after Hallie went to bed. When Hallie inquired the next morning how Francesca's "date" went, Francesca rolled her eyes and muttered, "Next time I'll buy my own dinner."

"My husband is going to propose on a gondola in Venice," Portia continued, her eyes flashing. "He's going to give me a diamond ring as big as a walnut. We'll get married in a castle on Lake Como, and our guests will drink champagne and eat chocolate cake."

"My grandmother says you have to get married in a church," Hallie said, frowning. "She says God can't hear you unless you're in His house."

"God is always in my father's house." Portia sighed dramatically. "God is at school, God sits above my bed. I'm going to keep my wedding private."

Hallie imagined a figure in a white robe floating above the bed. She glanced at Portia and started laughing. She buried her face under the sheets so no one would hear her.

Every Sunday Hallie attended church with Constance. She wore her best dress and black Mary Janes and let Louisa pin her hair up. Hallie prayed at bedtime, closing her eyes and asking God to keep her mother and grandmother safe. But otherwise God kept his distance. She couldn't imagine having to answer to Him for everything she did.

"Poor Portia." Hallie sighed. "She's not going to be happy in her old bedroom. She always said she felt like Rapunzel. If she wore the wrong clothes, old Sophia would lock her up and throw away the key."

"Sophia is concerned about appearances." Constance nodded. "The Tesoro family is revered in Italy. She couldn't afford to have her granddaughter riding on a motorcycle with a thug in a black leather jacket."

"Portia was eighteen!" Hallie laughed, remembering the photo spread in *HELLO!* that featured a teenage Portia wearing boots and a tube top, clinging to the back of a man on a motorcycle. Hallie had been a junior at St. Ignatius when Portia sent the clipping, scribbling her signature like an autograph. Hallie passed the magazine around to her friends, proud that she had such a scandalous half sibling.

"Sophia heads the most important Catholic charities in Italy." Constance walked to the sideboard and replenished her glass. "She has the ear of the Pope; it's going to be very embarrassing."

"I thought San Francisco society was harsh," Hallie mused. "When Dick Palmer left his wife for a manicurist, they kicked him out of the Bohemian Club."

"At least Dina kept the mansion in Presidio Heights." Constance dropped two ice cubes in her glass. "Portia has to go live with her father. I wish Francesca would go see her. At times like this a girl needs her mother."

"Sophia still makes her break out in hives. Francesca's allergic to everything Italian. She won't even eat pizza."

"Francesca eats like a bird." Constance sat on the sofa. "The last time she came to dinner she brought a jar of seeds she wanted Louisa to cook. I tossed them in the garden."

"I'm glad I don't live with her anymore." Hallie giggled. "She made me bean sprout sandwiches all through high school. I threw them away and ate Melinda's bologna on white bread."

"I'd go to Como, but the doctor doesn't think I'm well enough to fly." Constance sniffed. "I walk every day, I've never felt better."

"Dr. Michaels has a crush on you," Hallie replied. "If you flounce off to Europe, he can't make house calls and drink your imported brandy."

"Sophia will find a way to blame Portia: she didn't attend to Riccardo's needs, she spent too much time in Milan at the fashion shows," Constance said, frowning. "Portia needs a friendly face. You could fly over."

"I'd love to spend August lolling around the villa," Hallie replied, picturing the turquoise lake, the little town that fell down to the shore. "But Kendra just signed two new clients."

"I heard she's decorating Patsy Mane's cabin in Tahoe."

"That was supposed to be a secret!" Hallie exclaimed.

"Lottie Mane called last night. Apparently Patsy's cabin is ten-thousand square feet and on the lake. Apparently the wedding was the event of the season. Fabergé eggs, Parisian silk tablecloths, lobster and filet mignon."

Hallie flinched. She hadn't thought about the wedding since Peter left on his bicycle ride. Suddenly she flashed on Kendra's hand slipping beneath Peter's shirt. She saw her gold Cartier watch pressed against Peter's back.

"The waiters poured champagne nonstop," Hallie mumbled. "I got a terrible headache."

"Pacing is everything," Constance agreed. "If your guests get drunk they won't remember the food or the music, and someone will behave badly."

"I think I've attended too many weddings this summer." Hallie sighed. "I see crepe bags of Jordan almonds when I close my eyes at night."

"None of them are going to hold a candle to your wedding." Constance got up and walked through the circular foyer. "I've already made a few enquiries on what dates Stanlee is available."

"Peter hasn't asked yet!" Hallie followed her grandmother into the dining room. The long mahogany table was set with two porcelain place settings. There were crystal water glasses and platinum silverware. A vase of irises stood in the middle of the table, and there was a basket of fragrant bread rolls.

"Stanlee is good at keeping secrets." Constance smiled like a Cheshire cat. "We wouldn't want Jenny Bach or Kelly Hampton to get the best date in June. Peter will propose soon. He's a good man and he worships you."

Hallie sat on a tall velvet chair and broke a bread roll in half. She pushed the image of Peter's crumpled tuxedo out of her mind. Kendra had been a tigress, trapping him in her lair. She bit into the warm, tangy bread, suddenly dreading seeing Kendra at the store in the morning.

Louisa served asparagus soup with dollops of sour cream. The soup was followed by stuffed Cornish hens and golden potatoes sprinkled with chives. Dessert was poached pears drizzled in a sweet liqueur.

"Food tastes better when it's shared." Constance drank a demitasse of espresso. "I do miss the dinners and galas. My Carolina Herrera gowns are gathering dust."

"You could ask Dr. Michaels if you could attend one event a month." Hallie wiped her mouth with a linen napkin.

"He says all the fatty food and alcohol is bad for the heart," Constance complained. "Once Peter proposes I'll have to come out of retirement. You'll need an engagement party, a shower, a rehearsal dinner."

"Don't you think we're jumping the gun?" Hallie asked.

Constance smiled. "I want you to have the most beautiful wedding the city has seen in years: a Vera Wang dress, Paula LeDuc catering, Stanlee doing the flowers. We'll take your grandfather's Bentley out of retirement. He would have been so proud of you."

Hallie knew Constance had never forgiven Francesca for getting married in Italy. Constance had been waiting thirty years to throw a grand San Francisco wedding. Sometimes Hallie felt it was her duty to walk down the aisle balancing a diamond tiara and carrying two dozen English roses.

"I should go." Hallie dropped her napkin on the table. "I have a client meeting tomorrow morning and I need to prepare."

Constance walked Hallie to the foyer and kissed her on both cheeks.

"Ask your mother to go see Portia." Constance opened the front door. "And bring Peter next week. He loves Louisa's beef bourguignon. She'll serve it with green beans and slivered almonds. We'll have Pavlova for dessert."

"Try not to cause Dr. Michaels too much trouble." Hallie hugged her grandmother. "You'll give him a heart attack."

Hallie got in the car and drove to Fillmore Street. She'd stop at the market and buy dinner. When Peter came home from cycling he was always starving. He sat in the kitchen like a teenager, wolfing down ham and cheese on sourdough bread. She'd buy a crisp Chardonnay, a raspberry tart, and a carton of chocolate ice cream.

Fillmore Street was teeming with couples sauntering past cafés and clothing boutiques. The fog had retreated and the sky was blue. Men wore sports shirts and girls wore sleeveless dresses and low-heeled summer sandals. Hallie put her purchases in the car and crossed the street to the design store.

Hallie admired the black-and-white awnings, the sign that announced KENDRA LARSEN INTERIORS in glossy black letters. The window was done all in white: a fringed sleigh bed upholstered in ivory satin, a white orchid in a white ceramic pot, a white wool rug threaded with narrow lines of gold.

Kendra changed the window every Monday. Last week she let Hallie pick out the display. Hallie had drawn from one of her favorite designers, Syrie Maugham, who was famous for creating the first white room. Hallie had added one emerald silk pillow for a splash of color, and a beige end table with spindly legs.

Hallie put her key in the lock and turned the brass handle. She flicked the light switch and glanced around the showroom. The floors were dark wood planks. The walls were canary yellow and hung with prints by Matisse and Picasso. A floral love seat was flanked by two potted palms.

Hallie loved walking into the showroom, imagining she was seeing it for the first time. There were so many items of beauty: Louis XIV end tables, Laredo statues, Venetian mirrors framed in twenty-four-karat gold. Kendra regularly visited castles in France and Italy, bringing back pieces that were exquisite and functional. She had a wonderful eye. A piece that looked forlorn when it arrived was brought to life by a coat of varnish or a touch of paint.

Hallie walked to her desk to retrieve some color samples and heard a sound in the back room. Kendra never came in on Sundays. She said she needed one day off to clear her head. On Monday mornings she arrived at eight, armed with black coffee and a notepad full of new ideas.

Hallie cautiously opened the door to the back room. Kendra was sitting cross-legged on the floor, surrounded by fabric swatches. She wore black leggings and a black leotard and her hair was pulled into a high ponytail. Her face was free of makeup and her feet were bare.

Kendra looked up sharply. "Hallie! You scared me. What are you doing here on Sunday?"

"I wanted to pick up some color samples for my meeting at Libby Taylor's. I thought you never came in on Sundays," Hallie replied defensively. She suddenly felt like her nerves were being pulled by an invisible string. Her body tensed, as if preparing for flight.

All day she had tried to keep the image of Kendra and Peter at bay. She hadn't known how she would react when she saw Kendra. She had hoped she would just shrug it off; Kendra had been drunk, it meant nothing. But now that Kendra was here, serene and smelling of Obsession, she wanted to take a fabric swatch and smack her across the face.

"I couldn't stand the gym." Kendra flipped through swatches with her long French-manicured nails. "I couldn't even run around the Marina Green. The sun was so bright, I got a headache. I thought I'd stay here until I regain my equilibrium."

"What's wrong?" Hallie asked. The desire to smack Kendra faded. Up close Kendra's skin looked yellow and there were deep circles under her eyes.

"I drank too much at the wedding." Kendra groaned, stretching her long legs. "Usually I switch to water, but I didn't have a chance. The waiter kept refilling my glass."

"It was pretty over the top," Hallie agreed warily.

"I don't remember anything after dinner," Kendra continued. "One minute I was searching for Jennifer Newsom, the next I was in the foyer of my apartment building. I don't know how I got there."

Hallie was silent. The room was so quiet she could hear her own breathing. She could pretend she didn't know anything. The whole episode could fade away.

"I found this in my purse." Kendra rummaged through her bag and brought out a black tux tie. "This is so embarrassing. What if I offended one of our clients? What if someone saw me?"

"I'm sure nothing happened." Hallie gazed at the tie as if it was a snake. "Probably a guest left it on a table and you put it in your purse. You were going to return it and you forgot."

"I just walked away with some guy's tie! What if this ends up in *San Francisco* magazine or on the *Gate*?" Kendra exclaimed.

"I wouldn't worry," Hallie soothed. "There were four hundred people at the wedding. Everyone was hammered. People were reeling all over the dance floor, no one would have noticed."

"Do you really think so?" Kendra smoothed her hair. Her color was coming back and she looked a bit more like herself.

"I'm sure even drunk you were in perfect control," Hallie murmured. "You're always the picture of elegance."

Kendra's shoulders relaxed. She studied the fabric swatches as if she was mesmerized by the patterns. She glanced at Hallie, her brown eyes wide and sincere.

"You're right," she said, smiling. "I'm going to go home and drink a pot of ginseng tea. I'll see you in the morning."

Hallie entered the apartment and put the groceries in the kitchen. Peter wasn't home and the rooms were bathed in late-afternoon light. Hallie walked onto the balcony, feeling the breeze graze her cheek. The sun was playing hide-and-seek with the clouds, and the city looked like an illustration from a picture book.

Hallie leaned on the railing, watching a girl play hopscotch on the sidewalk. She saw a couple sitting on the stoop, exchanging sections of the Sunday *New York Times*. She saw Peter ride down the street, his body supple as a greyhound. He hopped off the bicycle and rolled it into the garage.

Hallie went into the kitchen and put the Chardonnay in the fridge and the ice cream in the freezer. She felt lighter than she had since before Patsy's wedding. Constance was right: Peter was a good man and he worshipped her. She went into the dining room and lit the gold candles. She pictured eating a romantic dinner, sharing raspberry tart and ice cream, and climbing into bed. She watched the candles flicker and walked into the kitchen to prepare the salad.

chapter three

Hallie stood in the back room of the design store, picking at a carton of Chinese chicken salad. It had been a busy week; she hadn't once taken a lunch hour or gone to the gym in the evening. Kendra was preparing to go to Tahoe and sent Hallie on errands all over the city. Hallie spent the morning at the Design Center searching for a house-warming present for Patsy and her new husband.

"Find something unique," Kendra instructed. "I want Patsy to know I have a vision for her house."

Hallie finally settled on a ceramic vase with silk flowers. She put it on Kendra's desk and ate a few forkfuls of salad. Her phone buzzed and she saw Peter's number on the screen.

"Hi, stranger," Peter said. "Breakfast was lonely this morning."

"I'm sorry." Hallie put the lid on the salad and stuck it in the small fridge. "Kendra sent me to the Design Center at the crack of dawn."

"Then she should let you off early for good behavior," Peter replied. "I made dinner reservations tonight."

"I can't." Hallie sighed. "She wants to go over her notes for Tahoe and fill me in on deliveries for two other clients. I'm probably stuck here till eight o'clock."

"I've called Mr. Chow's for takeout every night this week," Peter complained mildly. "Tell Kendra you'll come early in the morning."

"She wants me here early anyway. I have to go to the flower market and buy bunches of sunflowers. Next week's window is going to be a Sun King theme."

"I need you tonight," Peter replied. "I have a really important dinner."

"Dinner with who?" Hallie checked her hair in the mirror and walked into the showroom.

"I got an interview with Marissa Mayer. I'm going to grill her about being the first female CEO at Yahoo!" Peter explained. "If you're there she'll open up more. You can ask her about her favorite designers."

"I'd love to," Hallie said. "But Kendra gets frantic before she goes away."

"Please, Hallie." Peter's voice was soft and coaxing. "I've been after Marissa Mayer for months. I made reservations at Gary Danko."

"Isn't that a little pricey?" Hallie asked.

Hallie had only been to Gary Danko once, when Peter was wooing financial backers for *Spilled*. It was one of San Francisco's most-admired restaurants. The maître d' had been poached from a Michelin three-star restaurant in Paris. An army of waiters filled wineglasses, replaced breadbaskets, and rolled out lobsters on sterling silver trays.

"It's a very important evening," Peter pleaded. "I had to call in a couple of favors to get the reservation."

"Okay." Hallie nodded, arranging a stack of magazines. "I'll meet you there at seven o'clock."

Hallie approached the restaurant and checked her reflection in the window. She wore a black-and-white lace dress with a full skirt. Her hair bounced on her shoulders and she wore coral lip gloss and thick brown mascara.

Kendra hadn't been happy about her leaving early, but softened when Hallie explained she was having dinner with Marissa Mayer.

"I heard she's buying a place in Aspen." Kendra had sat at her desk, sorting through papers. "Mention I'm doing Patsy Mane's place in Tahoe. She'll be impressed."

"I'll try." Hallie had smiled, changing into a dress she kept in the back room. Sometimes she had to attend a cocktail party or an opening and didn't have time to go home and change. She stored a couple of little black dresses and a pair of Ferragamos in the closet.

Hallie opened the double oak doors and stepped inside. The interior was breathtaking. The taupe walls were covered with paintings by Erin Parish and Hunt Slonem. The sleek tables were illuminated by colored pinpoint lighting. The room was vibrant and alive like a movie set.

"Am I late?" Hallie approached Peter, who sat at a tall, leather banquette.

"I'm early." Peter stood up and kissed Hallie on the cheek. He wore a navy pinstriped suit and black leather shoes. Hallie could smell his cologne and see the starch on his shirt collar.

"Where's Marissa?" Hallie slipped into the booth opposite him. She gazed around the room. Men wore slacks and soft leather jackets. Women wore bright cocktail dresses and thin gold sandals. They nursed cocktails and leaned into one another, laughing and exchanging gossip.

"She couldn't make it." Peter shrugged. "She had a scheduling conflict."

"Should we leave?" Hallie frowned. "This place costs a fortune."

"I already ordered a bottle of Jacuzzi Sauvignon Blanc," Peter replied. "I spent all day walking Jim Johnson through our first-quarter earnings."

"How do they look?" Hallie asked, dipping a baguette in olive oil. The bread was warm and tasted of parsley and olives.

"Print is in the red, but online advertising is solid. I tried to explain we need the paper version. If people see the magazine at the newsstand they're more likely to buy it on their tablets." Peter waited for the sommelier to fill his wineglass. He swirled the wine, sniffing the rim and nodding appreciatively.

"I'm sure you'll turn print around," Hallie replied. "New magazines take awhile to gain their readership."

"I don't want to talk about *Spilled*," Peter said, smiling. "I want to eat scallops and gaze at my stunning girlfriend."

"I don't feel stunning." Hallie grimaced. "I feel like I've been sold into slave labor. Kendra has me running like a gerbil on a treadmill."

"Wouldn't it be great to take a vacation?" Peter mused. "Sit on a sandy beach and drink mai tais and suck on pineapple wedges?"

"I can't get a Saturday off." Hallie ate another bite of her baguette. Suddenly she was starving. She studied the spidery calligraphy on the menu.

"I was thinking about next summer," Peter replied. "We could go to Como, I could finally meet Marcus and the scandalous Portia."

"Poor Portia." Hallie sighed. "I've been calling all week but a maid answers and says she's not home. She's probably in her room sticking pins in a Riccardo doll."

"We could paddleboat on the lake, take day trips to Milan and Lugano." Peter sipped his wine. "I haven't used my Italian since Lucia's closed in North Beach."

"I'd love to go." Hallie glanced at Peter. She flashed on what a wonderful honeymoon destination Lake Como would be. They could stay at the Tesoro villa and explore the lake by speedboat. Peter would take long bicycle rides on the shore, and Hallie and Portia would sit in outdoor cafés, eating slippery gelato.

"Good." Peter nodded. "Now let's eat. The menu reads like hieroglyphics; I'll ask the waiter to decipher it."

The meal resembled a Roman feast. Hallie started with the salad of figs with Gorgonzola dolce and pecan-raisin crostini. It was followed by quail stuffed with quinoa and cornbread pudding. Peter ordered sweet corn soup with pancetta and seared sea scallops in a zucchini-basil puree.

"The waiters must have graduate degrees to remember all that." Hallie grinned as she studied the brightly colored vegetables. "And Ph.D.'s to understand it."

"We're lucky, we just have to eat it." Peter ate a forkful of seared sea scallops. "My publisher said *Paul Johns Unplugged* went into its seventh printing."

"I'm proud of you." Hallie heaped mushrooms and foie gras onto her spoon.

"I'm just a yellow journalist who happened to be in the right place at the right time." Peter shrugged. "I hit the jackpot when I met you. You've got style and class, and the most beautiful smile in the city."

Hallie and Peter ate silently, sterling silverware scraping against white china. Hallie felt like there were unsaid words hanging in the air. Was Peter going to bring up what happened with Kendra? Should Hallie mention that Kendra didn't remember the entire episode?

The waiters cleared the plates and brought the dessert menu. Hallie gazed at the elaborate crêpes and soufflés and groaned.

"I can't have dessert." She shook her head. "I'll have to spend the next day horizontal."

"In that case you have to have dessert," Peter replied. "I'll choose for both of us."

Peter ordered the graham cracker–pecan streusel and coconut sorbet. "They prepare it at the table; you'll love it."

Two waiters reset their place settings. They rolled a sterling silver cart next to the table and took the rich streusel out of a warming tray.

"The sorbet is served separately," the waiter explained. "The warm and the cold function as yin and yang for your palate. Allow me." The waiter served Hallie a slice of streusel and a bowl of white sorbet.

Hallie put her spoon in the sorbet and blinked. On top of the ice cream, like a glistening cherry, was a large diamond-and-ruby ring. Hallie glanced at Peter, her heart thudding in her chest.

"I meant what I said." Peter took her hand across the table. "Without you I'm just a Southern boy who can scribble. You make me excited to get up in the morning. You make me want to fly high and see how far we can go. You're beautiful and bright and generous. I love you, Hallie. Will you marry me?"

Hallie stared at the ring. It was an oval diamond, flanked by two rubies. It was so breathtaking she was afraid to pick it up.

"Put it on." Peter scooped it up and held it in his palm. The pinpoint lighting made the diamond sparkle, as if it was flirting.

Hallie slipped the ring on her finger. The platinum band was sticky from the sorbet. The waiters applauded as if they were at the theater.

"Say yes," Peter prompted her.

Hallie gazed at Peter. She pictured walking down the aisle in a satin wedding dress. She saw her friends clapping. She imagined Constance swathed in vintage Valentino, smiling and nodding at the guests.

"Yes," she murmured.

The waiter brought a bottle of champagne and two crystal flutes. He popped the cork and poured hundreds of tiny bubbles.

"You proposed," Hallie mumbled. The ring made her finger feel heavy. She poked the streusel with her fork, unable to take a bite.

"I've been wanting to propose all summer," Peter said, grinning. He looked like a boy who had won the spelling bee. "I wanted to pick the perfect time."

"You were going to propose in front of Marissa Mayer?" Hallie frowned.

"I didn't really have an interview with Marissa," Peter admitted. "I used her as a decoy. I wanted to take you somewhere special without making you suspicious."

Hallie put down her fork. Suddenly her throat closed up and she couldn't swallow.

"You lied about the interview?"

"It's an old trick in journalism," Peter explained. "Offer your subject an opportunity they can't resist: theater tickets, box seats at a sporting event. They show up even when they don't want to do the interview."

"I'm not a subject." Hallie tried to keep her voice light.

"You're my gorgeous, talented fiancée," Peter replied. "I asked you to have dinner but you refused. You said Kendra had you running in circles."

"I guess I did." Hallie glanced at the smooth, round diamond.

"I didn't want to wait till you found time in your schedule."

Peter leaned across the table and kissed Hallie on the lips. She tasted the sweet coconut sorbet and the rich streusel; she felt the soft imprint of Peter's mouth. He sat back, his hands sweeping across the table, and Hallie's bowl of sorbet tipped over and dribbled on her skirt.

"I'm all thumbs!" Peter exclaimed, reaching for his napkin.

"I'll dab it in the bathroom." Hallie glanced at the spot that was spreading over black-and-white lace.

Hallie stood in front of the bathroom mirror. She felt like her breath was caught in her lungs and she had forgotten how to exhale. Everything was moving so fast. She was still reeling from Patsy's wedding and now she had a diamond ring on her finger.

Hallie rubbed the smooth stone, imagining announcing their engagement. Constance would immediately take out her calendar and circle the Saturdays in June. She'd call St. Dominic's and mull over reception locations. Should they have a black-tie affair in the city or a casually elegant event in Napa? Constance would make endless lists, ticking off their choices with her gold fountain pen.

Francesca would hug Hallie and say she was glad she'd found someone who made her happy. Kendra would plan a small soiree, possibly in the store. Peter was a minor celebrity and her clients would be impressed by Hallie and Peter's engagement.

Hallie dabbed water on the stain and checked her hair and lip gloss. She pictured flickering candles and stained-glass windows. She imagined Peter slipping the ring on her finger. She could hear his vows, like the ones she listened to all summer.

Peter would promise to make her eggs sunny-side up, and to be there for her every day. Hallie would say "I do" and the guests would smile and clap. They'd leave the church in a white Bentley, sipping champagne and peering out the window. It was going to be a gorgeous wedding and they were going to be a golden couple.

Hallie walked back to the table and saw a tall man leaning against the banquette. He had red hair and freckles and he was punching Peter on the shoulder.

"Hallie, this is Rex Meany. He was a couple of years ahead of me at Stanford. He was a brilliant math major with a brain like Einstein."

"Seems like you're the smart one." Rex winked at Peter approvingly. "Yesterday I saw you at lunch with that ravishing brunette and tonight you're at dinner with a classy blonde. I should quit finance and become a journalist."

Hallie froze. She looked from Rex to Peter. She slid into the banquette, her heart beating fiercely.

"Hallie is my fiancée," Peter explained. "We got engaged this evening."

"In that case, you better give me the brunette's phone number." Rex pounded Peter on the back. "I haven't seen Peter in years. Obviously I've been hanging out in the wrong places."

"I'd like to go," Hallie said quietly.

"I don't want to interrupt the celebration." Rex shook Peter's hand. "Congratulations, send me an invitation to the wedding."

Hallie watched Rex walk to the bar. She glanced at Peter, but it was as if she was peering down a tunnel. His face came in and out of focus and his voice seemed far away.

"Hallie," Peter repeated. "Did you hear me?"

"Hear what?" Hallie tried to concentrate on Peter's mouth.

"I met Kendra for lunch to show her your ring." Peter rested his elbows on the table.

"My ring." Hallie glanced at her finger as if she'd forgotten she was wearing it. "Why would you want to show her my ring?"

"She works with you, she knows your taste." Peter was almost shouting.

"I can hear you," Hallie murmured. "I don't quite understand."

"I met Kendra at Perry's on Union Street," Peter said in a rush. "I needed a woman's perspective. I wanted to make sure I chose the perfect ring."

Hallie blinked. "Don't they have women at the jewelry store? Aren't there such things as salesgirls?"

"I needed to ask someone who knew you and could keep a secret. The ring is really important to me," Peter pleaded. "You're going to wear it forever."

"I don't think I am." Hallie wriggled it off her finger and dropped it on the table. "Maybe you and Kendra are a better match. You're both really good at keeping secrets."

"Hallie, stop." Peter grabbed her hand. "I love you. I want to marry you."

"And you're both excellent liars." Hallie stood up. She slipped out of the booth and ran to the door.

"You have to believe me." Peter followed her outside. "I can't live without you."

Peter grabbed her and squeezed her shoulders. He pulled her face to his and kissed her hard on the mouth. Hallie tasted wine and sorbet. She felt his chest shielding her from the fog.

"I don't know what to believe." Hallie pulled away and ran down the street.

"Wait!" Peter called desperately. "I have to pay the bill."

Hallie ran until Peter's voice was swallowed up by the fog and she could only hear her heels clicking on the sidewalk.

Hallie ran four blocks before she realized she didn't know where she was going. She couldn't face Peter back at the apartment. She couldn't go to her grandmother's. Constance thought the world of Peter. It would break her heart to see chinks in his armor. Hallie checked the money in her purse. She flagged a cab and gave the driver her mother's address.

Hallie buzzed Francesca's apartment and waited. Francesca was probably at the bakery. She shared a commercial kitchen with another baker and rarely came home before ten o'clock. Other single women relaxed with an episode of *CSI* and a bowl of popcorn. Francesca's idea of fun was making buttercream rosettes.

Hallie let herself in and climbed the three floors to her mother's apartment. The living room had wood floors and plaster walls. A floral sofa faced a bookshelf lined with cookbooks. The oak dining table was heaped with bills. A coffee cup was left on the table, making a ring on the wood. Hallie took it into the kitchen, depositing it in the sink.

Hallie sat on a stool, gazing at the brightly colored jars and containers. The counters were crammed with ingredients: brown sugar, honey, cinnamon, molasses. There were baskets of fresh peaches and bowls of strawberries. Everything in the kitchen would eventually end up in a cake. Francesca stockpiled ingredients like a squirrel hoarding nuts. She wore jeans and sneakers and splurged on imported vanilla extract.

Hallie finally let the tears come. They rolled down her cheeks, falling on the counter. She rocked back and forth, hugging her chest. She cried until her body felt like it would fold up like a pack of cards. Exhausted, she got up and walked into the living room.

Hallie and Francesca moved into the apartment when Hallie was in high school. Hallie had loved jogging on the green, watching the boats in the marina, but she missed the glittering rooms of Constance's house. Hallie found tables and chairs at garage sales and brightened them up with tablecloths and pillows. She painted the walls eggshell yellow and sewed lace curtains for the windows.

Francesca had acted more like a sister than a mother. On Friday nights, if Hallie didn't have a date, they painted each other's toenails. On Sundays they put on matching aprons and prepared dinner. Hallie tossed spinach salad and Francesca baked German chocolate cake.

Hallie wished for a moment she had a mother who would smooth her hair and promise her everything would be all right. She wanted a father who would hold her and tell her Peter wasn't worth crying about.

Hallie never knew her father. When she was nine years old, Francesca had found Hallie in Constance's kitchen, piling brownies on a plate.

"What are you doing?" Francesca had asked, frowning.

Hallie had stood on a stepstool, straining to reach the top shelf in the fridge. "Jenny's mother said I'm illegitimate and I'm going to burn in hell. I'm going to bring God some brownies so he forgives me."

"Sit down." Francesca had motioned for Hallie to sit at the kitchen table.

"What does illegitimate mean? Didn't you get a receipt for me at the hospital?"

"Illegitimate means you were more loved and wanted than any baby in the world."

"Jenny said illegitimate means I don't know who my father is. She says my father must be a pirate or a pop star." Hallie had inspected her nails. She had bitten her fingernails to the quick and covered them with bright pink nail polish.

"Your father was a student named Phillip Elliot." Francesca had nibbled a brownie. She had dark brown hair and large brown eyes. Her hair was cut short to frame her face and she had thick, curly eyelashes. The only features she shared with Hallie were a small nose and a round, rosebud mouth.

"That's my last name!" Hallie had chimed in.

"We met in Rome, when I was returning to America. I was very sad because I had to leave Portia and Marcus, and I spent a whole day crying at the Trevi Fountain."

Hallie had chewed her fingernail, waiting expectantly for the rest of the story.

"Phillip was a few years older than me, maybe twenty-five. He was backpacking across Europe, studying architecture. We spent the day together, exploring the Vatican, running down the steps of the Coliseum. I felt young and free, and by nighttime I was in love with him."

"You fell in love in one day?" Hallie had tried to remember if any of the heroines of her books fell in love so quickly.

"That can happen if you meet the right person." Francesca had smiled. "It started pouring, buckets and buckets flooding the sidewalk. We huddled under his backpack, trying to hail a taxi. But everyone was stranded and there were no cabs."

"I read about a flood in Sunday school. Noah led the animals on the ark two-by-two."

"We didn't have an ark, but there was a little pensione near the Coliseum. We ran in to wait out the storm."

"Is that where I was born?" Hallie had asked.

"It was where you were conceived," Francesca had murmured. "Phillip and I stayed up all night, talking. He was very handsome: tall, curly blond hair, pale blue eyes. My flight left in the morning and he was on his way to Pompeii. We exchanged phone numbers and kissed good-bye."

"Why didn't you marry him?" Most of her friends had parents who were married. A few had parents who were divorced and they met their fathers every Sunday at Pizza Hut or McDonald's. Hallie had wondered if she could meet Phillip at McDonald's and get one of those Happy Meal dolls with a pink miniskirt and straw hair.

"I was still married to Pliny and I was on my way home. It was complicated."

"Why didn't you marry him later, when it was simple?" Hallie had asked.

"We lost touch." Francesca had shrugged. "We didn't have the Internet or e-mail."

"I knew my father was special. Jenny's jealous because her father smells like garlic."

"Plus you have a grandmother who adores you and a half brother and half sister in Italy." Francesca had stood up and took a carton of milk from the fridge.

"It's like we have our own ark!" Hallie had beamed. "Can I ask Constance for a goat or a pig?"

"I don't think they allow goats in the city." Francesca had poured Hallie a glass of milk. "But you might ask for a guinea pig."

"I'll name him P. Elliot," Hallie had decided. "Do you think God would mind if I ate the brownies?"

"I think they were put in the fridge for that purpose." Francesca had put a brownie on a plate and passed it to Hallie.

The love story of Francesca and Phillip made Hallie popular at school, but sometimes she wished she had a father who smelled like garlic and asked her to pass the peas at dinner.

When Peter came home from cycling he was covered in sweat, but Hallie loved to bury her face in his chest. She didn't mind stocking the fridge with pretzels and beer nuts. She liked the masculine traces he left around the apartment: an *Esquire* on the coffee table, blobs of shaving cream in the bathroom sink.

"Hallie!" Francesca opened the door and entered the living room. She wore faded jeans and a pastel sweater. Francesca was slender as a boy, with small breasts and narrow hips. She never seemed to care how she dressed, but she had an innate sophistication. Even in her frayed sneakers, she looked casually elegant.

"I let myself in." Hallie slumped on the sofa. She had slipped off her Ferragamos and tucked her feet under the cushion.

"What a beautiful dress." Francesca set a pink cake box on the coffee table. "I'm glad you took after Constance instead of me in fashion. You have such a classic style, like a young Grace Kelly."

Hallie tried to smile. Her head felt heavy and there was a pain deep in her chest. "Peter took me to dinner at Gary Danko."

"I adore their lemon soufflé cake, I can't make mine as fluffy." Francesca dropped onto the sofa. She moved with the ease of a dancer. Only the streaks of gray in her hair hinted that she had three grown children.

"Peter proposed." Hallie tried to keep her voice steady.

"That's wonderful!" Francesca beamed. "You've been planning your wedding since you were eight years old. Do you remember when you used to walk your My Little Ponies down the aisle? And the year you wrote three letters to Santa Claus asking for a bride Barbie, in case there was a blizzard and your first letter didn't make it to the North Pole?"

"I still have bride Barbie," Hallie mumbled. "She has her own drawer in my dresser."

"Have you told Constance?" Francesca asked. "Finally she'll get to plan her dream wedding. Try to remind her it's your day."

"There's not going to be a wedding," Hallie murmured.

Francesca paused. "You can't elope. It would break your grandmother's heart."

"Peter and I aren't getting married." Hallie felt like she was pushing the words up a steep hill.

"You've been talking about getting married all summer," Francesca protested. "All those weddings you attended, all the bridal showers and gift registries. You said you were prepping for your own big day."

"I thought Peter was going to propose." Hallie flinched. She remembered the espresso makers and panini presses, the sets of Waterford china and Christofle silverware. Each time she walked into Gump's she drooled over the Swarovski crystal, and added a piece to the gift registry she kept in her head.

"And he did propose," Francesca said slowly, as if Hallie had the flu and needed to be coaxed into taking her medicine. "Did you say yes?"

Hallie nodded, blinking away the tears that threatened to spill down her cheeks.

"Let me see the ring!" Francesca brightened. "Knowing Peter, he bought up Tiffany."

"I gave it back." Hallie sobbed. She put her head in her hands and recited the whole story: Kendra tearing at Peter's tuxedo jacket on the steps of City Hall, Peter's hands on Kendra's skirt. The fake interview with Marissa Mayer, the diamond-and-ruby ring in the sorbet, and Peter's old school friend, Rex Meany.

"Rex asked Peter for Kendra's phone number," Hallie cried, wiping her eyes with her skirt.

Francesca opened the cake box and took out a pink-and-yellow marzipan mouse. She admired the pointed ears and sharp nose. "Peter might be telling the truth."

"What do you mean?" Hallie frowned.

"I've seen a bride run down a hotel lobby in stockings and a push-up bra. I've seen the mother of the bride sing 'Unforgettable' while doing a striptease. People behave worse at weddings than they do in Vegas." Francesca paced around the room, warming to her point. "Kendra was plastered and Peter was trying to be a gentleman."

"She says she doesn't remember the whole evening," Hallie murmured.

"And Kendra does have exquisite taste in jewelry," Francesca mused.

"Peter lied about the interview with Marissa Mayer." Hallie leaned back against the cushions. "He could lie about anything."

"Everyone lies a little, I bet even the Pope shades the truth now and then." Francesca nibbled the mouse's nose. "Has Peter ever hurt you?"

"No." Hallie shook her head. "He treats me like a goddess."

"When Portia met Riccardo he was engaged to another woman." Francesca took another mouse out of the cake box and handed it to Hallie. "He was seeing both women at the same time. It's no surprise he cheated on Portia; men rarely change."

"Poor Portia." Hallie bit into pink icing. "I keep calling but I can't get through to her."

"I suggested Portia come to America," Francesca replied. "But Sophia is afraid if Portia disappears, Riccardo will flaunt his mistress in public."

"Constance thinks you should go see Portia," Hallie replied. The marzipan was sweet and smooth and slipped past the lump in her throat.

Francesca took another marzipan mouse out of the box and held it in her palm. "You should go! You know the expression 'When the cat is away, the mice will play.'" She nodded at the pink-and-yellow mouse excitedly. "If Peter behaves while you're away, you'll know you can trust him."

"How will I know if he's cheating?" Hallie asked.

"San Francisco is a small town," Francesca replied. "We'll know."

"I couldn't go to Lake Como." Hallie sighed. She remembered the first time she visited, the summer after she graduated from St. Ignatius. She had seen pictures of the lake. She read about the splendid villas and ancient churches. Portia had told her about the cafés, the boutiques, the cute boys who rode vespas around the village.

But she wasn't prepared for the breathtaking beauty of the mountains sweeping down to the shore. She had never seen water a blue-green so glorious it belonged on a painting. She had never experienced the Italian love of life, the late dinners, the early-morning espressos, the feeling that life was one big happy party.

"Why not?" Francesca demanded. "Constance is right, it would be great for Portia to have company."

"Kendra would never let me take time off," Hallie replied. "We're inundated with new clients."

"Kendra knows that Constance sits on every important board in the city." Francesca picked her words carefully. "If members of Encore! or the Symphony Gala heard about Kendra's 'public stumble' they may think twice about hiring her as a designer."

"How Machiavellian." Hallie giggled.

"I may not have been the best mother when it came to homework and being a member of the PTA"—Francesca sat next to Hallie—"but you're my baby and I want you to be happy."

"Maybe I shouldn't get married." Hallie suddenly felt like a little girl, wanting to climb into her mother's lap. "You hated being a wife."

"I was so young." Francesca shrugged. "Sophia was a tyrant and Pliny did whatever she said. It seemed like a fairy tale but it became a nightmare. You and Peter are both bright professionals, you want the same things."

Hallie thought about how her married friends were buying houses in Pacific Heights. They hosted dinner parties with their new crystal and silverware. She didn't want to be the only couple with different last names and separate checking accounts.

"I want to believe him." Hallie's mind flashed on Peter standing on the sidewalk outside Gary Danko.

"Don't decide tonight." Francesca squeezed Hallie's hand. "I'll move some boxes in your old room. Everything will be clearer in the morning."

Francesca led Hallie to the small bedroom, which was piled with cake boxes of every shape and color. Hallie put on a pair of her mother's pajamas, the legs too short and the top barely covering her midriff. She climbed into bed, hoping when she woke up it would all have been a bad dream.

chapter four

Hallie paid the cab and stood at the entrance of their apartment building. The fog had cleared and the city was bathed in warm morning light. Summer was everywhere: rose bushes bloomed on the sidewalk; women drank iced espressos; and children licked chocolate ice-cream cones. Hallie gazed at the bay, watching the boats slide along the glass surface.

Hallie had woken up and pulled on a pair of leggings and a T-shirt she found in the closet. Her mother had left a pot of coffee, two slices of toast, and a note apologizing for not having more food. Hallie sat at the bay window, her feet cold on the wood floor. She missed Peter's eggs, the wet kiss he planted on her lips as he ran out the door.

Hallie entered the building and climbed three floors to their apartment. Peter lay on the purple sofa, dressed in slacks and a crumpled white shirt. His shoes were tossed under the coffee table, and his suit jacket was draped over a chair. His eyes were closed and he had new stubble on his chin.

"Hi." Hallie closed the front door quietly.

Peter's eyes flew open as if he'd been shot. "Christ, Hallie. I waited up all night."

"I texted you that I was going to stay at my mother's." Hallie sat on the low orange chair opposite him.

"I couldn't sleep in our bed without you." Peter rubbed his chin. He had circles under his eyes and his cheeks were pale.

"I talked with my mother," Hallie began.

"Nothing happened with Kendra," Peter interrupted. "Not at the wedding and not at lunch."

"I'm not interested." Hallie shook her head.

Peter stood up and smoothed his shirt. He brushed his hair with his hands and kneeled on the rug. "Maybe I shouldn't have proposed at dinner, maybe I should have buried the carpet in rose petals and proposed here."

"Peter." Hallie tried to get up, but Peter grabbed her hand and pulled her down in the chair.

"You left this at the restaurant." Peter took the ring out of his pocket and slipped it on Hallie's finger.

Hallie glanced at the clear diamond, the deep red rubies. She could keep the ring snug on her finger, and call Constance to announce the good news. She could make appointments at bridal salons and floral designers and calligraphers. She only had to nod and the future would roll out like a red carpet.

"I can't wear it yet." Hallie pulled it off her finger.

"What do you mean 'yet'?" Peter asked.

"I need time to think." Hallie tried to sound confident.

"I love you and I want to spend my life with you." Peter squeezed her hand. "We're going to wake up every morning and have hot sex and eat waffles and read *The New York Times*."

"I talked to Portia this morning." Hallie stood up and walked to the balcony. "Sophia wants her to take Riccardo back. Portia said the only way she wants to see Riccardo is pulled apart limb for limb by wild horses."

"Portia sounds like someone you don't want to cross," Peter replied.

"I'm going to Lake Como; I'm going to spend August with her."

Peter frowned. "I can't take time off now. Jim's fears have made the other investors anxious. I need to score a major interview to calm their nerves."

"What about Frank Marshall?" Hallie asked.

"Not big enough." Peter grimaced. "I've got an inside track at Apple. They haven't given an interview since Steve Jobs died. No one knows what goes on in there; it's like a black hole. I have a guy who's ready to talk, I just need to loosen him up a little."

"Like Deep Throat," Hallie murmured. "I'm going to Lake Como alone."

"Let's go to Como next year on our honeymoon," Peter suggested. "We'll feed the pigeons in Venice and eat pasta Alfredo in Rome."

"I need to get away." Hallie glanced at the rug. She thought Peter's eyes saw through her like an X-ray.

"You said Kendra wouldn't let you have a day off," Peter exclaimed. "How can you jet off to Europe for a month?"

"Kendra has been courting Charlotte Schulz and Dede Wilsey for months. Constance is having lunch with them at the Mark Hopkins on Wednesday. I was going to ask Constance to put in a good word."

Peter let her words sink in. His body was rigid and his eyes flashed. "Nothing happened! Kendra's not even a woman; she's a robot in a skirt and heels."

Hallie kept her shoulders back the way she had learned in ballroom dancing lessons when she was twelve. She walked over to Peter and handed him the ring.

"I just need some time."

Peter put the ring in his pocket. He grabbed Hallie's hand and kissed her fingers. He pulled her close and kissed her neck. He slid his hand under her T-shirt and rubbed her nipples.

Hallie felt as if her body was lit by a match. She kissed him back, tasting the familiar flavor of his mouth, the scent of cologne mixed with sleep. Peter pulled her down on the sofa, rolling off her leggings and tugging at her panties. He stripped off his shirt and slacks and lay beside her.

Hallie felt her body meld into his. She felt his mouth on her breasts, his fingers probing, teasing, making her wet. She held on to his back, opening her legs, wanting him to fill her up. But he waited, digging his fingers deeper inside her, watching her rise and peak and shudder. Finally he climbed on top of her and pushed so deep she thought she would break. They came together, moaning, whimpering, holding each other, exchanging kisses and trickles of sweat.

Peter turned on his side and draped his hand over Hallie's breasts. Hallie felt her heart beat under his touch; his thigh rubbing against hers. She glanced at the photographs over the fireplace and her portrait on the wall. She wriggled off the sofa and pulled on her clothes.

Hallie slid open the glass doors and stood on the balcony. It was noon and the street was full of people on their lunch break. She watched women carrying cartons of salad, hurrying back to boutiques and galleries. She saw men in shirts and slacks eating slices of pizza and drinking cans of Coke. She saw a couple holding hands, sharing a cup of gelato.

Hallie walked inside. She went into the small study and turned on the computer. She clicked on Alitalia and searched flights. She chose a flight to Rome, continuing to Milan. She entered the numbers of her credit card and clicked BUY.

Hallie walked briskly down Fillmore Street, checking her reflection in a shop window. Kendra would be livid that she took the morning off and furious that she intended to go to Italy.

Hallie wore a camel-colored cashmere dress with a brown Gucci belt and matching pumps. She couldn't show any weakness or Kendra would have her sweeping the back room, promising not to take another day off until Christmas.

"Hallie!" Kendra looked up from arranging silk pillows on a velvet daybed. "I've been calling your phone all morning. I'm leaving for Tahoe tomorrow and there are a million things to do. I need you to pick up some fabric swatches from Britex and stop by Floramor and get one of those gorgeous wreaths."

"I have to talk to you," Hallie said, tapping her fingers on a Chippendale rolltop desk.

"You cannot take another morning off." Kendra moved around the store, smoothing fabrics and plumping pillows. "I'm relying on you to keep the store running smoothly while I'm away."

"Peter proposed last night," Hallie replied. She kept her voice calm but her hands were shaking.

"That's wonderful!" Kendra barely paused, pulling stems from a bunch of yellow roses. "Let me see the ring."

"I thought you've seen it," Hallie said icily. "Peter said he asked your opinion."

"I want to see it on your finger," Kendra replied. "He was so concerned that you love it. You struck gold with Peter. There aren't many men who are successful and sensitive."

Hallie's shoulders relaxed. She glanced at her reflection in the gilt mirror. Her cheeks were dusted with powder, and she wore thick mascara and shimmering eye shadow. She had pulled her hair back with a gold clip and doused herself in Obsession.

"I haven't given Peter an answer yet." Hallie eyed Kendra carefully. "Portia's husband left her. I'm going to Lake Como to spend some time with her."

"You're doing what?" Kendra stopped dusting silver candelabras. "We've got deliveries all month and I'm going to be buried in Patsy's new place. You'll have to babysit some of my clients and run the store."

"I'll be in Lake Como for August," Hallie continued. "I'll be home on Labor Day."

"If you and Peter had a lover's quarrel, work it out on your own time," Kendra snapped. "I need you in the store every day."

"Did I mention Constance is having lunch with Charlotte Shulz and Dede Wilsey on Wednesday? Dede is about to choose a designer to do her house in Napa," Hallie said. "It's thirty-thousand square feet with a private gym and championship tennis courts."

Kendra ran her long French-manicured nails over a Fabergé jewelry box. The muscles in her neck tightened but her expression remained calm. "I've been dying to go on a buying trip to Italy. So many ancient families are strapped for cash and are selling off the family treasures. You could do some buying while you're in Italy; pick up some bolts of silk from Milan and glass in Murano."

"That's a wonderful idea." Hallie matched Kendra's smooth tone. Her stomach tightened as if she was on an elliptical machine.

"I'm glad that's settled." Kendra resumed straightening magazines. "I'll ask Stefan if one of his artists can mind the store. They don't know much about interior design, but they look good with the furniture."

"I'll make a list of deliveries I'm expecting for Libby Taylor's house." Hallie walked to the backroom. "I'll be accessible by e-mail and phone."

"Let me know if you'd like me to do anything while you're gone," Kendra called. "Water your plants, bring in the newspaper."

Hallie felt a chill run up her spine. She turned to Kendra and smiled graciously. "That's very thoughtful, but Peter is perfectly capable."

Hallie rang the doorbell of Constance's house, desperate for something cold to drink. The afternoon in the store had been interminable; she and Kendra moved like jousters playing an invisible fencing match. Kendra issued endless instructions and Hallie flinched as if she was ducking blows. Now and then Hallie looked up from her paperwork to see if she could read Kendra's expression, but her face was as inscrutable as a Chinese warrior.

"Hallie!" Constance beamed. "What a pleasure to see you twice in one week. I was fixing a gin and tonic."

"Where's Louisa?" Hallie stepped into the marble foyer.

"I sent her to buy *Vanity Fair*," Constance replied. "Dr. Michaels disapproves of my evening cocktail, so I have to invent reasons for Louisa to leave the house."

"Outsmarting your doctor isn't the way to get well," Hallie said, smiling.

"He shouldn't make my own employee spy on me," Constance huffed. She wore a beige wool skirt and a yellow silk shirt. "Why don't you go into the kitchen and open a jar of macadamia nuts? Dr. Michaels won't let me near them."

Hallie walked to the kitchen, pausing at the twelve-foot double doors. If she had to choose a favorite room in Constance's house, it would be the kitchen. When she was a girl she sat at the long oak table, her head in a copy of *Persuasion*, and imagined the room full of maids scrubbing potatoes and shining silverware. The floors were polished stone and the counters were creamy marble. A fireplace took up one wall and French doors opened onto a vegetable garden.

"Is that a Lanvin?" Constance pointed at Hallie's dress when she walked back into the salon. "Cashmere is such a clever choice for summer in San Francisco, and the cut is sublime."

Hallie sipped the gin and tonic. She rarely drank during the week and it tasted strong and bitter. "I talked to Francesca last night."

"Did you convince her to go to Como?" Constance asked, nibbling a macadamia nut.

"I'm going to Lake Como," Hallie replied.

"I thought Kendra had you chained to the store." Constance raised her eyebrows.

"I'm going to buy some things for the store while I'm there," Hallie said, scooping up macadamia nuts.

"Then it's a wonderful idea." Constance smiled. "You and Peter can explore the lake. Show him Villa del Balbienello, it's one of my favorite spots."

"Peter's not going," Hallie murmured. "He's busy with *Spilled*."

"You're leaving your job and your boyfriend?" Constance frowned.

"Peter and Kendra can manage without me for a month," Hallie replied lightly.

"Peter has been dropping hints all summer." Constance poured another gin and tonic. "How is he going to propose if you're on the other side of the ocean?"

Hallie fiddled with her drink. She had never lied to her grandmother. When Hallie was thirteen and Constance discovered a dog-eared *Cosmopolitan* in her backpack, Hallie was tempted to say it belonged to a friend. But she saw Constance's expression, stern and regal as Queen Elizabeth, and confessed she had bought it at a newsstand.

"Peter proposed last night," Hallie said.

"I must call Reverend Xavier at St. Dominic's," Constance exclaimed, walking over to the house phone. "Dates in June fill up so quickly."

"I didn't say yes."

"Did you and Peter have a disagreement?" Constance asked, reluctantly putting the phone down.

"Peter took me to dinner at Gary Danko and hid the ring in the coconut sorbet," Hallie replied. "It's an oval diamond flanked by rubies."

"Why aren't you wearing it?"

"Francesca's marriage ended so badly," Hallie began. "And now Portia and Riccardo."

"It's not about marriage, it's about the person you marry," Constance interrupted. "Your mother married a prince she met on a ski slope; they didn't even speak the same language. Portia always had a wild streak. She had to learn the hard way that bad boys make terrible husbands."

"I don't want to make a mistake." Hallie wanted to tell Constance about Patsy's wedding, about Peter's lunch date with Kendra, but the words stuck in her throat.

"When you were six I took you to a pet store to pick out a puppy. I was sure you would choose a sweet little cocker spaniel. He had floppy ears and a silky coat; he was the perfect dog for a young girl. But you marched right over to a cage that held a lanky golden retriever. He was already six months old, with paws as big as your hands. I asked why you chose the golden retriever and you said you were going to keep growing. One day you'd be the same size and be best friends."

"Miles." Hallie smiled, remembering. "He slept at the foot of my bed."

"God took my Theodore early." Constance lowered her eyes. "But we had thirty-five good years because he was my best friend. Marry your best friend and you'll never have a single regret."

Hallie drained her glass. She couldn't tell Constance that Peter had shaken her trust; that she needed to put some distance between them. Suddenly Constance looked older; her shoulders hunched, her hand shook as she added ice to her gin and tonic.

"Portia and I are going to spend August gorging ourselves on fruit from the outdoor markets. We'll buy shoes and bags in

Milan, and visit the Uffizi Gallery in Florence. When I come home, Peter and I will announce our engagement."

"I'll host a Labor Day party!" Constance exclaimed. "It will have a white theme—white flowers, white food, the invitations will say white attire requested. We'll hire Dick Bright Orchestra. It would be lovely to see people dancing again."

Constance placed the lid on the jar of macadamia nuts and put the gin under the bar.

"You must stay for dinner. I'll ask Louisa to set an extra place."

"I'd love to." Hallie noticed the sparkle in Constance's eyes, the pink blush in her cheeks. "But I haven't packed and I'm leaving in the morning."

"You need two sets of clothes," Constance instructed. "Cotton dresses for daytime and silk gowns for the evening. Sophia doesn't allow women to wear pants in the villa, and you must wear at least two-inch heels at dinner."

"Does she still keep such strict rules?" Hallie frowned. "She must be close to eighty."

"Sophia Tesoro will be buried in a Marchioni gown, clutching a diamond cross," Constance replied. "I would like you to give her something for me."

Hallie waited while Constance disappeared into the library. She pictured the Tesoro villa and felt a pinprick of excitement. She remembered the gardens of roses and fruit trees, the rooms with stone floors and massive pieces of furniture, the view of the lake so intoxicating that it filled Hallie's lungs like oxygen.

The last time Hallie visited Lake Como was six years ago for Portia's wedding. It had been two weeks of nonstop celebration. They held lakeside picnics that started at breakfast and ended as the sun set behind the mountains. They attended all-night parties that featured clowns and acrobats, exotic birds in gilt cages, discos with glittering balls of light.

Hallie met racecar drivers, polo players, princes, and counts with names that seemed straight out of *Romeo and Juliet.* Young men with olive skin and green eyes whirled her around the dance floor and whispered poetry in her ear. They fed her profiteroles and poured Italian wines into crystal goblets.

"Antonio Picata wants to marry you," Portia had said as they lay in Portia's bedroom after a party that ended at dawn.

"He doesn't speak a word of English. He talked with his hands all night."

"Did you see his hands?" Portia had sighed, hugging her chest. "They were made for lovemaking."

"You're getting married in three days." Hallie had smiled. "You shouldn't be thinking about another man's hands."

"In Italy you never stop thinking about another man's hands. That's what keeps marriage alive. Every time Riccardo touches me I imagine he is a stranger; it sends shivers down my spine."

"Americans are boring," Hallie had murmured sleepily.

"Who wants a boring life?" Portia had sat up in bed. "You should move to Italy. You'll marry a count and we'll have speedboat races across the lake."

"I just graduated from UCLA, I want to have my own design firm and create fabulous rooms clients adore," Hallie had mumbled.

"You'll get tired of working for other people." Portia had waved her hand airily. "For Italians there are no sweeter words than '*la dolce vita.*'"

"*La dolce vita,*" Hallie said the words aloud as Louisa cleared the glasses.

Hallie would drag Portia out of her turret bedroom and they would swim and bicycle, hike and paddleboat, shop and walk along the promenade. Portia would kick and scream and curse Riccardo. Hallie would try to forget the scene at Patsy's wedding and remember the things she loved about Peter: his curious mind, his bright, boyish charm.

Constance walked into the salon clutching a parcel wrapped in gold paper.

"Did you know Sophia has never been on an airplane?" Constance handed the package to Hallie. "She says she only wants to touch the clouds when she's on her way to heaven."

"Sophia probably arranged with the Pope for a private escort to bring her to the pearly gates." Hallie turned the parcel over in her hand. It was a thick rectangle tied with red ribbon.

"She put your mother through the circles of hell, but that was decades ago." Constance kissed Hallie on both cheeks. "Tell Peter to come for dinner on Sunday; we'll miss you together."

Hallie walked down the steps to her car. She peered up at Constance's mansion. She could see the chandeliers twinkling behind velvet curtains and imagined Constance sitting down at the mahogany dining table. She tried to quiet the butterflies in her stomach. She was leaving Peter, Constance, her mother, and her job. She murmured, *"La dolce vita,"* and turned the car toward Russian Hill.

chapter five

Hallie stood in the arrivals terminal of the Milan airport, waiting for her luggage. It seemed like days since she boarded the plane in San Francisco. Francesca had driven her to the airport, ladening her with pastries for Portia and Sophia and a selection of baby clothes for Marcus's wife, Angelica.

"Tell Marcus to call the minute the baby arrives." Francesca hugged Hallie at the security check-in. "And give Angelica lots of hugs; at least I have one child whose life isn't full of drama."

"I can't believe Marcus is going to be a father," Hallie agreed, picturing a dark-haired baby with round fists and feet. Marcus managed the Tesoro business interests in Milan and his wife was newly pregnant.

"Tell Angelica to save the clothes for you." Francesca squeezed Hallie's hand. "In a couple of years you'll need them."

"I hope so." Hallie blinked away tears. She refused to let Peter take her to the airport, and he barely glanced up from his laptop when she lugged her suitcase to the door. She put her bag in her mother's Volkswagen and hugged the cake box against her chest.

———

Hallie watched her bag come off the carousel. Portia wanted to meet her in Milan but Hallie insisted she could get to Lake Como by herself. Suddenly she felt tired and alone. The Italian men and women resembled film stars with their glossy black hair and smooth olive skin.

Until Hallie landed in Rome, she felt chic and sophisticated. She wore yellow Kate Spade capris with a matching hoodie and flat Tory Burch sandals. She carried a cavernous Michael Kors tote and wore white Oliver Peoples sunglasses.

But stepping off the plane in Rome, Hallie felt like a teenager crashing her first adult cocktail party. The women wore pencil-thin skirts and carried Gucci clutches. Their skin glowed as if they emerged from a spa instead of an international flight.

Milan was worse. Hallie saw bright silk dresses that belonged on a runway and four-inch stilettos encrusted with jewels. The men wore shirts open to the waist and leather loafers without socks.

"*Potrebbe aivatani con le valige?*" a man asked, pointing to her suitcase.

Hallie jumped. No one had spoken to her since the flight attendant announced their arrival in Milan.

"My Italian is rusty," she apologized, shrugging her shoulders.

"Would you like help with your luggage?" the man asked in accented English. "You are too pretty to handle such a big suitcase."

Hallie blushed. The man was tall, with curly black hair and black eyes. He had a dimple on his chin and carried a suit bag over his shoulder.

"No, thank you. I'm taking the shuttle bus to the train station."

"I will take you to the train station." The man rolled her bag toward the exit. "A shuttle bus is no place for a beautiful American."

"Really, I've done it before." Hallie ran after him. "I'm going to Lake Como to visit my half sister."

"Ah, Como." The man sighed. "A playground of miraculous beauty."

"My grandmother has a villa there," Hallie replied. "Sophia Tesoro."

"I do business with Marcus Tesoro! I manufacture silk." He unzipped his bag and extracted a silk scarf with a floral design. "You must have this, it brings out the blue in your eyes."

"I can't take it." Hallie pushed the scarf into his hands.

"I insist." The man draped it around her neck. "Here is my card. I am Alfonso Diamante. I will check you are wearing it the next time I am in Como."

Hallie sat on the bus, the fine silk caressing her shoulders. She felt grimy from the long flight and unsettled by the encounter at the airport. She wasn't used to talking to dark, handsome strangers. She tore up the card and stuffed the scarf into her suitcase. She closed her eyes, wishing Peter was in the seat next to her, and that she wore his oval diamond on her finger.

Sitting on the express train to Como, Hallie remembered why she wanted to travel alone to the villa. The scenery was so spectacular: the villages with tall church spires, the fields of brightly colored flowers, the green mountains capped with snow. Hallie didn't want to miss a minute of it by conversing with Portia.

By the time Hallie arrived in Como, her jet lag was replaced by the excitement of being on holiday. Tourists chatted in German and French. They pointed out landmarks, craning their heads as the train pulled into the station.

Hallie jumped off the train and breathed the perfumed air. She could smell jasmine and roses and oleander. The cobblestoned streets baked under the noon sun and the lake glittered like a sheet of new pennies. Hallie rolled her suitcase toward the ferry, passing cafés and gelato stands.

The black and white boats sat in the harbor, waiting to take passengers to villages around the lake. Hallie was going to Bellagio, one of the most popular destinations. The line was full of families licking ice-cream cones, young lovers holding hands, nannies trying to round up their charges while the parents sipped a last aperitif in the bar next to the dock.

A red speedboat pulled up to the dock and a man jumped out. He had curly black hair peppered with gray and a sharp, angular chin. His eyes were pale blue and his profile belonged on a Roman statue. He wore silk shorts and a navy shirt and a gold cross hung around his neck. He took off his sunglasses and searched the terminal, suddenly waving at Hallie.

"Pliny?" Hallie squinted in the sun. She dragged her suitcase to the side to get a closer look. The speedboat was built like a bullet, sharp and snub-nosed, and it had the Tesoro crest painted on the side.

"Sophia sent me to pick you up." Pliny made a little bow. "No guest of the Tesoros arrives in Bellagio by passenger ferry."

"You didn't have to." Hallie slipped out of the line. "I like playing tourist."

"Sophia is pleased you are here." Pliny grabbed Hallie's suitcase. "She thinks you will talk some sense into Portia."

"Me?" Hallie let Pliny help her into the speedboat. Pliny started the motor and Hallie sat back against the soft leather upholstery.

"Constance told Sophia you have a good head on your shoulders," Pliny said in careful English. "I am glad you are here, too, you have grown into a beautiful woman."

"Thank you," Hallie mumbled, letting her hair cover her cheeks so Pliny wouldn't see her blush.

She glanced at Pliny curiously, trying to imagine Pliny and Francesca together. There were fines lines around his eyes and mouth, but Hallie could imagine him as the young man on the ski slope. She pictured Francesca falling in fresh powder and looking up to see an Italian prince offering her his hand.

"It is very difficult for Sophia," Pliny explained over the roar of the engine. "They are about to erect a statue of my great-grandfather in the Piazza San Giacomo. Sophia has worked on this for many years; the bishop and the cardinal have given it their blessing."

"How wonderful!" Hallie exclaimed.

"A scandal involving Portia and Riccardo could ruin everything." Pliny's eyebrows knotted together.

"It's not Portia's fault Riccardo left her," Hallie said doubtfully. She wasn't used to talking to Pliny. At Portia's wedding he had been busy toasting the bride, and on her previous visit she and Portia had been teenagers trying to stay beneath his radar.

"Italy is different from America," Pliny replied. "Men are never at fault."

"That's Victorian!" Hallie bristled.

"That is the way it is." Pliny shrugged. "Sophia hopes you will convince Portia to take Riccardo back."

"Don't you want Portia to be happy?" Hallie asked.

"There are many ways to be happy." Pliny guided the boat between two sailboats with bright billowing sails. "I was devastated when your mother left. But my children made me happy; my home, Bellagio, Italy."

"I'm sure Portia will make the right decision," Hallie murmured.

"It must be the right decision for the Tesoro name," Pliny insisted, guiding the boat into a small harbor.

Hallie shivered under the hot sun. She couldn't understand how Sophia and Pliny cared more about the Tesoro name than the members of the family. She remembered how Sophia refused to allow Portia and Marcus to go with their mother. She pictured Marcus, a small boy with his father's blue eyes and Portia practically a baby, forced to stay when Francesca returned to America.

"I want you to enjoy your holiday," Pliny said, smiling. "Lake Como in August is for lovers and dreamers. Sophia is holding a feast tonight in your honor."

Hallie watched the village of Bellagio appear beyond the curve of the lake. The promenade was lined with olive trees and the villas were surrounded by gardens as large as parks. Hallie saw the Hotel Metropole perched above the dock, and a string of cafés where smartly dressed tourists ate shrimp and paella.

Hallie turned to Pliny. "I'd be happy with a plate of antipasto and a bowl of fresh berries."

"There will be antipasto and prosciutto and every kind of fruit. The cooks have been preparing for days and Sophia sent Lea to the market twice this morning." Pliny steered the boat into a small cove.

The chatter of tourists and the *put-put* of motors were replaced by silence. A fish poked its head above the water and dived back under the surface. Hallie glanced up at the Tesoro villa and saw grand balconies with wrought-iron railings, stone walls covered in ivy, and glimpses of marble through open windows.

"Sophia has invited Riccardo and all their friends." Pliny tied the boat up at the private dock. "He wouldn't dream of refusing the invitation. Sophia is hoping for a reconciliation."

"Hallie!" a young woman with raven black hair and large green eyes ran down to the dock. She wore an orange chiffon skirt and a white halter top. She had gold hoop earrings in her ears and leather sandals with colored ribbons on her feet.

"Portia." Hallie hugged her sister. Hallie felt sharp bones through the halter top and could see the outline of Portia's ribcage.

"Infidelity is wonderful for the diet." Portia laughed. "I look like a prison camp survivor."

"You're gorgeous," Hallie replied. Even with the skin pulled tight on her cheeks and the sharp angles of her hips, Portia was strikingly beautiful. Her hair was glossy as paint and her mouth was an invitation to be kissed.

"Sophia hired a hairdresser and a masseuse." Portia grimaced. "She wants me to look my best tonight. I'm like a can of meat trying to push back its sell-by date."

"In America you'd be a supermodel." Hallie followed Portia up the winding path to the house.

"Apparently Riccardo likes more buxom women." Portia shrugged. "His mistress has the hips of a Venetian courtesan."

"Pliny told me that Sophia wants you to take Riccardo back." Hallie put her hand on Portia's arm. "You don't have to settle, you can have any man."

Portia was about to speak, but looked up and saw her grandmother appear on the balcony. Sophia was dressed in black silk and her white hair framed her face like a helmet. She stood with her arms on the railing, a diamond-and-ruby bracelet glinting in the sun.

Hallie saw a flicker in Portia's green eyes, like a flame trying to ignite. Portia slipped her arm through Hallie's and skipped toward the house.

"I feel better already," Portia whispered as they approached the stairs. "After lunch we'll go to the garden. I'll show you my new archery set."

"Sounds dangerous." Hallie giggled. "I wonder who's the target."

Hallie and Portia climbed the stone steps to the balcony, where Sophia waited to greet them. Sophia was petite like Portia, with a tiny waist and small hands and feet. Her face was lined and blue veins covered her wrists, but her eyes belonged on a Siamese cat. She looked at Hallie closely, as if inspecting a new couture gown.

"You are a true beauty," Sophia said finally. "I see little resemblance to your mother."

Hallie bit back a reply and smiled graciously. "Francesca says I take after my grandmother."

"Constance is a formidable foe but a fine woman." Sophia nodded. "I haven't seen her since she and her husband stayed at the villa years ago. Theodore liked to play cards and Constance was fond of a glass of drambuie after dinner."

Hallie tried to keep her face expressionless. She knew Constance had visited Lake Como when Portia and Marcus were young, but she never said she stayed at the villa. Hallie imagined Constance and Theodore dining with Sophia and Pliny and shivered.

"I gather Constance never told Francesca she was our guest." Sophia smiled as if she could read Hallie's mind.

"Hallie's been on a plane for hours," Portia interrupted. "Let her shower and change."

"Lea has prepared brunch." Sophia moved toward the house. "We will eat and then you can take a siesta before the evening's celebration."

Hallie followed Sophia through the double glass doors into the foyer. She had forgotten the scope of the house: the sweeping marble staircase, the intricate murals painted on the ceiling. Every chair, love seat, and ottoman was covered in thick gold brocade. It was like standing inside a jewelry box.

"Portia tells me you have taken up interior design," Sophia said.

"I work for one of the premier designers in San Francisco," Hallie replied.

"Maybe you can teach Portia." Sophia walked through double oak doors into the family dining room. "If she had an interest she wouldn't concern herself with Riccardo's peccadilloes."

"Veronica is not a peccadillo. She's a twenty-two-year-old actress with breasts like hot-air balloons and the hair of Medusa," Portia muttered, putting a celery stick and a baby carrot on a dessert plate.

"Riccardo will tire of her." Sophia shrugged. "They always do."

The table was covered with a burgundy tablecloth and set with inlaid china. Crystal pitchers held fresh juice and stone platters overflowed with fruits and vegetables. There were eggs simmering under silver domes, whipped mashed potatoes in warming trays, grilled mushrooms and tomatoes.

"It is healthy to eat a large midday meal." Sophia handed Hallie a plate. "Tonight you will dance it off."

Hallie felt the jet lag return, crushing her like a boulder. She filled the plate with melon balls, strips of ham, and green olives. She poured a glass of cranberry juice and sat in one of the ornate brocade chairs. She tried to bring the fork to her mouth but suddenly she grew dizzy.

"I'm sorry." Hallie gulped, trying to stop the room from spinning. "The jet lag caught up with me."

"Are you feeling ill?" Pliny appeared from the foyer. He walked over to the table and touched Hallie's arm. "My mother has never been on an airplane, she doesn't understand how travel can affect you."

"I could use a glass of water," Hallie murmured.

"You need to put something solid in your stomach," Pliny insisted. "I will fix you a plate."

Portia ran to the kitchen to get a glass of water. Pliny strode quickly around the table and set a full plate in front of Hallie.

"Eat, you will feel better," he prompted.

Hallie's head tipped forward and she knocked the plate on the floor. Eggs and prosciutto spilled onto the ceramic tile and the plate shattered into pieces. She slumped in the chair, and the stained-glass windows, the plastered walls, and the gold drapes disappeared. She let the cool blackness swallow her up like Alice falling down the rabbit hole.

chapter six

"How am I going to go to the feast with a lump the size of an Easter egg?" Hallie lay back against the pillows in Portia's bedroom.

After Hallie fainted, Pliny had carried her upstairs and laid her on the canopied bed. Hallie woke up with a cold cloth pressed against her forehead and a brandy snifter held under her nose.

"Alcohol is the last thing I need." Hallie pushed the snifter away. "I feel like I've been hit by a train."

Portia set the glass on the bedside table. "We'll put some powder on the bump and you'll be brand new."

"Will Sophia forgive me?" Hallie groaned. "I ruined brunch and broke a family heirloom."

"You distracted her from worrying about me." Portia sat on the edge of the bed. "All day long she plots how to get Riccardo and me back together."

"Do you want Riccardo back?" Hallie asked, flinching as she reached for a glass of water.

"I'm almost thirty years old and I'm living in my childhood bedroom." Portia shrugged her narrow shoulders. "I used to play this guitar when I was seven, and this is the lacrosse stick I used at boarding school in Switzerland. That was a terrible year." Portia shuddered. "I smoked a whole pack of Virginia Slims on the roof of the chalet before they sent me home."

"You never told me you smoked." Hallie frowned.

"I didn't." Portia swung the lacrosse stick in the air. "I missed Lake Como so much I tried everything to get expelled."

"I would love a bedroom like this," Hallie mused. The floor was covered in a thick white carpet and the walls were yards of yellow silk. A king-sized canopy bed occupied the center of the room and a satin love seat sat near the window.

"I told Sophia I wanted an *Arabian Nights* theme." Portia grimaced. "I think I was six at the time."

"We could redecorate," Hallie said excitedly. "I'd love to prowl around the furniture stores in Milan."

"I don't want to live in this room or this house," Portia said, and sighed. "Riccardo and I have a gorgeous villa in Menaggio, and a high-rise apartment in Milan."

"Why don't you stay in your villa?" Hallie asked.

"If I live there alone, everyone will know Riccardo deserted me. Sophia has told people I moved home because I was 'overworked' and 'needed rest.'" Portia chuckled.

"You can't worry about what other people think." Hallie shook her head.

"Spoken like an American," Portia said, smiling. "If the truth gets out, the whole family will be shamed. I can't do that to Sophia."

"That doesn't sound like the girl who wore her father's suit to get into a disco." Hallie grinned.

"I made you wear one of Sophia's gowns," Portia exclaimed, her face breaking into an impish smile. "We pretended we were newlyweds."

"We stuffed socks in my bra because my chest was flat as a board," Hallie said, laughing.

"I was sixteen." Portia grew serious. "Now I have to consider the Tesoro name."

"You agree with Sophia?" Hallie asked.

"Remember before my wedding, you asked how I could think about other men? I said in Italy you always think about other men, even after you're married. I don't want a lover." Portia sighed. "But Riccardo has hot Italian blood. One wife was not enough."

"Then take him back." Hallie shivered. She flashed on Kendra pressed against the column at City Hall, and Peter's hands on her skirt.

"That's what Sophia doesn't understand," Portia replied. "Riccardo is in love with Veronica. He wants to divorce me and marry her."

"What are you going to do?" Hallie swung her legs off the bed.

"I'm going to let the hairdresser tease my hair and the masseuse massage my neck." Portia spun around the room like a dancer on top of a music box. "Then I'll put on my low-cut Elie Saab gown and try to seduce my husband."

"Kendra was all over Peter at Patsy Mane's wedding," Hallie said, walking out on the balcony.

Hallie gazed at the villa gardens. Fountains dotted the lawns, and stone benches sat under ivy-covered trellises. Hallie saw a large sundial on the main lawn, decorated with roses. The afternoon air was warm and fragrant and Hallie wanted to slip on a swimsuit and sit by the pool. She wanted to forget about Peter and Riccardo, and dip her feet in clear blue water.

"You didn't tell me!" Portia joined Hallie on the balcony. "I can't imagine Peter cheating on you; you're like Grace Kelly."

"He says Kendra was drunk and attacked him," Hallie replied. "When I saw them, he was trying to pull away."

"Do you believe him?"

"He was very upset." Hallie's stomach twisted in knots. "He took me out to dinner and gave me an oval diamond ring."

"Peter proposed?" Portia's eyes grew wide.

"I didn't say yes." Hallie walked to the railing. "I told him I was going to come here and think about it."

"Do you love him?" Portia asked.

"Peter asked me to move in with him two months after we met. We never even went on a date." Hallie hesitated. "Constance is dying to plan my wedding and all my friends think he's perfect for me. But I don't know if I can trust him."

"In Italy it is different." Portia grabbed the railing, bending into a deep plié. "You trust your heart that you are in love, that's all that matters."

"*La dolce vita*," Hallie said, smiling.

"Let's go for a swim before the party," Portia said grimly. "We need to forget about men."

Hallie gazed at the sun dancing on the lake. "That's exactly what I was thinking."

Hallie and Portia descended a flight of white marble steps to the pool area. The pool was pale blue and surrounded by marble busts. A pool house was equipped with a sauna, exercise room, granite bar, and giant flat-screen television.

"Sophia won't allow television in the villa," Portia explained, grabbing robes and towels. "It's okay for Riccardo to cheat, but she thinks television is immoral."

"I would love to redo this room." Hallie glanced at the bamboo furniture. "I've always wanted to decorate a pool house in greens and blues, with shag carpeting and windows shaped like portals."

"You think too much about work," Portia said, shaking her head. "That's almost as bad as obsessing about men."

"When I was eight I sat in my room every afternoon"—Hallie

followed Portia to the pool—"sketching my dream house with a box of colored pencils."

"When I was nine I packed my overnight case with three pairs of ballet shoes, two leotards, and my diary." Portia adjusted the straps on her bikini. "I left a note for Sophia and Pliny that I was going to join La Scala. My plan was to take the bus to Milan and become a member of the ballet school."

"What happened?" Hallie imagined Portia, small and slim as a pixie, darting through the gardens to the bus stop.

"One of the cooks was sitting at the bus stop," Portia replied. "She turned me around and marched me straight back to Sophia. I had to eat stale bread and stinky cheese for a week."

"Why didn't you dance when you were older?" Hallie wondered.

"Being a dancer is more scandalous than having a cheating husband." Portia shrugged. "Tesoro women are wives, mothers, and leaders of the church."

"That sounds medieval." Hallie dipped her toe in the water. The bottom of the pool was made of mosaic tile like shards of colored confetti.

"The Tesoros have owned the villa since the eighteenth century. In 1763, Augustus Tesoro was given a plot of land for his service to the Duke of Milan. His wife was homesick. She wanted to sell the land and return to her family in Naples," Portia began.

"Augustus brought her to this spot and placed his sword on the ground. He said if she insisted they sell he would pierce both their hearts with the sword. She relented and Augustus commissioned Piero Adamo to build the villa."

"That's a terrible story!" Hallie jumped into the pool, splashing Portia.

"The Tesoro men have always been hot-headed." Portia dove into the water, her body sleek as a seal. "My father can explode like a firecracker and then be gentle as a lamb."

"They do have exquisite taste in architecture." Hallie grinned, swimming the length of the pool.

Hallie and Portia played in the pool like children on summer vacation. They swam races, they dove for pennies, they did jack-knives from the diving board. They climbed out, tired and breathless, and dried themselves with plush, cotton towels.

"Being a Tesoro woman seems to have certain advantages." Hallie wrapped herself in a silk robe.

"We enjoy the finest cuisine," Portia agreed, picking at a pro-sciutto sandwich from the tray Lea had prepared. "We have a wine cellar stocked with the best wines. I can drive to Milan and order any gown I want." Portia sighed. "But I can't hold on to my own husband. Do you know what they did to deserted wives in ancient Rome?"

"No." Hallie bit into a sweet, firm peach.

"They fed them to the lions in the Colosseum," Portia replied.

"They did not." Hallie laughed, wiping peach juice from her chin.

"They may as well have." Portia sighed, lying back on the lounge. "If Riccardo doesn't come back, my life is over."

Hallie searched through her dresses, looking for the perfect outfit for tonight's festivities. Sophia had assigned her the bedroom next to Portia's, and Lea had hung her clothes in the cavernous walk-in closet. It felt wonderfully decadent to have her own room, to rub her feet on the leopard-skin rug, to stretch out on the four-poster bed, surrounded by fat down pillows.

Hallie selected a yellow silk Fendi dress and slipped it over her head. She hardly ever wore yellow. Kendra insisted Hallie wear classic, subdued colors to social events in San Francisco.

Hallie's wardrobe consisted mostly of Donna Karan navies, Jill St. John browns, and little black dresses by Dior and Chanel.

Hallie's cell phone rang and she jumped. She hadn't talked to anyone in San Francisco since she arrived in Milan. She'd sent her mother a text that she arrived safely, and replied to a long text from Peter with three *x*'s and *o*'s. Hallie saw Constance's number appear on the screen and pressed answer.

"Hallie, dear, what time is it in Italy?" Constance asked.

"It's evening," Hallie replied, imagining Constance in her breakfast room, eating a sliced grapefruit.

"How does Portia look?" Constance asked. "Has she been eating?"

"Sophia is holding a feast tonight. I'll make sure Portia eats sirloin tips and roast potatoes."

"How is Sophia?" Constance asked. "Did you give her my present?"

"I'll give it to her tonight." Hallie searched her suitcase for the gold package. "You never told me you stayed at the villa."

"That was decades ago." Constance sniffed. "Francesca was miserable. It was time Portia and Marcus were allowed to visit America."

"How did you convince Sophia?" Hallie asked.

"I applied a little pressure," Constance said. "Sophia is an intelligent woman, a little hard around the edges."

"Like a pointed dagger!" Hallie shivered.

"Peter came for dinner last night," Constance said. "We discussed the Labor Day party. He suggested we have two bands, one for the older crowd and one for the young people."

"Peter was there?" Hallie clutched the corner of the dressing table. Suddenly she missed his bright green eyes, his hard chest and long, sinewy legs. She wished she could conjure him up and they could stand on the balcony, watching the sunset over the lake.

"He had great suggestions for the band," Constance continued. "He's been researching them for your wedding."

"Our wedding," Hallie repeated.

"I told him we would announce your engagement at the party," Constance said.

"You told Peter I was going to say yes?" Hallie asked.

"You are going to say yes," Constance replied. "He is so charming and madly in love with you."

"I just," Hallie began. She pictured Constance alone in her mansion, sneaking gin and tonics when Louisa wasn't looking. "Wanted to tell him myself," she finished lamely.

"You're very lucky," Constance said. "Peter worships you."

"I know." Hallie closed her eyes and pictured Kendra, cool as ice, asking to see Hallie's diamond ring. She saw Peter standing outside Gary Danko, pleading with her to believe him. "I have to go." Hallie blinked. "I can't be late, I'm the guest of honor."

"It's wonderful to talk to you," Constance replied. "I feel like you're just next door."

Hallie hung up and gazed at the lake. The sky was dark and stars glittered like diamonds. Suddenly she missed her own bed with its suede headboard and cream satin sheets. She felt far away from home, but she didn't know if the world she and Peter shared, riding the cable car to Fisherman's Wharf, climbing the hill to Coit Tower, would be there when she returned.

Hallie descended the marble staircase, feeling like she was walking into a Fellini movie. Uniformed waiters passed trays of prawns and scampi. Bartenders mixed martinis and champagne cocktails. Hallie stepped outside and saw the balcony lit up like a Christmas tree. Paper lanterns swayed above and fairy lights were wrapped around tall plane trees.

But it was the guests that made Hallie stop and stare. In San Francisco, cocktail parties were conducted with unspoken rules of decorum. Women wore gowns that did not show their cleavage. Men and women stood far apart, discussing the opera or the stock market until the hosts called them into dinner.

Hallie slipped past women wearing metallic dresses and see-through chiffon. She saw men with heavy chains around their necks and gold rings on every finger. The men held cocktails in one hand and used the other to touch a woman's cheek, caress her hair, run his fingers down her back.

"I see Sophia invited the youngest and brightest." Portia stood beside her. She wore a siren-red gown with a plunging neckline. Her hair cascaded down her back, and her eyes were painted like an Egyptian queen. She wore a large ruby around her neck and sparkling diamonds in her ears.

"You look amazing," Hallie murmured, feeling suddenly like a staid San Francisco socialite.

"Sophia insisted on the jewels." Portia shrugged. "She wants to remind Riccardo why he married into the Tesoro family."

"Riccardo didn't marry you for your money," Hallie replied.

"Oh, Riccardo has plenty of money." Portia wound her way to the bar. "But in Italy money can't buy a title or a family tree. He'll be here any minute. I need a double shot, no ice."

"I thought Sophia was a strict Catholic." Hallie gazed at a woman whose dress was slit so high Hallie could see lace panties. "This is like a scene from *The Decameron*."

"In Italy the mating dance is conducted in the open." Portia drained her glass. "Sex is nothing to be ashamed of."

"The women aren't wearing any clothing," Hallie mumbled.

"They wear their family jewels, their titles, and their ancestry. Half the women in this room are countesses or princesses. The men are princes and dukes. They have known one another since they were babies in their birthday suits."

"In San Francisco, even babies wear rompers or onesies," Hallie replied, sipping a fizzy champagne cocktail.

"Portia, Hallie, you shine brighter than any woman in the room." Pliny strode toward them. He was freshly shaved and wore pleated navy slacks and a white silk shirt.

"Sophia's hairdresser spent two hours on my hair." Portia touched the tendrils that framed her large green eyes. "I hope she got her money's worth."

"Do not be angry with your grandmother," Pliny said, frowning. "She wants what is best for you."

"Sophia wants a fairy tale." Portia grimaced. "Oh, God! I see Riccardo."

Hallie followed Portia's gaze. Riccardo stood in a corner, flirting with two girls wearing neon miniskirts and stiletto heels.

"Riccardo is like a game hunter." Portia rattled her glass. "He only likes young meat."

"Your father is right," Hallie piped in. "You are the most beautiful woman in the room."

"That's why I have family." Portia smiled at Pliny and Hallie. "They always say the right thing. I may as well take the bull by the horns." She set off in Riccardo's direction. "May the best matador win."

"And you?" Pliny turned warm eyes to Hallie. "Did you recover from your fainting spell?"

"I hope Sophia doesn't hate me for ruining brunch." Hallie blushed.

"Sophia will be grateful if you convince Portia to take Riccardo back," Pliny murmured.

Hallie watched Riccardo kiss Portia briefly on both cheeks. She saw Portia lean in to him, her body fluttering like a bird. She wanted to tell Pliny that Riccardo didn't want to come back, that Portia should be encouraged to move on. But she saw Pliny's proud Roman profile, and knew he wasn't used to not getting what he wanted.

Sophia joined them. "I see Portia and Riccardo found each other." She wore a green satin dress and gold slippers. A ruby ring as large as a bird's egg dwarfed her ring finger.

"The Tesoro ruby." Pliny glanced at the ring. "Isn't that a little excessive?"

"It will be Portia's one day." Sophia shrugged. "It doesn't hurt to wear it in public."

"Find your enemy's weak spot and go in for the kill." Pliny chuckled. "You would have done well in the Medici court."

"Constance asked me to give you a gift," Hallie broke in, handing Sophia the rectangular package.

"Your grandmother is so thoughtful." Sophia smiled. "I will open it later. I must make sure the Rothschild Sauvignon Blanc is chilled."

Sophia and Pliny drifted off and Hallie nursed her cocktail. Suddenly she felt alone and hungry. A dark-haired man strode toward her. He wore a patterned silk shirt and his face looked familiar.

"You are not wearing the silk scarf I gave you." He made a little bow. "I am crestfallen."

"You are the man at the airport!" Hallie exclaimed, recognizing the dark curly hair and sharp black eyes.

"Alfonso Diamante." He took Hallie's hand and brought it to his lips. "I see you arrived in Como safely."

"It feels like a century ago," Hallie said, and sighed. "What are you doing here?"

"I have business in Lenno," Alfonso replied. "The Tesoros are known for their feasts and I am always hungry."

"I forgot how late Italians eat," Hallie said. "I'm starving."

"I like an American who can eat." Alfonso nodded approvingly. "Sophia would not like her guest to go hungry; we will fill you up."

Hallie followed Alfonso through the living room. They passed the dining room where a small army of waiters put the finishing touches on the table. They walked through a conservatory with a grand piano, and a gallery hung with watercolors.

Alfonso opened the door to the kitchen and Hallie gasped. The kitchens she read about in the Hamptons and Dubai, the kitchens she dreamed about when she climbed into bed, could not compare with the Tesoro kitchen. The floors were antique wood, made smooth and shiny with pine oil. The counters were pink and white marble, luminous as seashells. Hallie's eyes rested on the backsplash behind the industrial-size range. It was made of tiny mosaic tiles and depicted the Last Supper.

"Sophia takes great pride in design, but now is not the time to study art." Alfonso walked toward the pots simmering on the stove. "It is time to eat."

Alfonso heaped plates with risotto, asparagus, sweet potato, bruschetta, and olive pesto. He slipped a bottle of wine and two glasses under his arm and motioned Hallie to follow him.

"We will go to the gardens," he explained. "We will get in trouble if the cook finds the risotto missing."

"You know the villa very well." Hallie followed Alfonso across the lawn.

"I have known Marcus since university," Alfonso replied. "I spent many summers swimming in the pool and sailing on the lake. The Tesoros are excellent hosts as long as you compliment Sophia on her wines and know how to dress for dinner."

Alfonso opened the door of the long, low greenhouse and turned on the lights. Hallie saw rows of azaleas and rhododendrons, heads of lettuce, bundles of asparagus, and bunches of baby carrots.

"Here we will be warm, like the plants." Alfonso found a tarp and spread it on the ground. "Marcus didn't tell me he had a sister in America."

"My mother was married to Pliny, but they separated when Portia was a baby," Hallie replied. "She's my half sister."

"Poor Portia." Alfonso dropped his eyes. "I would like to take a skein of silk and wrap it around Riccardo's neck."

"You know Riccardo?" Hallie raised her eyebrows.

"Riccardo's father owns a fleet of supermarkets from Naples to Milan, but Riccardo has the soul of a shopkeeper." Alfonso frowned. "You don't display your mistress like a side of beef."

"Portia is having a rough time," Hallie conceded, scooping up a forkful of risotto.

"She always had bad taste in men. Marcus and I used to tease her about the boys riding motorcycles she brought to the villa." Alfonso swirled his wine in the wineglass. "Does the American half sister have better luck with men?"

Hallie choked on the spicy rice and fish. "I have a boyfriend."

"But no ring." Alfonso touched her hand. "American men remain children too long. An Italian would have put a ring on that finger."

Hallie dropped her fork on the plate. "We should go, I feel much better."

"You are right." Alfonso gathered the plates and glasses. "Sophia will throw one of her famous tantrums if her guests are late to the table."

"I can't imagine Sophia losing control," Hallie replied when they walked outside. She breathed the crisp night air, relieved to get away from the sweet scent of hothouse flowers.

"All the Tesoros have terrible tempers. I have seen Portia slice the tires of a motorcycle and shred a leather jacket into pieces."

"I hope no one was wearing the jacket at the time," Hallie said, laughing.

"If I remember, she had already kicked him out of the villa." Alfonso grinned.

Hallie followed him down a gravel path to the house. She caught her heel in the pebbles and grabbed a bush to steady herself. Her hand fell through the leaves, and she landed on the ground, her knees scraped by the stones.

"Are you hurt?" Alfonso crouched beside her.

"I'll be fine." Hallie struggled to get up. "It's just a scratch."

Alfonso took a silk handkerchief from his pocket and dabbed the blood on her knee. He pulled her up, brushing the dirt from her dress. He put one arm around her shoulder and guided her toward the balcony.

Hallie paused at the bottom step and turned to thank him. He touched her cheek, and then he pulled her close and kissed her on the lips. Hallie froze, watching the paper lanterns sway above them. She broke away and slipped through the double glass doors.

"Hallie, wait." Alfonso ran ahead, blocking her path.

"What do you think you're doing?" Hallie sputtered. Her knee throbbed and there was blood on the hem of her dress.

"You are so beautiful," Alfonso pleaded. "I thought we could make music together."

"I have a boyfriend." Hallie glanced around the room to see if Sophia or Pliny were watching. She didn't want to make a scene but she was anxious to get away from Alfonso.

"Across a wide ocean." He put his hand on her arm.

"Leave me alone," Hallie whispered. "Or I will tell Sophia."

"It will not happen again. Keep the handkerchief." Alfonso slipped the silk square into her hand. "A token of friendship."

Hallie wanted to run upstairs and close the door to her room. She wanted to get away from the women displaying high, round breasts and the men whispering endearments. But she saw Sophia ringing the dinner bell. She followed the guests into the dining room and sat at the long table, staring at the naked cherubs painted on the ceiling.

chapter seven

Hallie sat at an outdoor café in the Piazza San Giacamo, sipping an orange soda. It was early afternoon and the town was alive with tourists. They were everywhere: prowling the designer boutiques, flipping through postcard stands, buying glass hedgehogs and stacks of silk scarves. Hallie hadn't moved in an hour but the scene kept changing like a kaleidoscope.

Hallie had suffered through last night's feast and stumbled up to bed at two in the morning. She managed to avoid Alfonso and made small talk with the count and marquis, who were seated on either side of her. By the time the waiters had served five courses—goat cheese salad drizzled in olive oil, salmon served on a bed of rice, figs in a sweet wine sauce, and hazelnut gelato for dessert—Hallie thought she was going to fall asleep at the table. She slipped upstairs and tumbled into bed. When she woke, she didn't know what day it was.

Hallie stayed in bed for a long time, listening to the silence. There were no taxis honking their horns, no cars screeching to a stop, no Muni buses chugging up Russian Hill. Hallie touched her lips, remembering Alfonso's kiss, and thought how easy it was to find oneself in an awkward situation.

She picked up her phone and called Peter, smiling at the familiar ring tone.

"How is my *molto bella* girlfriend?" Peter answered on the second ring.

"You don't have to speak Italian." Hallie grinned.

"I bought a phrase book," Peter replied. "I'm thinking of coming over there."

"I thought you had to hold Jim Johnson's hand," Hallie said.

"I heard about a think tank outside Paris. They put five gifted teenagers in a house for two years and teach them computer programming. It's an incubator for geniuses."

"Sounds interesting," Hallie replied.

"They're about to graduate their first batch; I might check it out."

Hallie hesitated. "I'll be home in a month."

"How is Lake Como?" Peter asked. "Have you met many princes and princesses?"

Hallie gulped. She wanted to tell Peter about Alfonso but she couldn't do it over the phone. She had to see his face so she knew he believed her.

"I've only been here twenty-four hours," Hallie said, sighing. "The food is amazing and the scenery is breathtaking."

"We'll return next year on our honeymoon," Peter replied.

"Peter." Hallie's stomach suddenly felt queasy. "I'm still thinking."

"I love you," Peter interrupted. "I'll call you tomorrow."

Hallie hung up and watched the sailboats cut across the lake. She pictured Kendra peeling off Peter's tux jacket. She thought about the diamond-and-ruby engagement ring, and realized her brush with Alfonso didn't make the scene between Peter and Kendra any clearer.

By the time Hallie walked downstairs, wearing a Lilly Pulitzer dress and leather espadrilles, the breakfast dishes had been cleared and the main rooms were empty. Lea told her that Pliny had taken the boat to Verenna, and Sophia was upstairs writing letters. Hallie asked if Lea had seen Portia but Lea shrugged, as if suddenly her English failed her.

The last time Hallie had seen Portia she was sitting on Riccardo's lap, sipping a glass of sambuca. The last guests were clustered on the balcony; men smoked cigars and women curled up against their partners like kittens. Portia had shot Hallie a look that was part victory and part anguish. Hallie wanted to pull Portia aside, but Riccardo's hand gripped Portia's waist as if she was his property.

Hallie had tapped on Portia's door in the morning but there was no answer. She imagined Portia and Riccardo lying under the silk canopy, or perhaps Riccardo had driven Portia back to their villa in Menaggio. Hallie decided to walk into town, thinking Portia hadn't looked like a woman in love, she looked like someone who was desperate.

Sitting in the piazza, nibbling a plate of bruschetta with olive oil, Hallie didn't think about Peter or Portia or Riccardo. She watched the women passing by: fashion plates wearing Pucci dresses and sandals by Prada and Gucci. After lunch she would explore the shoe boutiques and pick up something for Francesca and Constance.

"Lake Como makes the best olive oil in Italy," a voice said behind her. "Tourists think Como is just spectacular gardens and villas, but it is also a center of manufacturing."

Hallie spun around and saw Alfonso. "What are you doing here?" He held a bottle of mineral water in one hand and a plate of polenta in the other.

"I am eating lunch. May I join you?"

"I have a boyfriend." Hallie started to get up. "I don't have lunch with strange men."

"I would never chase a woman who did not want to be caught." Alfonso placed his plate on the table.

"Then why are you here?" Hallie demanded.

"To apologize." Alfonso put a linen napkin in his lap and ate a spoonful of polenta. "The Tesoro family is important to me, I do not want friction between us."

Hallie watched Alfonso eat. He took large bites, wiping his mouth with the napkin and washing it down with mineral water.

"I accept your apology," Hallie said finally.

"*Bennissimo!*" Alfonso's black eyes sparkled. "We will be great friends. Try the polenta, it is the best in Bellagio."

Hallie ate a few spoonfuls of polenta and they chatted about the feast.

"I think Portia left with Riccardo," Hallie mused. "I was too tired, I went to bed."

"He better treat her well or I will slit his throat." Alfonso's eyebrows drew together.

"I thought you said the Tesoros had bad tempers," Hallie said, laughing.

"Marcus gave me my first silk order years ago," Alfonso replied. "And you? Do you have a career like all American women?"

"I'm an interior designer," Hallie replied. "I work at an exclusive design store in San Francisco."

"Today I deliver silk to the finest private villa in Lake Como." Alfonso rested his elbows on the table. "You will come with me."

"Why would I do that?" Hallie asked.

"Because you will see rooms more beautiful than Versailles. The gardens are finer than any in England, and the view will make your heart shiver."

"I'm not sure I trust you," Hallie murmured.

"I gave you my word," Alfonso said seriously. "The villa is in Lenno, we will take a motorboat."

"My grandmother said I should go to Lenno to see the Villa Balbianello," Hallie mused.

"The Villa Balbianello is like a servant's quarters compared to where we are going." Alfonso stood up.

"Okay." She nodded.

"You will not be sorry." Alfonso beamed. "And you can tell me about your work. Perhaps I will export my silk to America."

"Does everybody in Lake Como commute by boat?" Hallie asked.

Hallie sat next to Alfonso in a royal blue speedboat. From the middle of the lake, the villages looked like a collection of dollhouses and the mountain was a sleeping giant.

"It is faster than driving." Alfonso used one hand to navigate and the other to point out landmarks. "By boat, Lenno is ten minutes from Bellagio. By car, we would have to drive around the whole lake."

Hallie closed her eyes and let the wind blow through her hair. Suddenly the boat slowed and the water grew completely calm. Hallie opened her eyes and saw a villa sitting on its own promontory. It was at least four stories with stained-glass windows set high in the walls. There were several separate buildings covered in ivy. It looked like a castle in a fairy tale.

"The Villa Luce." Alfonso steered the boat to the landing. "It was built in 1654 by Cardinal Donato as a monastery. In 1792, it was sold to a French nobleman and his wife who escaped the French revolution. They brought all their furnishings from France and lived in complete seclusion. Lenno is the most private village, it does not have the bustle of Bellagio."

"Who owns it now?" Hallie gazed at the tall turrets, the stone crosses on the smaller buildings, and the green hill studded with olive trees.

"An American billionaire." Alfonso hopped out of the boat. "I have never met him, but he has excellent taste in silk. He has ordered silk curtains for the whole villa."

"I feel like I'm in a James Bond movie." Hallie grinned, following Alfonso up a flight of stone steps.

Alfonso paused at the top step and motioned for Hallie to turn around. "Look." He pointed. "The most beautiful view in Lake Como."

Hallie could see the whole lake from Como to the northern tip. Bellagio was directly opposite them, its steep streets and narrow houses like a child's sketch. The village of Tremezzo lay to the north and Aregeno to the south, cradling Lenno like an infant.

Inside, the house was vast as a museum. While the Tesoro villa was decorated in rich brocades, the Villa Luce was almost austere in design. Hallie followed Alfonso from one long room to another, awed by thick plank floors and beamed ceilings. The furniture was dark and heavy and religious paintings covered the walls.

"You said it looked like Versailles," Hallie said, frowning.

"The French nobleman thought this part of the house was unlucky and closed it up," Alfonso explained. "This is the original monastery furnishings. Wait till you see the main wing."

"There's more?" Hallie asked, feeling like Alice in Wonderland.

"I must go upstairs and take some measurements," Alfonso replied. "Wait here and I will give you a tour."

Hallie walked through a narrow hall lined with figures on the cross. She opened an oak door and suddenly felt like she had slipped into another century. The chandeliers looked so heavy; Hallie wondered how the ceiling supported them. The floor was gold parquet and gold statues lined the room, like guests at a cocktail party.

"You goddamned paparazzi never stop! How did you get in here?" a voice demanded. "If you have a camera I'm going to smash it to bits, and then I'll toss you into the lake."

"I'm not a photographer," Hallie stuttered, afraid to move.

"Journalist?" The man strode toward her. "If you're hiding a tape recorder, I'll shake you till I find it."

"I'm an interior designer," Hallie replied meekly.

"An interior designer?" The man stopped. He was tall with reddish brown hair and almond-shaped hazel eyes. He wore cotton shorts and leather sandals and he had a broad American accent.

"I'm here with a friend, Alfonso Diamante," Hallie explained. "He went upstairs to take some measurements. I was supposed to wait in the monastery."

"Instead you barged in here," the man spluttered. "No one is allowed in the hall of mirrors."

"It is exactly like Versailles," Hallie whispered, glancing at the huge mirrors that stood against the walls.

"It's beautiful, isn't it?" The man's shoulders relaxed. "Are you sure you're not from *OK!* or *HELLO!*"

"I don't even read *OK!*" Hallie opened her purse and took out an embossed card. "Here's my business card. I work for a designer in San Francisco."

"Hallie Elliot," the man read aloud. "I still don't know what you're doing here."

"I'm staying at a villa in Bellagio," Hallie explained. "Alfonso insisted this was the finest villa in Lake Como. He said I had to see it."

"He's right." The man nodded. "But visitors aren't allowed. He shouldn't have brought you."

"I'm sorry." Hallie walked toward the exit. "I can wait outside."

"You're here now." The man extended his hand. "I'm Angus Barlow."

"Are you the owner?" Hallie asked.

"I'm Max Rodale's estate manager." He shoved his hands in his pockets. "My job is to keep out people like you."

"I don't want to get you in trouble," Hallie said, frowning.

"Mr. Rodale is in Florence," Angus said. "The Uffizi Gallery is interested in his Renaissance art collection."

"I studied Renaissance paintings at UCLA," Hallie breathed. "Can I see them?"

"Are you sure you don't have a camera in your buttonhole?" Angus asked.

"I don't even have a button hole." Hallie grinned. "You can search me."

"You have an honest face," Angus relented. "I better not be wrong, or I'll get fired."

Hallie followed Angus through a succession of rooms with polished floors and stately furniture. Every piece was exciting: the authentic Louis XIV chairs, the lacquered cabinets, the gold candelabras. Hallie glanced at the ceiling and saw planets circling the solar system.

"Mr. Rodale has one of the finest private Renaissance collections in Italy." Angus directed Hallie to a small room past the library. "It includes one of Botticelli's earliest works and several little-known paintings by Bellini."

"These are original?" Hallie asked.

Angus nodded. "It's been his life's work for the past decade. Mr. Rodale keeps a very low profile. I'm the only person who sees him."

"The only one?" Hallie repeated.

"He buys his art through dealers and I take care of his personal life," Angus explained. "One of the hardest things is keeping the paparazzi away. You'd think they'd stay busy with George Clooney, but when they smell money they attack like vultures."

"I'm sorry I barged in," Hallie apologized.

"It's nice to have company." Angus smiled. "I only see the gardener and the cook and the butcher every Thursday."

"Can I see more of the villa?" Hallie asked tentatively.

Angus paused, scratching his forehead. "Just the first floor," he said finally. "But please don't touch anything."

Angus showed Hallie the indoor fountains, the grand circular staircase, the bathrooms with marble floors and gold-plated bidets.

"How long has he lived here?" Hallie asked when they stepped onto the balcony. There were a series of terraced gardens leading down to the lake, and a grove of apple trees.

"Four years." Angus leaned on the railing. "He wanted a place where he could build his collection in private. Sometimes I think I should carry a stick and pepper spray. I once found a photographer hiding in an apple tree. He almost landed on my head."

"Collecting priceless art isn't the best way to avoid attention." Hallie grinned.

"I guess it's hard to escape one's passion." Angus shrugged. "I should ask you to leave. Mr. Rodale could return at any time."

"He should display the paintings in a better space," Hallie said as they retraced their steps. "Each painting should have its own wall and be flooded with light."

"Hallie!" Alfonso rushed down the hall. "I thought you vanished."

"I did a little sightseeing on my own," Hallie replied, glancing nervously at the floor.

"I found her in the hall of mirrors," Angus explained. "I thought she was paparazzi. I was about to throw her into the lake."

"I apologize." Alfonso bowed his head. "I wanted to show her the beauty of Villa Luce."

"Don't bring anyone again," Angus replied, suddenly abrupt.

"You have my word," Alfonso mumbled. "But so much beauty should be shared."

"That's not for us to decide," Angus said gruffly. "I'll let you show yourselves out."

Hallie and Alfonso were silent on the trip back to Bellagio. Alfonso was angry that she wandered off, and Hallie's head was spinning at the villa's grandeur. She sat backward in the boat, watching the Villa Luce disappear across the lake. She wanted to call Constance and tell her about the paintings. She opened her purse to take out her phone and realized Angus had kept her business card.

chapter eight

Hallie sat in the front parlor flicking through an *Italian Ar-chitectural Digest*. She hadn't seen Portia since the feast and she was worried about her. Portia's phone went straight to voice mail and her room was empty, the bedspread unruffled.

Hallie's phone buzzed and she answered it without checking the caller ID.

"Hallie, darling," Francesca said. "How is Italy?"

"I thought you were Portia." Hallie frowned. "I haven't seen her in two days."

"Portia's missing?" Francesca replied. "I thought you were going to keep an eye on her."

"Sophia held a feast to celebrate my arrival and Portia left with Riccardo. I haven't seen her since."

"Well, if she's with Riccardo." Francesca hesitated. "That's great news."

Hallie thought about Riccardo's mistress stashed in Milan, about his declaration that he wanted to divorce Portia and marry Veronica.

"I hope so," Hallie murmured, fiddling with the gold tassels on the sofa.

"Tell me everything." Francesca's voice was warm and engaging. "Are Sophia and Pliny treating you well? Have you seen Marcus?"

"Marcus and Angelica are visiting her parents in Tuscany," Hallie replied. "Sophia is still a dragon, but Pliny has been very kind."

"He does have a charming side," Francesca agreed. "I can't imagine Sophia mellowing with age. That would be like the Pope becoming less Catholic."

"I saw the most beautiful villa," Hallie mused. "It's in Lenno and it looks exactly like Versailles."

Since she returned from Villa Luce she hadn't been able to think about anything else. When she closed her eyes she saw the glittering chandeliers and the elaborate frescos. She pictured the bubbling fountains and magnificent chestnut trees.

"Have you thought about Peter?"

"San Francisco seems so far away," Hallie replied. "I don't know how I'll feel when I see him."

"Distances can seem very great or terribly small," Francesca said thoughtfully. "I must go; I have a six-tier vanilla custard wedding cake to deliver."

"How do you fit that into your car?" Hallie giggled, suddenly missing her mother's light vanilla custard and rich chocolate icing.

"Very carefully." Francesca laughed. "Give my love to Portia."

Hallie hung up and flipped through the magazine. She wished she could go for a run on the Marina Green or buy dinner at Safeway; do all the normal things that filled her life. Without Portia, the day stretched ahead like a blank sheet of paper.

"Hallie!" Portia blew in the door. She wore a silver Versace dress and gold Gucci sandals. Her cheeks were tan and her hair tumbled down her back.

"You look very elegant for eleven o'clock in the morning." Hallie smiled. "I take it you didn't run away to the ballet school in Milan."

"I'm sorry I didn't call." Portia threw herself on the sofa. "Riccardo took me to the Villa d'Este. It was such a whirlwind; I didn't even have any clothes. I had to buy this in the gift shop."

Hallie raised her eyebrows. The Villa d'Este was one of the most famous hotels in the world, patronized by kings and rock stars. Hallie had seen pictures and Alfonso had pointed it out from the boat, but she had never been inside.

"We wanted to be together after the feast," Portia explained. "I couldn't take him up to my bedroom."

"Why didn't you go to your villa?"

"Riccardo wanted to do something more romantic." Portia fell back against the cushions. "We ate on the terrace overlooking the floating pool, we danced under the stars. It was like being on honeymoon."

"Are you back together?"

"Riccardo doesn't think we should live together yet," Portia replied evasively.

"You mean he's keeping his mistress in Milan, and humoring you on the side?" Hallie asked, suddenly angry.

"At least he still wants to be married to me," Portia argued. "He didn't mention divorce."

"Villa d'Este is hardly the place you take someone to discuss divorce," Hallie muttered. "Do you want to date your own husband?"

"If Riccardo leaves, no man will want to marry a divorced woman."

"This isn't the Dark Ages." Hallie sighed. "Remember your vows: in sickness and in health, through good times and bad. They didn't say anything about two nights at a five-star resort when you're horny."

"It wasn't just sex." Portia pouted.

"You deserve better; Alfonso agrees."

"When did you see Alfonso?" Portia asked.

"I ran into him in Bellagio yesterday. He took me to see the most amazing private villa. He said you always brought home bad boys."

"Alfonso and Marcus think they know everything." Portia shrugged. "Men are like little boys, they are good and bad at the same time."

"A husband isn't a child." Hallie closed the magazine. "Let's go exploring. I'd love to see the castle at Varenna."

"Are you trying to get my mind off Riccardo?" Portia asked suspiciously. "You think I'll meet some romantic Frenchman and fly off to the City of Lights?"

"It could happen." Hallie grinned.

Portia shook her head. "A Tesoro has to marry an Italian."

"Pliny married Francesca," Hallie protested.

"When he was a university student on a ski vacation." Portia sighed. "Sophia didn't know about it until he carried Francesca over the threshold."

"It's your life," Hallie argued.

"But it's the Tesoro name," Portia mumbled. "I'll go upstairs and change and then we'll sightsee. Promise that you won't say anything bad about Riccardo."

Hallie looked at Portia's narrow cheekbones, her dark luminous eyes. She saw pain and joy flit across her face. She crossed her fingers behind her back and nodded.

Hallie and Portia sat in the Piazza San Giorgio, sharing a wood-fired pizza. They spent all day exploring Varenna, climbing higher until they reached the ruins of the Castello di Vezio. They learned about Queen Theodolina who was sentenced to death in the seventh century, and imagined what it would be like to know your days were numbered when you were surrounded by so much beauty.

Hallie thought maybe Portia was right about Riccardo. Portia was almost her old self. When they reached the Castello di Vezio, Hallie was breathless from the long hike, but Portia twirled around the ruins like it was a stage. Portia ran all the way down to the Piazza San Giorgio like a child testing a new bicycle, while Hallie navigated the uneven cobblestones, trying not to feel dizzy.

Now, sitting in the charming square surrounded by its medieval buildings and stone fountain, Portia devoured her pizza like a teenager. She washed it down with a glass of wine and licked olive oil and tomato sauce from her fingers.

"I had forgotten what sex does for the appetite." Portia smiled wickedly. "I'm going to have a double scoop of gelato for dessert."

"I'm glad Riccardo is good for something," Hallie said warily.

"You promised you wouldn't say anything bad about Riccardo." Portia scowled. "Tell me about the fabulous villa you saw yesterday."

"It's owned by a man named Max Rodale. He's a complete recluse. The dimensions of the rooms were overwhelming," Hallie replied, picturing the smooth gold floors and dramatic ceilings.

"Lake Como is full of mysterious villas," Portia said, and shrugged. "I'm going to get a gelato, would you like some?"

Hallie shook her head and waited for Portia to return. She sipped sparkling water and watched tourists try on souvenir T-shirts. She saw a tall man flipping through magazines at the newsstand. He paid for the magazine and walked toward her, his hands stuffed in his pockets.

"You're the intruder." He stopped at her table, frowning in the late-afternoon sun.

Hallie noticed that his eyes had yellow flecks, and his hair was the color of chestnuts. "Interior designer, not intruder," she mumbled, swallowing a bite of pizza.

"Are you sure you're not following me?" Angus smiled. He wore beige shorts and a plain black T-shirt and carried a cloth shopping bag.

"I'm sightseeing," Hallie replied. "What are you doing here?"

"Max likes a special olive oil they only sell in Varenna," Angus explained. "I take the opportunity to stock up on American magazines. I miss reading about the Red Sox."

"I love everything Italian." Hallie wiped her mouth with a napkin. "They don't sell pizza like this in North Beach."

"May I sit down?" Angus pointed to the empty chair. "I want to ask you something."

"Sure." Hallie nodded. "But I promise I didn't take any pictures of Villa Luce, you can search my phone."

Angus sat opposite her, cramming his long legs under the table. "I mentioned to Max your suggestion about the paintings."

"What suggestion?"

"About housing them in a bigger space," Angus replied.

"I'm gone two minutes and you give away my chair?" Portia demanded, licking a cone of rainbow gelato.

Hallie blushed. "This is Angus Barlow. I met him yesterday at the Villa Luce."

"You didn't tell me the villa came with a sexy estate manager." Portia fluttered dark eyelashes.

"Am I interrupting?" Angus started to get up.

"Please stay." Portia pulled up another chair. "I love to listen to American accents."

"Max thought it was a great idea; he's been thinking about redoing the monastery wing for some time," Angus continued.

"Alfonso said the original owner closed it up because it was unlucky," Hallie said, frowning.

"There is a story about an unfaithful noblewoman buried under the floor." Angus shrugged.

"Italian men." Portia shivered. "Treating their wives like chattel."

"That was four centuries ago." Hallie turned to Angus. "I think that's a wonderful idea."

"Max wondered if you'd be interested in designing the whole wing," Angus replied.

"Me?" Hallie stammered.

"He checked out your work online," Angus continued. "You could set your own budget and make all the decisions."

Hallie pictured the villa perched above the lake like Sleeping Beauty's castle. She saw the endless halls like reflections in a funhouse mirror. She imagined combing stores in Milan for fine silks, traveling to Paris for Louis XIV armoires.

"That's a huge job," she said finally. "It would take months."

"And Hallie would love to do it," Portia broke in. "She has nothing but time."

"It's a tremendous opportunity," Hallie murmured. "But I didn't plan on staying that long."

"Will you think about it?" Angus asked.

Hallie watched a couple walk by sharing a slice of pizza. She saw a boy and girl fight over an ice-cream cone, two scoops falling on the cobblestones. She watched a young man in a leather jacket buy a dozen roses at a flower stall.

Hallie turned to Angus and nodded. "I'll think about it."

"I've got your card." Angus pushed his chair back, smiling. "I'll call you."

"Did you forget that I have a job and a boyfriend at home?" Hallie asked when Angus disappeared down the alley to the boat dock.

"You've been saying for years you want your own design firm," Portia replied. "If you have the Villa Luce on your resumé, clients will line up to work with you."

Hallie pictured showing Libby Taylor or Patsy Mane photos of Villa Luce. She imagined them clamoring to use the same drapes and furniture in their Pacific Heights mansions.

"What about Peter?" Hallie demanded.

"You can Skype him every night." Portia shrugged. "If he wants to see you, he can hop on a plane and be here in ten hours."

The young man in the leather jacket approached their table. He presented Hallie and Portia with two red roses and murmured, *"Ciao, Bellissima."*

Portia picked up her rose and grinned. "It looks like you have a new admirer."

Hallie sat at the desk in her room, waiting for the dinner bell to sound. After they returned from Varenna, she took a long bath and slathered her skin with Acqua di Parma. She put on a navy silk dress with Gucci pumps and a white leather belt. Glancing in the mirror she felt young and sophisticated, but her stomach was filled with butterflies.

She opened her laptop, suddenly missing Peter's boyish smile. She clicked on Facebook and saw photos of Peter cycling, drinking a beer with his buddies after a race.

She clicked through to Kendra's page and saw pictures of the Symphony Summer Ball. She saw Patsy Mane and her new husband, Libby Taylor sporting a baby bump, Kendra wearing vintage Dior.

She scrolled through photos of San Francisco's young elite: Mark Zuckerberg and his fiancée, Marissa Mayer and her husband, Jennifer and Gavin Newsom. Suddenly she froze. There was a picture of Kendra and Peter, their heads tilted toward each other.

Hallie searched through the photos faster. There were pictures of Kendra with a dozen men, all in the same intimate poses. She flipped back to the picture of Kendra and Peter to see if she could read some signal in their eyes. They both looked directly into the camera, smiling clean white smiles.

Hallie shut the computer and paced around the room. Of course Peter had been at the ball, it was packed with Silicon Valley techno-celebrities. She inhaled sharply, trying to erase the seed of doubt that formed hard and jagged as a diamond.

She wanted to call Peter but it was five in the morning in San Francisco. Her phone buzzed and she answered, not recognizing the number.

"Hallie?" a man asked. "It's Angus. I wondered if you thought about the job."

Hallie walked onto the balcony. The lake was forest green and the villages hugged the shore like colored Lego sets. She breathed deeply, filling her lungs with cool, alpine air.

"I can't say no." She hugged her arms around her chest. "It sounds wonderful."

chapter nine

Hallie put down her tape measure and tapped notes into her computer. She had worked at the Villa Luce for a week, arriving each morning as Angus set out two cups of steaming hot espresso. She showed him her sketches and then he disappeared into the endless rooms of the villa. Hallie was left alone to mull over fabric and wallpaper swatches, to draw pictures of marble fireplaces and crystal chandeliers.

The ideas came so fast; Hallie had trouble getting them down. At night she kept a pad by her bed, scribbling designs before she was fully awake. She rose before Sophia or Pliny appeared downstairs and walked to the ferry terminal. Pliny offered to take her in the motorboat, but she loved the delicious quiet of the lake in the morning. She sat in the back of the ferry, straining to see Villa Luce as the mist cleared.

Constance had been distraught when Hallie called to tell her she was staying in Lake Como.

"Six months," Constance's voice wavered. "You'll miss the fall season. Who will I take to the opera?"

"You can ask Francesca," Hallie replied. She sat at her dressing table, brushing her straight, blond hair.

"Francesca won't see any opera that's performed in Italian." Constance sighed. "It sounds wonderful, but are you sure it's what you want to do?"

"You told me to come to Como and be with Portia," Hallie argued.

"But she's seeing Riccardo again," Constance replied. "Does Peter know you're staying so long?"

Hallie put the hairbrush down. "I'm going to call him next."

"I'll ask Peter to the opera," Constance decided. "We can discuss the wedding. We'll have to move quickly, if you want to get married next summer."

Hallie looked in the mirror, picturing a scooped neckline and a white gauze veil. "The villa is like a siren," she explained. "I have to do it."

"Then I'm proud of you," Constance replied. "Send me lots of pictures."

Hallie hung up, feeling guilty for not telling Constance that she still had doubts. Peter and the apartment on Russian Hill seemed so far away, as if they were part of a movie she had watched on the plane. When she closed her eyes to picture the Bay Bridge, she saw speedboats zipping across Lake Como. She craved paella and risotto instead of cheeseburgers and enchiladas.

"You're doing what?" Peter demanded. "Hallie, are you crazy?"

"Any designer would kill for this job," Hallie replied with more bravado than she felt. It took two cups of Lea's strong dark coffee for Hallie to get up the nerve to call him.

"You live in San Francisco," Peter snapped. "The job is in Italy."

"Would you turn down writing a biography of Bill Gates because he lives in Seattle?"

"Italy is another continent, another time zone," Peter pleaded. "I can't be without you."

"If you saw it you'd understand; it's a magnificent canvas and I can choose the materials." Hallie brushed her hair with slow, methodical strokes.

"I will come," Peter insisted. "Next month, after I wrap up my exposé of Apple."

Hallie couldn't sleep, thinking she had made a terrible mistake. But lying in bed staring at the angels painted on the ceiling, she knew that six months apart would be good for them. She would discover if she truly missed Peter or just the idea of him.

"Am I interrupting?" Angus poked his head in the door.

Hallie started. She never saw Angus during the workday. He was usually directing the staff or running errands in Tremezzo or Menaggio.

"I'm choosing colors for the anteroom," Hallie explained. "Powder blue walls and black-and-white marble floors."

"I like it." Angus nodded. "I wondered if you wanted to have lunch with me. The cook made shrimp paella, and it smells delicious."

Hallie hesitated. She planned a buying trip to Milan and was anxious to complete her sketches. But she hadn't eaten lunch and her morning espresso carved a hole in her stomach.

"I'm starving," Hallie admitted. "And I'm addicted to shrimp paella."

Hallie followed Angus out to the balcony. A table was set with a checkered tablecloth and white china. Silver tongs rested in a ceramic salad bowl. There was a loaf of bread, a jar of olive oil, and a plate of mixed berries.

Angus returned from the kitchen with two plates heaped with shrimp paella. Hallie ate greedily, mopping up rice with crusty bread and sprinkling brown sugar on the berries.

"This is delicious." Hallie put down her spoon. "I'll have to ask the cook for her recipe."

"I'm actually the cook." Angus tore off a chunk of bread and dipped it in olive oil. "When Bella has a day off, I love messing around in the kitchen. Max is a vegetarian, and I make too much food for one person."

"This is a curious place to be a vegetarian." Hallie gazed at the fishing boats out on the lake. "Am I going to meet Mr. Rodale?"

"Everyone asks that." Angus poured a glass of sparkling cider. "He's not the hunchback of Notre Dame, he's just very private."

"How did you meet him?" Hallie asked. All week she had wondered about her employer, searching the villa for clues to his personality. But there were no family photos, no worn books on the bookshelf, no framed awards or diplomas.

"On a train from Naples to Rome," Angus replied. "I grew up outside Boston, studied archaeology at a tiny New England college, and joined a dig in Athens. When that ended, I moved to a dig in Cyprus and then Pompeii. That's how I learned to cook. At the end of the day, it was every man for himself."

"I've always been fascinated by Pompeii," Hallie said. "All those children frozen in ashes."

"Archaeology is more fun in textbooks than in real life." Angus shrugged. "It's years of living in tents and sifting through dirt. If you're lucky you find one gold coin. I started craving indoor plumbing. Mr. Rodale was looking for an estate manager and I accepted."

"It must be an interesting job." Hallie glanced at Angus curiously. He seemed too educated, too intense, to spend his life picking up another man's laundry.

"Is that a nice way of saying I'm wasting my degree?" Angus grinned. "In Lake Como I'm surrounded by history. Lenno has churches that date back to the twelfth century." Angus paused. "How about you? Have you wanted to be a designer since you were a little girl in pigtails?"

"I used to draw on all my schoolbooks," Hallie said, smiling. "Lake Como is so beautiful, every villa is a work of art."

"It's Shangri-la." Angus nodded. "The mountains keep out the world, and the lake is bursting with life. You could eat locally grown foods every day."

"If I'm not careful, I'll get fat." Hallie pushed away her plate. "I should get back to work. Would you like to see what I've done?"

Angus cleared away the plates and Hallie turned on her computer. She clicked through plans for each room: ceilings the color of Wedgwood china, drapes like spun gold.

Angus was quiet and Hallie glanced up, nervous that he didn't like her designs. But when she saw his face, his red hair swept over his forehead, his hazel eyes and sharp nose, she realized he wasn't looking at the computer. He was staring at her. Hallie turned quickly away, and described how she was going to hang the Botticelli.

Portia called as Hallie waited for the ferry. It was early evening and the ferry terminal was full of families returning from the beach, carrying buckets full of sand.

"Meet me at the Hotel du Lac for dinner," Portia demanded before Hallie could say hello.

"When?" Hallie asked.

"Now," Portia replied. "I'm waiting in the bar."

"I'm not dressed for dinner." Hallie glanced at her cotton skirt and leather sandals. "And I ate too much shrimp paella at lunch."

"Please, Hallie, I need to talk to you."

"Where's Riccardo?" Hallie frowned. Hallie had barely seen Portia all week. Portia and Riccardo spent two nights at the

Gritti Palace in Venice. Portia returned with new diamond earrings and a bottle of expensive perfume.

"He's going to meet me after dinner," Portia replied.

"Can we talk at home?" Hallie sighed. "I'd love a hot bath."

"I'll order you a drink." Portia hung up before Hallie could protest.

Hallie entered the Hotel du Lac and glanced around the room. Women wore skimpy cocktail dresses and stiletto heels. Their skin was golden brown and their mouths were dark shades of red. She found Portia at the bar, sucking down a martini.

Portia spun around on the barstool. "I saved you a seat."

"It looks like you're on a liquid diet." Hallie pointed to the empty glasses lined up on the bar.

"I got a head start." Portia giggled. "But you can catch up."

"Is that a new dress?" Hallie asked. Portia wore a gray silk dress with an ivory sash. She had silver sandals on her feet and a diamond bracelet around her wrist.

"It's vintage Valentino." Portia caressed the folds of the skirt. "We spent one night at the W in Milan. Riccardo gave me the dress and the bracelet."

"You're running out of hotels." Hallie sipped an apple martini. "You should live together, like most married couples."

"Riccardo wants to live together." Portia glanced at Hallie with big, liquid eyes.

"And give up Veronica?" Hallie asked.

"I don't know. But he doesn't want a divorce."

"That's wonderful," Hallie said tentatively.

"Sophia and Pliny will be very happy," Portia mumbled.

"You don't look happy." Hallie frowned. "Maybe Riccardo's mistress does bother you. You're not as European as you think."

"I just lock Veronica up in a compartment that I don't let myself open." Portia shrugged. "There's something I haven't told you."

"You have a dashing Englishman who's going to carry you off to a remote castle on the moor?" Hallie giggled.

"You read too much Charlotte Brontë." Portia rolled her eyes. "Let's get a table. I need a plate of pasta."

Hallie and Portia sat at a table on the terrace. Hallie watched couples stroll along the promenade. The men smoked cigarettes and the women clicked narrow heels on the gravel.

Hallie ordered gnocchi in a cream sauce and Portia ate tagliarini with prawns. They shared a bottle of red wine and a loaf of garlic bread.

"It's hard to be unhappy with such good food and wine," Hallie mused.

"*La dolce vita.*" Portia raised her glass.

"May you and Riccardo live happily ever after and have many bambinos."

Portia put her glass down abruptly. She stabbed the pasta with her fork and looked at Hallie.

"Riccardo left me because I'm afraid of having children," Portia murmured. "He'll only stay married on the condition that we have a baby."

"I thought he was in love with Veronica."

"He always has a Veronica." Portia shrugged. "His women are like newspapers. He discards them when he's done."

"Then what's the problem?" Hallie frowned. "Children will give you gray hairs and ruin the furniture, but they are very rewarding."

"I'm afraid I'd be a terrible mother." Portia held her glass so tightly, Hallie thought it would snap. "I would run away like Francesca and abandon my children."

"Francesca was so young," Hallie replied. "She was far away from Constance and San Francisco. The Tesoro villa was like a prison, she had to escape."

"But what if I'm just like her?" Portia demanded. "What if the baby is ugly or cries too much and I can't stand it? I've always sworn I'd never have children. That's why I wanted to be a dancer."

"I don't understand."

"When Francesca left I was barely one. Marcus said I lay in my cot and cried for Mama every night. When I was three, I asked him where Mama went. Marcus told me she went to America because she didn't love us."

"Why would he do that?"

"It was the only way to shut me up," Portia replied. "I couldn't understand how a mother could live away from her children. I hated her for so long. If I did the same thing, my children would hate me. I could never live with myself."

Hallie pictured young Portia, big green eyes and hair like a gypsy, running around the villa searching for her mother. "You wouldn't do the same thing. You're almost thirty, you have a good husband. You have Pliny and your grandmother and all your friends."

"Sometimes I get so angry at Riccardo, I want to stab him in the chest." Portia's eyes flashed. "What if I got sick of his women and had to leave? I couldn't take my children with me. I'd do just what Francesca did, I'd desert them."

"I'm sorry," Hallie mumbled, her eyes filling with tears.

"You didn't have anything to do with it." Portia tried to smile. "I was nine when I saw Francesca. By then I was a little girl who never had a mother."

"You seemed so worldly," Hallie mused. "I remember the first time you stayed at Constance's; you told me about the discos in Rome you could go to when you were ten."

"I was going to be the most famous ballerina since Anna Pavlova," Portia replied. "They were going to name a cake after me."

"Chocolate cake with rich vanilla custard," Hallie said lightly. "Do Sophia and Pliny know?"

"They would chain me to the bed until Riccardo and I made a baby." Portia shook her head.

"Why didn't you tell Riccardo when you married him?" Hallie asked.

"No Italian man would marry a woman who didn't want children." Portia finished her wine. "I thought I would change my mind. I thought once we were married I would want a little Riccardo or Portia. But I just see a little girl running through a villa crying for her mother. I can't take the chance of ruining a child's life."

"What are you going to do?" Hallie asked.

Portia refilled her wineglass and slumped in her chair. "I have no idea."

Hallie and Portia shared a dark chocolate cake in raspberry sauce. They had been sitting for an hour, mulling over Portia's problem. They were both blurry with wine and full of pasta and bread.

Hallie watched a young couple stroll along the promenade. The woman wore a wedding dress: creamy white satin, pearl beads, and a large ivory bow. The groom wore a black tux, white tie, and shiny black shoes. A photographer trailed them, posing them on the steps of the hotel.

Hallie thought about the weddings she had attended this summer: the ballrooms lit with twinkling lights, the pink wedding cakes, the glasses of sparkling champagne. She remembered the thrill of arriving on Peter's arm, confident that next year it would be her and Peter standing before the priest.

"They make it look so easy." Hallie pointed to the bride and groom. "Smile for the camera and live happily ever after."

"Weddings are like theater," Portia agreed. "A magnificent stage, wonderful costumes, music, applause. Marriage is like the actors backstage, constantly arguing about their lines. We were better off when marriages were arranged."

"Constance is busy planning my wedding." Hallie sighed. "I don't have the heart to stop her."

"Did you tell Peter yes?"

"I haven't told him anything." Hallie watched the bride and groom kiss. "I saw a picture of him and Kendra on Facebook. I'm sure it was innocent but it ties my stomach in knots."

"We're going to have a slumber party." Portia suddenly jumped up. "We're going to pull out my Bangles CDs and dance and forget about men."

"What about Riccardo?" Hallie asked, remembering Portia as a girl with neon nail polish and white plastic go-go boots.

"I'll see him tomorrow." Portia threw a wad of euros on the table and waltzed down the steps. "Tonight I'm going to be a little girl dreaming about being a ballerina."

"Can we jump on the bed and play air guitar?" Hallie laughed.

"We'll put up my old Enrique Iglesias poster and cover it with lipstick kisses," Portia replied.

"I wish I brought my bridal Barbie." Hallie giggled, running to catch up with Portia on the promenade.

chapter ten

Hallie slipped on a green Tory Burch sundress and glanced in the mirror. She and Portia had stayed up all night, singing along to David Cassidy and Justin Timberlake. They passed around a bottle of raspberry cassis, finally falling asleep fully dressed on Portia's king-sized bed.

When Hallie woke, the French doors were wide open and Hallie could hear speedboats zipping across the lake. Portia had left a note saying that she was going for a spin in Riccardo's new Lamborghini. Lea knocked on the door and informed Hallie that Sophia would like to see her in her study.

Hallie brushed her hair, feeling like a young girl called to see the principal. She remembered sitting in the drab school hall, waiting to hear her punishment. Her infractions were never larger than chewing bubble gum or passing notes during chapel, but the headmistress, with her steel gray hair and flowing robes, filled Hallie with terror.

Hallie knocked on the door and waited for an invitation to enter. The room had dark wood floors and a high, beamed ceiling. A painting of the Madonna and a round-faced infant filled one wall.

"Is that a Raphael?" Hallie moved closer to the painting.

"When he was a student," Sophia affirmed. "Raphael is the greatest painter Italy ever produced. You must go to the Vatican and see the School of Athens."

"The villa I am designing has the most wonderful Renaissance art collection," Hallie murmured. "You would love the Botticelli."

"I have a Botticelli in the library, I will show it to you." Sophia took off her reading glasses and studied Hallie. "You are a good influence on Portia; I am pleased."

Hallie exhaled like a child who received a new doll when she was expecting to have her toys taken away.

"I'm afraid we kept you awake last night." Hallie smiled. "We're not very good singers."

"Singing is better than staying locked in one's room, refusing to eat." Sophia twisted a large sapphire ring around her finger. "Portia is seeing Riccardo."

"I know."

"They must move in together and this will all be forgotten," Sophia continued. "A blemish in the first flush of marriage."

"I'm not sure Portia is ready to live with Riccardo," Hallie stammered.

"This is not the time for courtship," Sophia replied. "Portia will be thirty, it is time to start a family."

Hallie remembered Portia's big, frightened eyes, her narrow, trembling shoulders. She wanted to say not all women wanted babies; some couples stayed happily married for decades without children. But Sophia's eyes were hard as thumbtacks.

"Portia should wait till Marcus's wife has her baby," Hallie suggested. "Angelica can teach her everything she learns."

"Tesoros have lived in Lake Como for four hundred years," Sophia replied as if Hallie hadn't spoken. "Portia knows her duty."

Hallie glanced around the room, looking for some way to change the subject. She saw Constance's present, sitting on the desk wrapped in gold paper.

"Did you like your gift?" Hallie asked.

"Your grandmother is very thoughtful." Sophia nodded. "We found we had much in common when she stayed at the villa. We both admire the poetry of Christina Rossetti."

Hallie blinked, trying to imagine Constance and Sophia sipping espresso and discussing Romantic poetry.

"I must write to Constance and thank her," Sophia continued. "It is curious that a woman as cultured as Constance could produce a wild child like Francesca."

Hallie clenched her hands. She sat up straight so Sophia wouldn't see her flinch. "That was thirty years ago. Francesca has a successful wedding cake business."

"A baker." Sophia's eyes narrowed. "Young people make mistakes, it is left to their elders to correct them."

Hallie kept her expression neutral. She wanted to get away from Sophia and breathe the fresh lake air. She wanted to run down to the shore and watch children play on the beach and see fishermen catch their dinner.

"Come." Sophia stood up. "I will show you the Botticelli."

Hallie followed Sophia down the grand staircase to the library. Every inch of wall was covered in books; they were stacked so high Hallie wondered how anyone reached them. Some were bound in leather; others were black with yellowed pages. There was a section of history books, art books, and thick, gold Bibles.

"My grandfather started his collection one hundred years ago." Sophia ran her knobby fingers over leather bindings. "He cataloged every book: French poetry, British drama, the Renaissance, the Middle Ages."

"I would love to borrow a book on the Renaissance," Hallie murmured, flipping through a coffee table book on Michelangelo.

Sophia shook her head. "The books do not leave this room. But you are welcome to sit and read. Return each volume where you found it."

Sophia placed the book of Rossetti's poems on the shelf next to Elizabeth Barrett Browning. She showed Hallie the Botticelli in its ornate gold frame.

"I must check in with Lea," Sophia announced. "Riccardo and Portia are joining us for dinner."

Hallie waited till Sophia's footsteps faded, and then she approached the bookshelf. She remembered the hours she spent in Constance's library, reading Nancy Drew and Judy Blume. She would curl up on the floral sofa and eat Jelly Bellys as she turned the pages.

Hallie took down books on Donatello and da Vinci. She poured over Michelangelo's sketches and pictures of Bellini's statues. She moved from shelf to shelf, forgetting that she hadn't eaten breakfast. There were volumes of Dante, Baudelaire, and Machiavelli. Hallie took down a book with a familiar gray cover. It was a dog-eared copy of *The Water Babies,* the only book Francesca read to her when she was a child.

Constance usually supervised Hallie's bedtime, reading a big book of Grimm's fairy tales. But every now and then Francesca would take over, and read the same book at the same page. Hallie never got tired of the adventures of the water babies, thrilled to have Francesca's complete attention.

Hallie slid *The Water Babies* back on the shelf but it wouldn't fit snugly into its place. Hallie put her hand in the empty space and felt a book spine pressed against the wood. She reached in and pulled out a notebook with a purple cover.

"Dear Diary" was written in cursive, and underneath, the words "Property of Francesca Playfair." Hallie turned the notebook over carefully. Her mother never wrote more than cake recipes; what inspired her to keep a diary?

Hallie wanted to open it, yet she felt as though she was spying. But she couldn't put it back on the shelf, even if it was just girlish scribble. She sat in the leather armchair, tucked her feet under her, and turned the page.

January 15, 1980

Dear Diary,

We are headed for Gstaad! I'm traveling with Dolly and Grazia and Mercedes and staying at Grazia's parents' chalet.

I have been at Madame Lille's Ecole for four months and this is our first ski trip. The girls say Gstaad is wall-to-wall men; they come from Zurich and Geneva and Rome and they drive Ferraris and dress like movie stars.

I must put you away, Dear Diary, Grazia's father's chauffeur is waiting in his Bentley.

The next entry was dated a week later and began with a red heart.

January 22, 1980

Dear Diary,

I am in love! His name is Pliny Tesoro, he is a friend of Grazia's brother, and he has dark skin and curly black hair. He wants to take me tobogganing tonight. He is so handsome, like Warren Beatty, I can't believe he wants to go out with me!

Hallie glanced up as if expecting Sophia or Pliny to stride into the room. She turned to the next entry, promising herself she would read just a few more pages, until Sophia rang the bell for lunch.

January 22, 1980

Dear Diary,

We had to cancel our tobogganing; a blizzard has blown in, making the village look like a scene in a snow globe. Pliny is arriving in a few minutes and we are going to walk into the village and eat cheese and pumpernickel bread. Diary, he is so gorgeous! If he kisses me, I'm going to melt like a brand-new snowflake.

January 22, 1980

Dear Diary,

What a night! First we strolled the shops, and Pliny in-sisted on buying me a Courrèges ski suit and a pair of après-ski boots. I told him Constance gave me enough Swiss francs to paper my bedroom, but he said a gentleman always buys a lady gifts.

We went to a bistro and shared cheese fondue and apricot strudel and he told me about his villa in Lake Como. It has a private beach and swimming pool and its own chapel. He said he must take me there; we'll jet ski on the lake and stroll along the promenade in Bellagio.

We walked back to the chalet and Mercedes was sitting in the parlor. She offered Pliny a cup of coffee and he was too polite to decline, so we sat and talked about the ski condi-tions. Finally I walked Pliny to the door and we stood outside and kissed. He is a wonderful kisser, I never wanted to stop! His lips are soft and he whispers in my ear in Italian.

January 23, 1980

Dear Diary,

We are officially snowed in! The lifts are shut down and the roads are closed. Grazia rolled up the rugs and invited everyone we know to dance and drink schnapps.

Pliny looked so handsome in black ski pants and a red ribbed sweater. He has reserved a room at the Palace Hotel! We are going to drink Courvoisier and roast chestnuts by the fire.

I am going to leave you here, Dear Diary; it would not be polite to spy. I am so in love, every time I look at him my heart expands. Pray that we have a wonderful, romantic night! I will give you a full report in the morning.

Hallie heard the bell announcing lunch and shut the notebook quickly. She closed her eyes, picturing Francesca in furry après-ski boots, walking into the Palace Hotel with Pliny. They were both young—younger than Hallie was now—both beautiful and rich.

For the first time Hallie wondered what would have happened if Pliny and Francesca stayed together. Hallie would never have been born but Portia wouldn't be so skittish, so dependent on approval from Sophia or Riccardo. Hallie imagined Francesca living in Lake Como, and thought about what could have happened to make her leave.

Hallie flipped through the last pages of the notebook. Perhaps Francesca became pregnant that night and Pliny had to marry her. Maybe they weren't in love; it was just a holiday romance. Hallie heard the lunch bell ring again. She would read the last entry, and then she would join the others at the table.

January 24, 1980

Dear Diary,

We are married! It was so sudden and romantic. I cannot tell anyone, not even Constance, until we tell Pliny's mother. Pliny and I are going to Lake Como as soon as the roads clear, and I will be presented to Sophia.

The Palace Hotel sits right on the mountain, I could see the slopes from our balcony. Pliny ordered room service and we ate truffles and salmon. For dessert we shared flambé and chocolate-covered cherries.

After dinner Pliny took my hand and said he never felt like this before. I am like a young Audrey Hepburn and he can't take his eyes off me. Can you imagine, Diary! The most beautiful man I've ever met in love with me.

He said all the girls he knows smoke cigarettes and wear false eyelashes, and I smell like toothpaste and my eyes are liquid pools.

I let him talk, he's so gorgeous to look at, and suddenly he got down on one knee and proposed. I protested that we've only known each other a few days, but he insisted the moment we met he knew he had to marry me. I laughed, but he just knelt there and I realized he was serious. I nodded yes, and he called the concierge and told them to send up a priest.

Pliny told me to wait and I sat looking at the snow, nervous and excited. He returned with a beautiful dress—white lace with pearl buttons—and white satin slippers like Cinderella.

He gave me the most exquisite diamond ring he bought at the hotel gift shop—he said Sophia would give me the Tesoro ruby when we arrived in Lake Como—but I couldn't get married without a ring.

So I am Princess Francesca Tesoro. Isn't it funny that my name sounds Italian? Maybe Constance knew when I was born I was destined to live in Italy. I can't believe we're married, but I know we will be deliriously happy.

I know you want to know if we "did it" last night after the priest performed the ceremony. Now that I am a princess, I must practice decorum; so I will just say I'm glad you were tucked away in my bedside drawer. There are some things I cannot describe.

Hallie closed the diary. She remembered Francesca's stories about Phillip Elliot and thought he had been the great love of her life. But reading the diary, it seemed like Francesca had given her whole heart to Pliny. Could Sophia have been such a dragon that she chased Francesca away?

Hallie tucked the diary back on the shelf, and her fingers bumped up against a pile of books. She pulled them out and discovered four more notebooks tied with a purple ribbon. Hallie untied the ribbon and quickly checked the dates. The diaries began in 1980 and ended in 1982—the years Francesca spent in Lake Como.

Hallie ran up to her room. She tucked the notebooks into the bottom of her suitcase and covered them with clothes. Then she walked downstairs to join Sophia and Pliny for lunch.

chapter eleven

Hallie sat on her bed and opened the diary. She had been reading all afternoon, only stopping to walk onto the balcony and breathe the balmy air. Portia had wanted her to go to the outdoor markets in Tremezzo, but Hallie couldn't pull herself away from the notebooks.

The first pages were full of descriptions of the lake and the villa. Francesca had been besotted by the quaint villages, the emerald waters, and the imposing mountains. There were pages and pages of meals in intimate trattorias, visits to castles and ruins high above the shore.

Francesca wrote that Sophia had been furious with Pliny and treated Francesca like an intruder. Sophia barely nodded when she passed Francesca in the halls, until Francesca started throwing up in the marble bathroom. The village doctor confirmed her pregnancy and Sophia grudgingly offered her congratulations.

The mood in the villa changed and Francesca became the center of attention. The local aristocracy came to pay their respects, and Sophia held a celebration to announce the marriage. She skipped over the fact that Francesca was American, and lauded her dark coloring and Catholic upbringing.

Even when Francesca wrote about heartburn and indigestion, clothes that were too tight, and the impossibility of the language, she seemed happy. Pliny brought her presents and Sophia kept her distance, making sure she drank tall glasses of milk before bed.

Francesca stopped writing when she was eight months pregnant. Her last entry said she could barely hold a pen because her fingers were so swollen, and all she wanted to do was sleep. She scribbled two pages of boy names in big, curly letters and added a few girl names at the bottom.

The second notebook began six weeks after Marcus was born and Francesca's tone was completely different. Sophia insisted she give birth at home and the labor had gone on for two days. When Francesca finally delivered Marcus, the doctor gave her Valium that knocked her out so quickly she didn't get to hold the baby.

Marcus was given to a wet nurse and Francesca wasn't allowed near him. She sobbed for days, complaining that her breasts would explode with milk. But Sophia was adamant. Tesoro women did not nurse their babies. Francesca implored Pliny to step in but he refused. Tesoro women had used wet nurses for centuries and it was not up to them to change the custom. Francesca's milk would subside. She would get her figure back quickly, come and go as she pleased, accompany Pliny to dinners and performances in Milan. Francesca wrote that she saw a new side of Pliny that disturbed her.

January 10, 1981

> *Dear Diary,*
> *I do not know this man who is my husband. He has become a little boy, squarely under the thumb of Sophia. She is like a figure out of the Middle Ages. She gives me lists of*

people I need to call on. She tells me how to dress, whether I should wear my hair up or down, how to sip my wine.

When I was pregnant Sophia left me alone, and Pliny was so solicitous, making sure I was comfortable. But now everything is about Marcus, the future prince, and how I must make a good impression on the residents of Bellagio.

The other day I went into the village and chatted with Gina, the woman who sells vegetables at the outdoor market. I showed her pictures of Marcus and she shared photos of her new baby.

Sophia accosted me the minute I returned to the villa. One of her friends had seen me talking to Gina. Sophia said I must never mingle with shopkeepers, and I was forbidden to share photos of Marcus without her permission.

I pulled Pliny into the salon and begged him to intervene. He looked from me to his mother and said nothing. Finally he turned to Sophia and apologized. He said he would teach me that the Tesoros were aristocracy and only conversed with people of their class.

Diary, I was speechless! I wanted to pack my bags and run home to Constance. Constance is on the Symphony Board and Friends of the Ballet, but I have seen her invite Louisa to sit down for tea. She always has kind words for the gardener and she gives him roses for his wife.

I understand if Sophia is rigid and set in her ways, but Pliny is my husband! He should have defended me.

Hallie walked onto the balcony and watched the gardeners clip the tops of the hedges. She pictured Francesca, young, inexperienced, a new mother in a foreign country. She imagined Sophia in a black silk dress, emerald necklace around her neck, her expression stern and forbidding. Francesca must have felt so alone without Pliny's support. She went back inside and continued to read.

April 15, 1981

Dear Diary,

It is getting worse! I am beginning to feel like the Villa Tesoro is a prison and Sophia is my warden. She now has a servant follow me when I go into town. She says it is to help carry my purchases, but I know it is to make sure I don't fraternize with the shopkeepers.

And Diary, I am only allowed to see my baby for an hour a day! Marcus is growing plump with thick fists and thighs and a sweet dimple on his chin. I love to see him blow bubbles, but I am not allowed to give him a bath.

Marcus has a nanny as well as a wet nurse, and they take care of him from morning to the early afternoon. He is brought to me so I can see that he has been fed and burped, and then he is whisked away until evening. I am allowed to spend an hour with him before dinner. I place him on the rug in the library and watch his eyes follow me. I want to tell him that I miss him, that I love him so much, but he wouldn't understand.

The night nanny takes him away and I join Pliny and Sophia for cocktails and dinner. Often we have company and I have to sit at the table for hours. Once I excused myself and snuck up to the nursery. The nanny stopped me before I entered. She said Marcus was asleep. Diary, I stood on the landing listening to my son cooing, and I couldn't go inside to see his face.

I complain to Pliny and it is driving a wedge between us. He doesn't understand why I am upset. He says I should be happy we can spend time together. He laughs, says that he loves my breasts and he is glad he has them to himself. I love Pliny but I am so angry, I am like a dam waiting to burst.

Yesterday Sophia called Pliny and me into her study. She said we needed to start thinking about having another baby. It would be wise to have "a spare." At first I didn't understand her English. I am like a horse to be bred! Now that I have produced an heir, Sophia wants me to produce another, to make sure the Tesoro line continues.

Pliny and I went up to our bedroom. I was so upset; I didn't want him to touch me. He said his mother was right. If we had a girl, we would try again, so we mustn't waste time.

I stared at him like he was a stranger. Was this really the prince I met on the ski slope, the man who was so impetuous he proposed on the spot? I told him I didn't feel like making love and he slept in his study.

I don't know if I even want another child. I dreamed I was in San Francisco, pushing Marcus in his stroller in Golden Gate Park. When I woke up, I was crying.

I called Constance but she says there is nothing she can do. The Italian aristocracy is strict and the matriarch is the head of the family. She said I should try to make Sophia my friend but that is like telling a dragon not to breathe fire.

Hallie skipped over entries about Francesca's Italian lessons, dress fittings in Milan, hours spent learning the Tesoro family tree. Sometimes she seemed happy: driving the speedboat on the lake, strolling with Pliny through the gardens. But mostly she wrote about her growing frustration with Pliny, her misery at being separated from Marcus. Hallie jumped to an entry written nine months later.

January 18, 1982

Dear Diary,
On Christmas Eve I gave birth to the most beautiful baby girl. I am sorry I didn't write when I was pregnant, but I

was sick from morning till night. Pliny reminded me I should be glad I didn't have to take care of Marcus. For once I didn't argue with him. I couldn't eat anything but dry toast. My feet were swollen and my back ached.

Now that Portia is born, I am distraught. It is even worse than the early days with Marcus. She is the most exquisite baby—with thick black hair and huge green eyes. I hardly see her and I feel like my heart has been cut out. I didn't realize what it would be like to have a girl; I want to cradle her in my arms and stroke her hair. The new wet nurse is like an ogre in a fairy tale. Sophia hired her just to scare me!

Hallie heard Portia run up the stairs. She knew she would knock on Hallie's door and suggest a swim before dinner. Hallie wanted to dive off the diving board and forget she discovered Francesca's diary. But she had to find out how Francesca could have abandoned Marcus and Portia.

Hallie scribbled a note saying she had a terrible headache. She slipped it under the door and picked up the notebook.

She found a Polaroid photo, blurred and faded around the edges. Pliny stood tall and handsome with Portia in his arms. Francesca wore slim black pants and a silk scarf around her neck. Marcus held his mother's hand, blue eyes smiling into the camera. They stood on the dock, a picnic basket at their feet, Lake Como glittering behind them.

Hallie examined the photo. Francesca looked happy, her eyes sparkling. Maybe she had resigned herself to the Italian lifestyle.

September 2, 1982

Dear Diary,
Today I overheard Sophia and Pliny discussing Marcus's education. Sophia was saying it was time to enroll him in Le Rosey. My ears pricked up because Le Rosey is a boarding

school in Switzerland. Some of my friends at Madame Lille's École had been students there.

Sophia explained that Tesoros had attended Le Rosey since it opened in 1880. Students there form friendships with royalty from all over Europe. Pliny attended Le Rosey, and so did his father. I smiled and said weren't they planning far in the future? Marcus was barely two.

Sophie looked at me as if I was a student who failed my geometry lesson. She explained that Tesoro children go to Le Rosey at the age of eight. Can you imagine! Marcus and my darling Portia being sent to Switzerland when they are eight years old.

I was so angry I was afraid I would break Sophia's precious china. I screamed that they were my children and I would decide when they left home. They could go to a day school in Milan, they could stay home with a tutor, but they would not go to boarding school until they were at least twelve.

I looked at Pliny for support but he just sat there sipping his tea. I wanted to throw it in his lap. I stormed upstairs and eventually Pliny followed me.

We had a major row. I screamed if Sophia insisted that Marcus attend Le Rosey I would pack Marcus and Portia up and take them to San Francisco. Pliny said I would never be allowed to do that. Sophia was a powerful woman and she would stop me.

I asked if Pliny was threatening me, I started shaking so badly my teeth chattered. Pliny tried to hold me but I punched his chest. I kept hitting him, like a hummingbird attacking its feeder. He held me tight, stroking my hair and murmuring, "Francesca, caro," until I calmed down.

We sat on the bed where we had been so happy. He explained how being recognized by other members of European aristocracy was so important to Sophia.

I said I couldn't bear the thought of Marcus and Portia being so far away. I would miss their whole childhood, they would barely know me. Finally we compromised. Pliny would tell Sophia they could attend Le Rosey when they turned twelve.

We lay down on the bed and made love like we haven't in months. For the first time I felt Pliny and I were a team. It felt so good to be in his arms and not have Sophia between us.

Hallie heard the dinner bell ring. She craved a bowl of soup or a warm bread roll. But she had to find out what ruined their reconciliation. She climbed into bed and turned the page.

October 4, 1982

Dear Diary,

Pliny has lied to me! I am so furious I want to catch the next plane to San Francisco. I cannot take another day at the Villa Tesoro.

This morning I returned some books to Sophia's library. I saw a letter on her desk with the Le Rosey insignia. I picked it up and read it quickly.

Sophia enrolled Marcus for the autumn of 1989—when he is eight years old! A receipt of her deposit fluttered to the floor. I was so incensed I tore through the villa looking for Pliny.

I found him on the boat dock and I demanded to know what was going on. Pliny said he tried to reason with Sophia, but she was adamant. If they waited till Marcus was twelve, he would be left behind. The other students would have bonded and Marcus would be an outsider.

I was so angry I almost pushed Pliny into the lake. How could he betray me? He shrugged and said it was far in the future. By the time Marcus was eight I would have adjusted to the idea. I would have Portia to keep me company, and perhaps another baby boy.

I stormed back to the villa and locked myself in my bedroom. I can't do this anymore. I can't live under Sophia's regime with a husband who is a child. I don't see my own children and one day soon they will be taken away.

I waited till everyone was asleep and I called Constance and told her I must come home. She warned me that Sophia would stop me, but I begged her to find the best lawyers in San Francisco.

Today I woke up with a terrible flu. My head is groggy and I threw up all morning. At least I have an excuse not to go down to lunch. I will stay in bed and try to figure out what to do.

The final entry was written in cramped letters, as if Francesca was in a hurry to get them on the page.

October 12, 1982

Dear Diary,

I am leaving in the morning. I told Pliny I have a dress fitting in Milan. I will take the train to Rome and then the plane to San Francisco.

I went to the doctor and confirmed what I feared. I don't have the flu; I'm pregnant. I cannot stay here and hand another baby over to wet nurses and nannies. I would try to smuggle Marcus and Portia onto the plane but we never go anywhere without two nannies.

The only thing I can do is go to San Francisco and pray Constance can rescue my children. I can't stand another minute in this house. And I can't imagine a life of dining with middle-aged duchesses while my children attend boarding school in Switzerland.

No one knows I am pregnant and I must leave before anyone finds out. Sophia will put me on bed rest or insist a servant accompanies me wherever I go.

I am going to leave you here, Dear Diary, tucked behind Marcus's favorite bedtime story. I will return for Marcus and Portia very soon. I will move heaven and earth to bring them to San Francisco.

Hallie lay back against the pillow. It was past midnight and the villa was quiet. She tried to imagine Francesca boarding the train to Milan, leaving her husband and children behind. She wandered what happened to the baby she was carrying. Perhaps Francesca had a miscarriage, and her hasty departure had been for nothing.

Hallie picked up the notebook and read the final entry again. She glanced at the date, suddenly mesmerized. She counted on her fingers, stopped, and counted backward. She counted again and then dropped the notebook, a chill running down her spine.

Suddenly she knew the truth as if the words were written on the page. There was no Phillip Elliot and no romantic tryst in a Rome hotel room. Hallie was the baby in Francesca and Pliny Tesoro was her father.

chapter twelve

Hallie sat in the garden of the Villa Luce, gazing at the lake. The cool breeze that blew down from the mountains had vanished, and the villa baked in a heat wave. Hallie had worked in the monastery wing all afternoon, but suddenly she felt dizzy. She ran outside and collapsed on a stone bench.

Hallie hadn't been able to think straight since she found the diary. Her first impulse was to call Constance. She wanted to yell and scream about how she could have kept a secret for almost thirty years. But before she finished dialing, she knew Constance didn't know Pliny was her father. Constance would never lie to her.

Hallie considered calling her mother but she was too angry to talk to her. She imagined her questions: How could Francesca deprive Hallie of a father? How could she let Hallie grow up without getting to know her brother and sister? How could she not tell her she was half Italian, a princess, a Tesoro? She couldn't think of a possible explanation that would make her rage subside.

Hallie thought of calling Peter, but he seemed part of another life. She pictured him holding her in his arms, stroking her hair. She couldn't tell him because she didn't know what she wanted him to say.

The only person Hallie could talk to was Portia. What Francesca had done to Portia—deserting her when she was still a baby—was almost as bad as what Francesca had done to Hallie. But Portia and Riccardo had gone for a week to Capri. Portia had knocked on Hallie's door as Hallie tucked the notebooks into her suitcase.

Portia had peeked in the door. "You look like death." She had worn a white sundress that showed off her tan. Her arms were covered with gold bangles and she had a new emerald ring on her finger.

"I have a terrible headache," Hallie had said dully. "I've been up all night."

"We missed you at dinner." Portia had perched on the edge of Hallie's bed. "Sophia was so thrilled Riccardo joined us she served fresh crab and caviar. Pliny and Riccardo smoked cigars and Sophia hovered over Riccardo as if he was an emissary from the Pope."

"I'm glad things are going well," Hallie had mumbled.

"We're leaving for Capri this afternoon." Portia had twirled the ring around her finger. "We're going to dive in the grottos and climb to Anna Capri." Portia had hesitated. "Riccardo swore if I had a baby he would stop seeing other women. I'm going to try to get pregnant, and when we come back we're going to live together."

Hallie had tried to listen to Portia but she couldn't concentrate.

"Hallie, are you okay?" Portia had frowned at Hallie's pale cheeks and listless eyes.

"I'm happy for you." Hallie had tried to smile. "I just need some sleep."

———

Now Hallie wished she had told Portia. But she had been in shock, like someone who had witnessed a car accident. She stayed in her room all morning, pacing like a tiger locked in its cage. Finally she slipped on a sundress and sandals and walked to the ferry terminal.

She sat on the ferry to Lenno, watching tourists on jet skis, families in paddleboats, couples racing flashy speedboats. Instead of savoring the holiday scene, she felt a deep ache. She was conceived here, she belonged here, but the lake was as foreign to her as it was to the English couple who sat beside her on the boat.

Hallie entered the Villa Luce and pulled out her laptop and tape measure. She tried to distract herself with sketches and measurements. But her ideas were buried under a thick fog. She finally zipped up her laptop and ran to the garden.

"You look like you could use a lime soda."

Hallie turned around and saw Angus holding two glass bottles. He wore tan shorts, a green T-shirt, and leather sandals.

"I'm going back to work," Hallie explained. "I just needed some air."

"It's too hot to be inside." Angus handed her a bottle. "I got these from the freezer, try one."

Hallie drank the cold fizzy liquid. It was sweet and tart at the same time. "It's delicious."

"Max orders them by the case." Angus drank his in one long gulp. "The villa needs a new air-conditioning system, but in the meantime this will have to do."

"I didn't know Lake Como got so hot."

"We rely on the mountains to cool us down." Angus frowned. "You look like you're going to faint."

"I'm fine." Hallie sipped her soda. She thought about the diaries, and tears welled in her eyes.

"If you pass out I'll feel responsible." Angus stretched his long legs in front of him. "I've provided unfit work conditions."

"It's nothing." Hallie blinked furiously. "I didn't sleep well last night."

"Boyfriend troubles?" Angus asked.

"How did you know I have a boyfriend?"

"You're too pretty not to have a boyfriend," Angus said, grinning.

"I do." Hallie nodded. "But he's not the problem."

"On archaeological digs we used to sit around the fire and tell stories," Angus replied. "I'm a good listener."

"It's too personal." Hallie shook her head. "And you'd never believe it."

"Have you ever heard the story of Romulus and Remus? They were twins abandoned at birth and raised by wolves. Romulus became Rome's first emperor, after killing his own brother."

"I thought that was a myth," Hallie replied.

"Archaeologists have dug up proof of their existence," Angus said. "Our job is to suspend belief long enough to unearth the past."

"My story doesn't involve any she-wolves." Hallie sighed. "Just a lot of lies."

"Come with me." Angus stood up. "I have the perfect antidote to the heat, and you can tell me the whole story."

Hallie glanced at Angus. Something about his height, his long arms and legs, made her feel safe.

"Okay. I wasn't getting much done anyway."

They walked down to the dock and Angus stepped into a wooden fishing boat. He helped Hallie onboard and directed her to a chipped green bench. Angus pushed the boat back from the dock and rowed to a small cove.

"This part of the lake is stocked with Lavarello," Angus explained, taking out two fishing rods and handing one to Hallie.

"I haven't fished since I was nine years old," Hallie mused. "My grandmother used to take me to Santa Cruz and I'd fish off the pier."

"I always wanted to be Tom Sawyer." Angus hooked a worm on the rod. "I wore the same checkered shirt every day and kept a piece of straw between my teeth."

"My grandmother would wait at the end of the dock," Hallie replied. "Once an old man noticed my bucket was empty and gave me all his fish. Constance was so proud, I didn't have the heart to tell her the truth."

"Truth can be a slippery business." Angus threw his line into the water.

"It's okay to fib when you're nine." Hallie flinched. "Not when you're a grown woman, hurting a lot of people."

"Sometimes the fish are lazy." Angus leaned against the side of the boat. "Why don't you tell me what's going on?"

Hallie blinked back tears. "I don't think I can."

"You'll feel better and it'll pass the time," Angus encouraged her. "It beats watching the paint peel."

Hallie opened her mouth and the words spilled out. She told Angus about her private girls' school, Constance's mansion, afternoons spent sketching in the library. She told him how her mother was wrapped up in her bakery and treated Hallie more like a sister than a daughter. She told him about Portia and Marcus's annual visits. Portia wore neon miniskirts and told stories of Lake Como that were sophisticated and worldly and wonderfully European.

Hallie told him about Phillip Elliot, the great love of her mother's life. She told him how she used to dream about her father but the fantasies ebbed as she became consumed by college and her career.

Finally she told him about the diaries, Sophia's strict regime, Pliny's failures and lies. She told him Francesca ran away from Lake Como because Sophia made her life a nightmare.

"She was pregnant with me when she left," Hallie finished. "My whole life, I thought I was the product of one rainy night in a hotel in Rome. Instead I have a family, a country I barely know."

"Your mother was afraid Sophia would take you from her. If she had known she would have demanded custody."

"I understand that." Hallie's shoulders sagged as if she was a balloon with a steady leak. "But she could have told me when I was fifteen or twenty or twenty-five."

"She must have a reason." Angus tugged on his fishing line.

"I can't talk to her." Hallie shook her head. "Every time I pick up the phone I start shaking."

"Why don't you ask your grandmother?"

"Constance had a series of strokes last year." Hallie felt a tug on her line. She reeled it in but the wire went slack. "The shock might give her a heart attack."

"It sounds like you love your grandmother," Angus mused. "And you had a pretty gifted childhood."

"Are you saying I shouldn't complain because I grew up on top of Pacific Heights and attended the opera and the ballet?" Hallie fumed. "I missed out on a father, I barely know my brother, and I could be even closer to Portia."

"I didn't mean that." Angus concentrated on his fishing pole.

"You're right." Hallie slumped onto the bench. "I love everything about San Francisco: the cable cars, sourdough bread, the botanical gardens at Golden Gate Park. And my mother is smart and bright and makes the most delicious German chocolate cake." Hallie sighed. "But she didn't give me a choice."

Angus frowned as something pulled on his line. He stood on the edge of the boat, his muscles tense. He pitched the line and reeled in a large orange fish.

"You're good luck." Angus let the fish thrash on the floor of the boat. "I haven't caught a big one in weeks."

"Thanks for listening," Hallie mumbled. She suddenly regretted telling her intimate secrets to a stranger.

"Have you told your boyfriend?" Angus asked.

"He's in San Francisco," Hallie replied, watching the fish's tail flap back and forth.

"Is he a serious boyfriend?"

"We're almost engaged."

"You're a long way from an almost-fiancé." Angus unhooked the fish's mouth.

"We were working through some things," Hallie replied, feeling her line tense. She leaned over the side of the boat, trying to locate the fish. Suddenly it leaped into the air, pulling her line and throwing her back in the boat. She slipped on the wood and landed on her back.

"Are you okay?" Angus reached down to help her up. Instead of lifting her to her feet, he crouched down and gathered her in an embrace. His mouth found hers, his lips sweet and tangy like lime soda.

Hallie knew kissing Angus was wrong. It was wrong the way the lie about Phillip Elliot was wrong, the way she still saw Peter's hands on Kendra's skirt was wrong, the way she, with her Grace Kelly blond hair, was a Tesoro, was wrong. Kissing Angus on a fishing boat in the middle of Lake Como was so wrong, it felt right. If she could stay in his arms, all the other wrongs would fade away.

"Angus." Hallie pulled away, missing his strong arms the moment she left them.

"I'm sorry, blame it on the heat." Angus straightened up. "Hey, you caught one." He pointed to the fish thrashing in the corner.

"It's huge," Hallie replied, trying to hide the blush that grazed her cheeks.

"I'll cook them for dinner." Angus held it up. "Over a bed of risotto with a tomato and mozzarella salad."

"I can't." Hallie shook her head.

"You don't want to go back to the villa and eat with your grandmother and your father." Angus steered the boat toward the Villa Luce.

Hallie could still feel his lips on her mouth. "Peter might call."

"You're beautiful and vulnerable and I took advantage of you," Angus said seriously. "I promise it won't happen again. Join me for dinner and I'll take you back to the villa in the speedboat. You can slip into bed and not have to face Pliny and Sophia."

Hallie pictured the long dining table set with fine bone china. She imagined Sophia grilling her about her headache, Pliny being solicitous and charming. She pictured sitting through five long courses without Portia to speed things along.

"Okay." Hallie nodded. "I've never eaten Lavarello before."

"It's delicious, and it's local to Lake Como." Angus tied the boat up at the dock. "If you're going to get to know your home, you have to eat the local fish."

"It's not my home," Hallie started saying.

"It is at the moment." Angus jumped out of the boat. "Your designs are fabulous, Max is pleased."

They stopped in the vegetable garden and picked tomatoes from the vine. They pulled green beans and asparagus and heads of sweet butter lettuce. Angus grabbed two lemons from the orchard and six long-stemmed roses from the rose garden.

"These are for you." He handed them to Hallie.

"I can't accept presents." Hallie inhaled the rich fragrance.

"You caught dinner," Angus protested. "And you're going to help me scale the fish."

"I am?" Hallie shuddered.

"I can't do it alone, I get queasy when I touch fish scales."

"I'm not handling raw fish!" Hallie exclaimed.

"Then you can slice tomatoes and cut the lemons," Angus suggested.

"Deal," Hallie said, clutching the roses against her chest.

———

Hallie and Angus stood in the kitchen, cooking fish on the industrial-sized grill. Angus produced round wheels of mozzarella from the fridge and virgin olive oil from the pantry. He stirred a pot of risotto, adding garlic and onions and thyme. Hallie found platters and bowls and set them on the table on the balcony.

Angus served the risotto and poured two glasses of red wine. "Everything tastes better when it's shared."

"Do you ever eat with Max?" Hallie asked. The sun was setting and Hallie could see the heat shimmering on the lake. The sky turned pink and gray, and the villages looked like a scene out of a picture book.

"Max travels a lot. He's in Pisa and from there he's going to Verona and Genoa."

"Does it feel odd, living in someone else's house?" Hallie tasted the fish. It was light and buttery and blended smoothly with the risotto.

"Archaeologists are squatters. We're always pitching tents on foreign real estate." Angus ate a large mouthful of rice and fish. "I keep Max's estate running smoothly, when intruders aren't sneaking into the hall of mirrors."

"I didn't mean to sneak in." Hallie grimaced.

"I'm glad you did." Angus sipped his wine. "It's nice to hear the sound of a woman's footsteps in the halls."

"Thank you for listening to me today." Hallie put down her fork. "But I—"

"I meant what I said earlier," Angus interrupted. "We can be friends, like Tom Sawyer and Becky Thatcher."

"I was never a tomboy." Hallie's shoulders relaxed. "I have a large Barbie doll collection."

"I don't expect you to wear blond braids and suspenders"— Angus refilled his wineglass—"but maybe we can fish together. I'll show you different parts of the lake."

Hallie concentrated on the tomatoes and mozzarella drizzled in olive oil. The mozzarella was sweet, not like any she'd eaten in San Francisco. She glanced at the mosaic tile floor, the Corinthian columns, the sweeping views from Como to Cenobio.

Hallie shivered, thinking she should be sitting in a café on Fillmore, sharing a plate of tapas with Peter. She should be drinking Napa Valley pinot noir instead of Italian cabernet. She should go home to her apartment on Russian Hill and climb into her king-sized bed. She should know who she was, where she belonged, instead of having a last name that was fiction.

"It's been a long day." Hallie tried to keep the tears from her eyes. "I can take the ferry back."

"And miss me showing off my boating skills?" Angus collected dishes and plates. "I've been practicing since I was a kid with a rubber dingy in the bathtub."

Hallie sat in the back of the speedboat, her arms hugging her chest. The lake shimmered like diamonds laid out on black velvet. Angus seemed very tall, his hands clasped around the steering wheel. His hair was thick reddish brown and his eyes had yellow flecks in the moonlight.

"Safe and sound." Angus jumped onto the dock. He reached for Hallie's hand and helped her out of the boat.

"Thanks for dinner, it was delicious," Hallie replied.

"If you ever need a shoulder to cry on"—Angus squeezed her hand—"mine are pretty big."

"I'll remember that." Hallie paused. Angus stood so close she could smell wine and garlic and thyme. He reached down to kiss her cheek and she turned and ran up the steps to the villa.

chapter thirteen

Hallie sat in the small salon, leafing through *House & Garden*. She had waited until she saw Pliny untie the boat from the dock, until she heard Sophia close the door of her study. Then she crept downstairs and filled a plate with berries, toast, and scrambled eggs. She managed to eat three bites of egg before the events of yesterday came rushing back to her. Then she abandoned the plate and sank into a sofa in the salon.

Hallie still didn't know what to do with her new knowledge. She gazed at the frescos on the ceiling, the silk curtains on the windows, and felt a ping deep inside her. She was a Tesoro and this magnificent villa with its history and gilt furniture were in some way part of her. She had come close to knocking on Pliny's door, but at the last minute she froze. He might be furious with Francesca and throw Hallie out. Or he might put his arms around Hallie and embrace her.

"A gentleman is asking for you." Lea stood at the door in her black uniform and white apron.

Hallie closed the magazine. It was probably Alfonso, returned from Milan with the silk swatches he promised her. She glanced in the mirror over the fireplace and frowned. It could be Angus offering her a ride to Villa Luce.

When she woke up she lay in bed, and thought about her evening with Angus. The kiss was wrong, even dinner was wrong. From now on she would keep their relationship strictly professional. But when she closed her eyes she saw his broad shoulders, pictured him reeling in the big orange fish, and was glad she spent time with him.

"Hey," a voice said behind her. "Or should I say, *buona sera*."

Hallie turned around and saw Peter standing at the door. He wore jeans and a Giants T-shirt and carried a khaki backpack. He looked young and clean and all-American.

"Peter!" Hallie exclaimed. "What are you doing here?"

"That's not much of a greeting." He grinned, walking over to Hallie and kissing her on the lips.

"I'm thrilled," Hallie said when he finally released her. He smelled like deodorant and airplane peanuts. "I just had no idea."

"I got the interview with the think tank in Paris," Peter explained. "I decided to stop here on the way."

"I could have picked you up in Milan," Hallie replied.

"I wanted to surprise you." Peter smiled. His teeth were white and straight and shiny. "You look gorgeous, almost Italian."

Hallie glanced at her orange Pucci dress and strapless Gucci sandals. Her arms and legs were tan and she wore an enamel clip in her hair.

"I've spent a lot of time on the lake," Hallie murmured.

"Lake Como is beautiful." Peter nodded, admiring the artwork on the wall and the bronze statue by the fireplace. "And the villa is amazing, I've never seen so much marble."

"All the villas on the lake are spectacular," Hallie agreed. Her stomach did little flips and her heart raced. Peter was like a ghost from another life. She couldn't believe they were standing together in the Tesoro salon.

"I want a full tour," Peter said. "But right now I'm starving. All I ate on the plane was cardboard pizza and Styrofoam coffee."

"I don't think Lea has removed breakfast yet." Hallie walked across the hall to the dining room.

Peter loaded his plate with waffles and berries and fresh whipped cream. He drank a tall glass of orange juice and a demi-tasse of coffee. He ate everything and went back for eggs, wheat toast, and slices of melon.

"The food is delicious." Peter wiped his mouth with a napkin. "Is this all just for breakfast?"

"Sophia takes pride in the Tesoro cuisine," Hallie said. "Dinner is at least five courses."

"Where is everyone?" Peter asked, refilling his coffee cup.

"Pliny is out on the lake and Sophia is in her study," Hallie replied. "Portia and Riccardo are in Capri. They're almost back together."

"Then you can come home!" Peter put down his coffee, his eyes sparkling. "We can return together after I come back from France."

"I can't leave now," Hallie murmured.

"You came to keep Portia company," Peter said tersely. "She's on holiday with her husband."

"I have a job," Hallie replied. "I have to finish it."

"There are hundreds of interior designers in Italy," Peter argued. "I want you to come home."

"Designing the Villa Luce is very important to me; it's a golden opportunity."

"Christ, Hallie," Peter grumbled, suddenly angry. "You've been here almost a month."

"If I finish this job, I can open my own firm." Hallie stood up and walked to the buffet.

"I thought you liked working for Kendra." Peter stood beside her. "Is this still about the wedding at City Hall? I haven't seen Kendra in weeks."

"It's not about Kendra." Hallie shook her head. "If you saw the Villa Luce, you'd understand. I'm going on my first buying trip next week, I'm so excited."

"I'd love to see it," Peter suggested. "Let's go after breakfast."

Hallie flinched. "I can't just show up with you. Max is a recluse, with a particular dislike for journalists and photographers."

"Sounds like the kind of guy I'd like to meet." Peter grinned mischievously.

Hallie glanced at her watch. "I'm late. I should get to work."

"You're not going to take a siesta with me?" Peter whispered. He put one arm around her waist and the other smoothly beneath her dress. He flicked the top of her underwear and slipped his hand underneath the thin fabric.

"Peter!" Hallie protested. His hand felt warm and familiar. "Lea could walk in any second."

"Show me where your bedroom is," Peter murmured. "I'm going to lie down and sleep for eight hours."

"You can't stay here." Hallie felt his hand pressed between her thighs. "Portia doesn't even bring Riccardo upstairs."

"I've flown three thousand miles to see you," Peter pleaded, caressing her with his fingers.

"We'll check you in to the Hotel Metropole. It's just above the ferry terminal."

"As long as you promise to join me after work." Peter slipped his fingers deep inside her. He searched for the sweet spot, probing, working, until he felt her body tense and shudder.

"I will." Hallie clung to his back, letting the long, delicious waves wash over her.

"And you don't have to wear these," Peter whispered, snapping the panties against her skin.

———

Hallie stood in her closet, selecting a dress to wear for dinner. She had been strangely nervous all day. She walked from room to room at the Villa Luce, questioning her design decisions. She didn't eat lunch, and found herself in the kitchen in the late afternoon, eating Angus's leftover risotto. She put the bowl back in the fridge, embarrassed that she ate his food without asking.

Angus had taken the boat to run errands and Hallie had the villa to herself. She wondered whether Max was upstairs or in Genoa. She had stopped asking Angus about meeting him. She was so wrapped up in creating the new space, she almost didn't want outside influences. Except today, when she seemed to forget everything she learned in design school.

Hallie picked out a red Valentino with a heart-shaped neckline. She added small diamond earrings and a diamond-and-ruby bracelet. Peter liked her to wear red; he said it made her eyes glitter.

When she saw Peter standing in the salon, she had felt a rush of relief. She would tell him about Francesca's diaries and he would know what to do. But as the day wore on, she doubted her decision. Peter was a journalist; he would want to learn the whole story. Hallie couldn't risk him telling Constance or even Francesca before she was ready.

Returning to Bellagio on the evening ferry, Hallie probed her feelings about Peter. Her body had instantly welcomed him. He flipped a switch that made her greedy for his touch.

But Hallie felt a hardness inside her, like a coat of armor around her heart. Peter wanted to take her back to San Francisco where she would continue to be Hallie Elliot, and perhaps Hallie Merrick. She gazed at the narrow villages climbing up to the mountains, the majestic villas lining the shore, and felt like she had been sprinkled with fairy dust. Lake Como was magic and she wasn't ready to leave its spell.

Hallie slipped on gold Prada sandals and grabbed a red Fendi clutch. She rubbed on lip gloss and ran down the staircase to the foyer.

"Hallie!" Pliny stood in the entryway. He wore brown linen slacks and a white silk shirt, and twirled a set of car keys in his hand. "I'm going to pick up the mayor of Bellagio. He's joining us for dinner to discuss the dedication of the statue."

"I have dinner plans tonight," Hallie stammered. She hadn't seen Pliny since she found the diaries. Her heart seemed to slow and her blood froze. He looked the same as he had yesterday: salt-and-pepper hair, chiseled cheeks, kind smile. But everything was different.

"Are you making friends in Lake Como?" Pliny inquired.

"A friend arrived from San Francisco." Hallie blushed, picking a piece of lint from her dress. "He's staying at the Hotel Metropole."

"A male friend flew from America to see you," Pliny mused. "Is it something serious?"

Hallie mumbled, "We've known each other a long time."

"You will have to bring him to the villa," Pliny suggested.

"He's not staying long," Hallie said. "He's on his way to Paris."

"Portia and Riccardo are moving back to their villa," Pliny began. "Sophia is grateful to you, and so am I."

"I didn't do anything." Hallie thought about Portia's fears of being a mother, about Riccardo's mistress. She prayed that Portia knew what she was doing.

"We want you to know that you are welcome to stay at the Villa Tesoro as long as you like," Pliny finished.

"Thank you." Hallie's eyes filled with tears. She turned away, searching for something in her purse. "I have to go, I'm late."

"You're a beautiful young woman." Pliny opened the front door. "Your mother must be proud."

Peter was waiting for Hallie in the hotel lobby. He wore a white shirt and a narrow black tie. His short hair was brushed back and he was freshly shaved.

"You look gorgeous." He kissed the side of her neck. "Like a European film star."

"I'm thirsty," Hallie replied. Suddenly it was all too much: Peter at her side as if they were grabbing a bite on Union Street, Pliny kind and courteous like a benevolent stranger. She wished she were with Portia in her bedroom, playing loud music and dancing on the bed like teenagers.

"I have a bottle of champagne waiting upstairs." Peter guided her toward the elevator.

"I thought we were having dinner," Hallie said. The hotel lobby was full of couples on holiday, sipping evening aperitifs. A smattering of Italians sat at the bar, talking quickly and popping nuts into their mouths.

"I have a surprise in the room." Peter's eyes sparkled.

Hallie followed Peter to the elevator. The hotel room was lit with candles and a table for two was set on the balcony. There were crystal champagne glasses, a silver ice bucket, and a vase holding a white lily.

"It's beautiful." Hallie sank into a chair. Peter poured her a glass of champagne, and she drank it quickly, the bubbles traveling straight to her toes.

"Not as beautiful as you." Peter sat opposite her. He sprinkled ground pepper on her salad and tossed it in a Caesar dressing. "I had room service send everything in advance, so we wouldn't be disturbed."

Hallie ate mechanically, listening to Peter talk about *Spilled,* about the interview with the Apple programmer that might become a book.

"Speaking of books." Peter got up and walked to his backpack. "I brought you a present."

Hallie glanced at the thick book tied with a red ribbon. A photo of Paul Johns was on the front, and on the back, Peter's author photo: young and handsome and brimming with confidence.

"It's the seventh printing of *Paul Johns Unplugged*," Peter explained. "It has a new dedication and a preface by Mark Zuckerberg."

"That's fantastic." Hallie beamed. "I'm proud of you."

"I was wrong wanting you to come home," Peter said meditatively. He removed their salads and produced two plates of salmon and vegetables from the warmer. The salmon was covered in a light cream sauce and the vegetables were sweet and buttery. "We should rent a car and drive around the lake. Maybe drive over the mountains to Switzerland."

"I'm working." Hallie put down her fork. "And I thought you were chained to the magazine."

"I hired a new editor." Peter refilled their champagne glasses. "He just graduated from Berkeley and he's brilliant. Kendra introduced me, he's the son of one of her clients."

"I thought you hadn't seen Kendra in weeks." Hallie's fingers wound tightly around her glass.

"I ran into her at some society thing." Peter shrugged. "The kid is amazing, like a young Carl Bernstein."

"I'm really busy. It's a huge project."

"I didn't come to interview some kids in a think tank, I came to see you." Peter grabbed her hand across the table. "I'm going crazy without you. I can survive a few months, but you have to promise you'll marry me."

"Peter, I . . ." Hallie stammered.

Peter reached into his pocket and brought out the blue Tiffany box. "Put this on." He opened it and took out the diamond-and-ruby ring. "In five months I'll pick you up from San

Francisco airport. We'll drive to Constance's and sift through her list of florists and caterers. We'll pick out flatware and plan our honeymoon."

"Peter." Hallie pulled her hand back but he slipped the ring on her finger. He pulled her up and kissed her mouth and her neck. He brushed her breasts with his fingers and ran his hands down her thighs. He led her into the bedroom, closed the French doors, and dimmed the light.

Peter stood next to the bed, holding her, until Hallie felt her heart hammer in her chest. Then he slowly unzipped her dress and let it fall to the floor. He put his mouth on her nipple, his other hand curled around her waist. He laid her on the bed, whispering her name like a mantra.

Hallie watched Peter unbutton his shirt, pull off his tie, unzip his pants. She remembered the way his chest brushed against hers, the way he pinned her to the bed, his legs opening her thighs.

She remembered dozens of nights of lovemaking, mornings waking up to fresh coffee and eggs, weekends spent in bed reading the paper. She suddenly missed him with an ache so strong, she almost leaped off the bed and pulled him on top of her. But Peter just stood there, his eyes roaming over her body, his lips playing in a half smile.

Finally he lay on top of her, and entered her so quickly she thought she would break. He held her tightly, until her body quieted. Then he pulled her arms over her head, and pushed deeper, like a swimmer crossing the finishing line. His body moved in an invisible rhythm until she was caught up in it, shuddering and crying.

Later, when Peter was asleep, she tried to wriggle free. But his breathing was steady and his arm was tucked securely behind her back. Hallie lay, eyes wide open, staring at the diamond ring glinting on her finger.

When Hallie woke in the morning, Peter was gone. He left a note saying he was going for a run, signed with hearts and kisses. Hallie folded the note and slowly got dressed. She put the ring in its box and left it on the bedside table. She opened the French doors and sat on the balcony, watching Bellagio wake up below her.

Hallie felt lazy and satiated, like a cat who drank a bowl of warm milk. Making love to Peter had been so natural. Their bodies fit like pieces of a jigsaw puzzle. He knew how to make her soar, how to hold her afterward.

Hallie watched the ferries chug across the lake. She saw the mist clear, revealing Lenno and Tremezzo and Menaggio. She repeated the names of the villages, like lines in a nursery rhyme. She could live here, she could get to know her father, she could open a little design store in Como or Varenna.

Hallie didn't know if that was what she wanted, but she didn't know it wasn't what she wanted. And she couldn't string Peter along while she figured it out. She was like a lizard shedding her skin. Maybe the new Hallie would still be a California girl who loved shopping in Union Square, but maybe she would be happiest exploring Bellagio with Portia.

"Hey, Sleeping Beauty." Peter entered the room carrying a tray of scrambled eggs, wheat toast, and sliced honeydew. He wore running shorts and Nikes and had a wadded-up newspaper under his arm. "I don't know how to say 'sunny-side up' in Italian." He put the tray on the table.

"I'm not hungry."

"Then we can go back to bed and eat later." Peter kissed her neck. "After we work up an appetite."

"Peter, we can't do this anymore," Hallie said.

"Do what?" Peter frowned, spreading *The New York Times* on the table.

"Be together," Hallie stammered.

"You're wearing my ring!" Peter exclaimed. "We're engaged."

"I put it back in the box." Hallie showed him her naked finger. "It's on the bedside table."

"You seemed happy wearing it last night," Peter stormed. "You seemed pretty content drinking champagne and fucking like rabbits."

"I might stay here a while." Hallie's eyes filled with tears. "Long-distance relationships don't work."

"I told you I can survive a few months." Peter's eyes narrowed.

"I might stay longer, I may move here." Hallie fiddled with the pages of the newspaper.

"That's crazy! Lake Como is for holidays. You have a job in San Francisco, family, me."

"I have family here, and a job," Hallie replied.

"Did you meet someone?" Peter demanded furiously. "Some Italian bastard with leather loafers and a red Maserati?"

"It's no one." Hallie shook her head. "It's just me."

"That's the biggest cliché in the book." Peter jumped up. "Christ, Hallie, we're not teenagers. I thought you wanted to get married. I thought that's why we attended more weddings this summer than Father Xavier."

"I'm sorry," Hallie murmured.

"You're serious!" Peter shoved his clothes in his backpack. He stuffed the Tiffany box in his pocket and grabbed his passport from the bedside table. "Here." He threw *Paul Johns Unplugged* on the table. "You might want to read the dedication."

Hallie flinched as Peter slammed the door behind him. She watched him run down the promenade toward the ferry terminal. She saw him stand in line, buy his ticket, board the ferry. She waited to see if he would look back, but he stared straight ahead. Finally he sat on the bench, his body crumpling like a hand puppet.

Hallie turned the book over and glanced at Peter's photo. She opened it and read the inscription:

To Hallie. A journalist's job is to keep moving, chasing the next story. When I met you, I discovered what being home meant. You are everything to me, and none of it is worth anything without you.

Hallie read the words again. Then she closed the book, so the tears running down her cheeks wouldn't ruin the pages.

chapter fourteen

Hallie entered the Villa Tesoro and closed the door quietly behind her. She didn't want to run into Sophia or Pliny while wearing her red silk dress and Prada sandals. She crept past the library and heard voices arguing in Italian. She saw Sophia through the slit in the door, her face as pale as a statue, and Pliny gesturing like an orchestra conductor.

Hallie dragged herself up the stairs, still reeling from Peter's angry departure. She felt like a tightrope walker whose safety net had been pulled from under her. She knew she had done the right thing, but her heart ached. She wanted to crawl into bed and sleep, until her eyes stopped misting over.

"Where have you been at eleven in the morning wearing red Valentino?" Portia demanded. She sat cross-legged on Hallie's bed. Her hair was wound in a thick braid, and she wore a turquoise peasant skirt and silver sandals.

"You're supposed to be in Capri!" Hallie exclaimed.

"I came back early," Portia mumbled.

"Where's Riccardo?"

"Probably still at the Hotel Quisisana, wondering why I cut up his credit card." Portia giggled, wrapping her hair around her fingers.

"Tell me what happened." Hallie sank onto the bed.

"First tell me why you're sneaking into your bedroom like a naughty choirgirl."

"Peter showed up." Hallie sighed. "We spent the night at the Hotel Metropole."

"Why don't you have that wonderful postcoital glow?" Portia asked.

"Because I broke up with him," Hallie replied. "Permanently."

"I thought you said he was good in bed. Or are you still worried about Kendra?"

"The sex is great, and I believe nothing was going on," Hallie said, realizing she did believe him. Peter had been so earnest and sincere, she felt like she could see straight through him. "I'm not ready to get married."

"You've subscribed to *Bride* magazine since you were sixteen!" Portia exclaimed.

"I'll explain, but first I want to know why you're not exploring the grottos with Riccardo?"

"We took a boat through the grottos." Portia threw herself back on the bed. "We ate scampi in the piazza and shopped at Gucci and Fendi and Prada. We climbed to the top of Ana Capri and strolled through Tiberius's villa. Capri was glorious and sexy and exhilarating."

"What happened?"

"The Quisisana is breathtaking, all white marble and turquoise sofas and cushions. It's like the Mediterranean brought indoors, and the service is exquisite. Two dozen yellow roses and a jar of Beluga caviar were waiting in our room."

"Doesn't sound like a place you'd want to leave early," Hallie mused.

"Riccardo was so attentive; he would leave the hotel and bring back dresses, shoes, bags, scarves. I felt like Julia Roberts in *Pretty Woman*," Portia continued. "Last night he made reservations at Quisi, the five-star restaurant. The waiters wear Armani tuxes and the champagne flutes are Baccarat crystal. After dinner he presented me with this." Portia thrust her hand in front of Hallie. On her ring finger was a huge sapphire sitting on a bed of sparkling diamonds.

"Wow." Hallie examined the ring closely. "That looks like it belongs in the Tower of London."

"He opened a bottle of Krug champagne and said how he longs for children," Portia said. "If it was a boy he wanted to name him Allesandro and buy him a pony and teach him how to play polo."

"I'll give him children if I get a rock like this," Hallie teased.

"After dinner we went upstairs and made love." Portia lay back against the pillows. "It was wonderful and romantic and I prayed that I conceived. I woke up in the middle of the night and the bed was empty. I thought maybe Riccardo went down to get a newspaper; sometimes he's a terrible sleeper. I had this sudden urge for a candy bar. I even laughed I was pregnant and it was my first craving." Portia's face puckered like she had eaten a sour lemon. "So I slipped on a robe and took the elevator down to the gift shop. I passed the bar and I saw Riccardo sitting in a corner, his hand on some strange woman's breast. She had copper hair and eyelashes like Sophia Loren. He was fondling her breast and his other hand was creeping up her skirt. I could see her underwear."

"Oh, Portia," Hallie breathed.

"I ran upstairs and sliced his silk shirts, his linen blazers, his cotton pants with a pair of scissors. Then I cut up his credit cards and took the money in his wallet. He's not going to be happy when it's time to pay his bill."

"You didn't." Hallie laughed.

"I ran out of the hotel and waited at the ferry until morning," Portia continued grimly. "I took the train from Naples and arrived home an hour ago."

"Is that why I heard Sophia shrieking like a Greek chorus?" Hallie asked.

"I don't care if I end up a spinster who wears her hair in a bun and the same black dress every day." Portia's lips quivered. "I can't have children with a man who runs from our bed to another woman's breast."

"You'll find another husband." Hallie put her hand on Portia's arm.

"Sophia may be furious but I can't live a lie." Portia jumped up and darted around the room. "What kind of man would my son grow up to be with Riccardo for a father?"

"There's nothing worse than lying," Hallie agreed, thinking about Francesca's notebooks in her suitcase.

Portia curled up on the ottoman like a tight ball of string. "I'm going to go to the chapel and pray I'm not pregnant."

"I'll go with you," Hallie replied. "Let me change out of this dress."

"First tell me why you broke up with Peter," Portia demanded. "He may be the last decent man out there."

"Let's talk about it later. We've spent enough energy talking about men this morning."

Hallie sat in the back of the tiny chapel while Portia kneeled in the front row, her hands pressed firmly together. Hallie had never seen Portia so distraught, like a child who had witnessed some terrible crime. Her eyes were red-rimmed, her shoulders sagged. Only the sapphire glittering on her finger reminded Hallie of the strong, effervescent Portia she knew.

"Let's not go back to the villa yet," Portia said when they emerged into the sunshine. "Let's go somewhere we'll be completely alone and no one will find us."

Hallie followed Portia through the gardens to the lake. They ran through thick weeds and beds of dandelions. Finally they reached a small cove hidden from the villa, and Portia stripped off her clothes down to her underwear.

"Marcus and I used to swim here when we were children." Portia waded into the lake. "We pretended we were stranded on a desert island, and ate dandelions when we got hungry. Sophia never knew where we went, but we always returned home with a terrible stomachache."

Hallie slipped out of her cotton dress and dipped her toes in the water. It was warm and clear and she could see schools of fish swimming past her. They took turns climbing onto a rock and jumping into the lake. Then they clambered back to shore and lay prone on the sand like starfish.

"I'm glad you didn't give Riccardo back the ring." Hallie stretched out next to Portia.

"And give him the satisfaction of presenting it to his new girlfriend?" Portia held the stone up to the sun. "I'm going to sell it and donate the proceeds to a home for unwed mothers."

"Have you thought about what you are going to do?" Hallie asked.

"I considered joining a convent, but I look terrible in brown." Portia sat up and hugged her knees. "And I'd hate to cut my hair."

"You could dance again," Hallie suggested.

"I'm too old to *sell* tickets at the ballet." Portia shrugged. "But I might visit Madame LaFarge. She owns the ballet school I used to attend in Como. She's been saying she's going to retire for twenty years, but the last time I was in Como she was still rapping young girls' knees with her cane."

"I might stay at Villa Tesoro a while longer," Hallie mused. "I could use the company."

"You broke up with Peter and you're staying in Lake Como?" Portia frowned. "Did I miss something while I was gone? Are you having a torrid affair with that sexy estate manager I met in Varenna?"

"I'm not having an affair." Hallie shook her head, remembering the kiss on the lake, Angus's strong arms and hazel eyes.

"It could be a Lady Chatterley's lover thing. People say Italians invented love, but the British write the best novels about smoldering love affairs."

"I broke up with Peter because I discovered some things about myself," Hallie said seriously. "I need to work them out before I can be in a relationship."

"Are you sick?" Portia asked.

"I found Francesca's diaries," Hallie replied. "She wrote them while she lived at the villa."

"Our mother wrote diaries?" Portia pressed her lips together.

"They were hidden behind *The Water Babies*," Hallie replied. "Four notebooks tied with purple ribbon."

"I don't want to hear what she wrote," Portia said quietly.

Hallie looked at Portia, who had wide eyes like a doe, thin shoulders, and glossy black hair. She remembered the picture taken at the lake, Pliny holding Portia in his arms and Marcus clutching his mother's hand.

"The diaries start when she and Pliny met." Hallie went on as if she hadn't heard her. "They were both head over heels in love. Pliny was ridiculously handsome, like a European film star. He proposed after they'd known each other for a few days. The priest married them in a hotel room in Gstaad."

"My father told me," Portia said icily. "It was quite the fairy tale."

"Everything was fine until Marcus was born. Then the Villa

Tesoro became a prison. Francesca was only allowed to see Marcus for an hour a day. He had a wet nurse and a nanny."

"All upper-class Italian families have nannies."

"Sophia dictated how Francesca dressed, who she saw. She told Pliny and Francesca when to have another baby. Pliny took Sophia's side in every argument. He acted like a child instead of a husband."

"That's no reason to desert your children. I was barely one when Francesca left." Portia's eyes flashed.

"She loved you so much," Hallie replied. "She wrote you were the most beautiful baby. One day she discovered that Sophia was going to send Marcus to boarding school in Switzerland when he was eight. Francesca flew into a rage and insisted Pliny stop her. Pliny promised he would tell Sophia that you and Marcus didn't go away until you were twelve." Hallie ran her hands through the sand. "Francesca found a receipt from Le Rosey confirming Marcus's enrollment for the autumn of 1989. She was furious at Pliny for betraying her."

"Sophia is a difficult woman," Portia conceded, shielding her eyes from the sun. "But Francesca hopped on a plane without looking back."

"Francesca discovered she was pregnant and thought if she waited Sophia would confine her to the villa. She couldn't bear the thought of turning another baby over to nannies. She was sure when she got to San Francisco, Constance would help her rescue you and Marcus."

"What happened to the baby?" Portia asked.

"She was born Hallie Constance Elliot and grew up in a mansion in Pacific Heights. She had white blond hair and blue eyes and a beautiful half sister named Portia."

"But your father is Phillip Elliot," Portia interrupted. "You told me all about him."

"All fiction." Hallie hunched over in the sand. "You can read the diaries; they're in my suitcase."

"Why didn't Francesca come back for us?" Portia asked vehemently. "She couldn't have fought very hard. I didn't see her again until I was nine years old."

"I don't know." Suddenly her own anger couldn't stand the weight of Portia's. Portia was four years old again, flashing eyes and wild black hair, demanding to know where her mother was.

"Did you tell Peter?"

Hallie shook her head. "He and Constance are very close. I haven't told anyone, except Angus."

"The sexy estate manager?" Portia raised her eyebrows.

"You were in Capri." Hallie sighed. "Saying it out loud made me realize I might belong here. I'm half Italian, like you and Marcus."

"We need to tell Pliny," Portia said decisively.

"What if he kicks me out?"

"You're beautiful and educated and accomplished, you're Princess Grace and California Barbie rolled into one. And you haven't done anything scandalous like divorce your husband."

"Pliny loves you," Hallie said.

Portia nodded. "It's the only thing I've been sure of my whole life."

"Maybe we should both join the convent." Hallie thought of the pain Francesca had caused Pliny, the hurt Riccardo inflicted on Portia, the wounded look in Peter's eyes, and the empty pit in her own stomach.

"I could live without men." Portia lay back on the sand. "But I'd miss our slumber parties."

Hallie and Portia put on their clothes and crept back to the villa. It was almost evening and they were starving. Portia joked they should build a campfire. They could catch a fish and scavenge for berries. They could make a bed out of twigs and branches and sleep under the stars.

They waited until Sophia was in the chapel saying her evening prayers, then they slipped into the kitchen. Portia foraged through the pantry and collected a jar of olives, a box of breadsticks, and a pot of hummus. She opened the fridge and brought out cold slices of pizza.

"Sophia thinks pizza is for peasants, but it's Pliny's favorite food." Portia wrapped them in a napkin. "Now all we need is a bottle of wine and we'll have a picnic."

"I don't want to go back to the lake. I'm covered in bug bites."

"I have a better idea." Portia smiled. "All we need is a flashlight."

Portia grabbed two flashlights and led Hallie up a stone path behind the villa. They climbed higher, until the lake fluttered below them like tissue paper. They reached a grove of olive trees and found a small hut. Inside there was a wooden table and two chairs painted dark green.

"Marcus and I begged a gardener to build this for us years ago." Portia squeezed through the narrow door. "We used to hold meetings of our secret society. You were only allowed in if you drank a teaspoon of castor oil."

"I'm guessing you didn't have many members." Hallie sat on the green chair. She unwrapped a piece of pizza and chewed it hungrily. She hadn't eaten since Peter stormed out of the hotel room.

"We're like the two girls in that movie *The Parent Trap*." Portia opened the jar of olives. "They meet at camp and discover they are identical twins. One had never known her mother and the other had never met her father."

"They were twelve." Hallie sighed. "I'm too old to be figuring out who I am."

"Remember the first summer I came to America and we made a pact that we would remain best friends, even with an ocean separating us?" Portia asked.

"We snuck into Constance's sewing room and pricked our thumbs with a needle," Hallie said, smiling. "Then we pressed our thumbs together and swore that we were blood sisters."

"We are sisters!" Portia exclaimed. "The same blood runs through our veins. Maybe I shouldn't be so angry with Francesca; she gave me the best present I could ask for."

"But she didn't tell us," Hallie murmured. "You can't enjoy a gift if you don't know it exists."

"You're right." Portia's eyes were wet and bright. "Maybe we're not angry enough."

"I don't know if Pliny likes his coffee black or white." Hallie sighed. "He doesn't know I love Agatha Christie novels, that my first pet was named Miles, and that I broke my front tooth in the fourth grade."

"We'll tell him tomorrow." Portia opened the bottle of wine.

"I hope he listens," Hallie said darkly.

"Tesoro women are strong." Portia's eyes glinted like a cat. "We won't give him a choice."

chapter fifteen

Hallie waited for Portia in the small salon. She had slept badly; her skin was sunburned and smattered with bug bites. She kept her phone beside the bed, but Peter hadn't called or texted. She knew he wouldn't—she recognized the wounded, determined look when he walked out the door. But she couldn't stop herself from checking the screen.

Hallie knew she must call Constance and tell her that she had broken up with Peter. Constance would be so upset—all her plans for a summer wedding, the lengthy discussions with Stanlee Gatti and Paula LeDuc, for nothing. But Hallie had to tell her the truth; she didn't want to be someone who kept secrets.

She tossed in bed, debating whether to call Francesca. Recounting the diaries to Portia, Hallie realized her mother wrote with little emotion. There were no scenes of weeping, no tortured nights lying awake, wondering if she made the right decision.

Hallie had to ask Francesca how she could bring herself to leave two tiny children, how she could have kept Pliny's relationship to Hallie a secret for so many years. She glanced at the phone illuminated in the dark, and knew if she didn't talk to her mother soon, she may never talk to her again.

Portia entered the salon carrying a large box. She wore a red tube top and a white miniskirt. Her nails were painted with pink polish and a sterling silver heart dangled at her neck.

"I'm donating all the clothes Riccardo gave me to charity." Portia set the box on the coffee table.

"What are you going to wear?" Hallie put down her magazine.

"I've got closets full of clothes I bought in Milan and Florence." Portia sifted through Valentino dresses, Dior silk blouses, Pucci slacks. "But I don't want to touch anything Riccardo touched again. He's lucky I don't toss it all into the lake."

"You're looking better." Hallie glanced at Portia. She walked with her old skip and held herself erect like a ballerina. Even her words came out faster, as if the numbing pain had subsided.

"I called Signor Berta, our family lawyer, and told him I want a divorce." Portia closed the box. "If I'm going to burn in hell, I may as well enjoy living. *La dolce vita!*"

"*La dolce vita,*" Hallie repeated.

"I told Pliny you wanted to go sightseeing and asked him to drive us," Portia said. "He's bringing the car around."

"I've never driven with him," Hallie murmured, catching her reflection in the mirror. She wore a blue cotton dress with a wide leather belt. Her hair was held back with a white ribbon, and she had applied mascara and shimmering lip gloss.

"You look beautiful." Portia squeezed her arm. "Wear your seat belt, he's a terrible driver."

Hallie stepped into the backseat of the red Fiat and Pliny roared down the driveway. He drove with one hand, using the other to point out historic gardens, stone statues, and ancient churches. Portia turned up the radio and sang along to Italian pop songs, encouraging Hallie to join in on the chorus.

The road was so narrow, Hallie held her breath whenever a car came in the other direction. Every now and then the Fiat entered a long tunnel. Hallie could almost feel the weight of the mountain above them, and closed her eyes until they emerged safely on the other side.

They arrived in Lecco at lunchtime and the central piazza was teeming with people. Lecco wasn't a tourist town like Bellagio, but somehow that made it more romantic. The inhabitants lived in small apartments and had ordinary jobs, but everywhere they turned was impossible beauty. The lake lapped the edge of Piazza Settembre and a tall clock tower stood in the town center. Behind, the Alps loomed like elder statesmen watching over their citizens.

Pliny showed Hallie and Portia the basilica of San Nicolo and the Viscontea Tower, crumbling ruins of the Roman Empire. They visited the villa of the nineteenth-century writer Alfredo Manzoni, and Hallie bought a copy of his novel in the bookstore.

They waited until the crowds thinned and the piazza lay serene in the afternoon sun. Pliny directed them to a restaurant facing the lake and they sat outside, drinking bottles of sparkling mineral water.

Pliny consulted the menu. "They make the best pizza in Lake Como." He had been animated and smiling all day. When workers whistled at Portia, he put his arm around her shoulder and murmured, *"Mia bambina."*

"Pliny used to bring me here when I was young." Portia sipped her water. "I always laughed and said we drove twenty kilometers so Sophia didn't know we ate pizza!"

"My mother thinks anything eaten with your fingers does not belong at the table," Pliny explained. "She has not tried their pizza margherita with olives and ricotta cheese."

"We wanted to discuss something with you," Portia said when the waiter had taken their order.

"Nothing has to be said." Pliny laid his hand on Portia's. He had large hands with oval nails and gold rings on each finger. He wore linen slacks and a camel-colored shirt and his sunglasses perched on his forehead. "If I see Riccardo again, I will throw him out of the villa."

"You're not angry with me?" Portia asked.

"You are a princess." Pliny scowled. "He treated you like chattel."

"But I thought you and Sophia were so upset," Portia stammered. "The disgrace to the family name, the statue."

"The statue will go up and the Tesoro name will continue." Pliny shrugged. "I saw your face when you returned from Capri, I cannot watch you suffer. My children's happiness is the most important thing."

Hallie watched Portia's eyes grow wide. Her mouth curled into a dazzling smile. She stood up and hugged her father, her slim arms barely encircling him.

"Come." Pliny brushed his hand over his eyes. "We must eat while the pizza is hot, to leave it sitting is a sin."

They ate slices crammed with tomatoes, onions, and creamy ricotta cheese. Hallie had never tasted such a delicious crust, such sweet tomatoes and savory spices. She watched Pliny and Portia chatter in Italian, waving their hands and wiping the sauce from their chins. They seemed like halves cut from the same whole, their gestures mirroring each other. Hallie felt like a child arriving on her first day at kindergarten, to find the other children already playing together.

They followed the pizza with chocolate sponge cake and cups of strong, dark coffee. Hallie turned her face up to the sun and felt sexy and sophisticated and almost Italian. Perhaps it was the caffeine, or the men who whistled admiringly, but she suddenly felt like she belonged.

Hallie could see herself owning a chic design store, with

beige silk walls and polished marble floors. She would stock modern pieces from Milan and Vienna and elegant antiques she discovered in Tuscany. Pliny would introduce her to the old families of Bellagio and Varenna, and she would decorate their homes with exquisite taste.

"Hallie has something exciting to tell you," Portia interrupted her thoughts.

"If you are going to turn your talents on the Villa Tesoro, I must warn you Sophia hasn't changed the furnishings in fifty years." Pliny smiled.

"I wouldn't dream of redecorating the villa." Hallie blushed. "Though I would love to get my hands on the pool house."

"What would you like to tell me?" Pliny inquired, sipping his coffee.

"It's about Francesca," Hallie stammered. The sun dipped behind a cloud and Hallie shivered. She could remain silent and enjoy the afternoon. Pliny would drive back too fast and Hallie's hair would blow in the breeze. They would join Sophia for dinner and Pliny and Portia would wink over the lasagna, never mentioning the pizza they shared.

"Is she coming when Marcus has his baby?" Pliny asked, his face clouding over. "One would think she would like to meet her first grandchild."

"I found her notebooks in the library," Hallie began. "She kept a diary when she lived at the villa."

"A diary?" Pliny's brows knotted together.

"It starts in Gstaad." Hallie blushed, remembering Francesca's girlish proclamations of love. "And it continues till she left."

"And what does she write in this diary?" Pliny scoffed. "That she had to learn Italian, that no television was allowed in the villa?"

"She wrote she was only allowed to see Marcus and Portia for an hour a day." Hallie's lips trembled. "Sophia told her how to dress and who to talk to. She was completely miserable and you sided with Sophia in every argument."

"Francesca and I were very young and from different cultures. She didn't understand the Italian way of doing things." Pliny sipped his coffee and gazed at Hallie. "I was a good son, perhaps too good a son. In Italy the matriarch rules the household, that's the way it is done."

"You lied to Francesca," Hallie continued boldly. "You told her you would stop Sophia from sending Marcus to boarding school. She found the letter from Le Rosey, she was devastated."

"I tried to make Francesca happy." Pliny twisted his gold ring. "We went to the opera, we boated on the lake. Francesca ate the finest foods, wore designer clothes. She lived in the most beautiful villa."

"She was barely allowed to see her children," Hallie insisted. "She was afraid she would miss their whole childhoods."

"In time Francesca would have gotten used to the Italian way of life." Pliny frowned. "She left so quickly. She went to Milan for a dress fitting and disappeared."

Hallie felt the wind blow off the lake. She took a deep breath and looked at Pliny.

"She was pregnant. She couldn't face watching her children being raised by nannies and sent to boarding school. She had to leave before her pregnancy was discovered."

"That is absurd!" Pliny suddenly grew angry. "Francesca wouldn't steal a Tesoro heir."

"I did the math," Hallie said quietly. "I'm the baby, I'm your daughter."

Pliny slammed his fists on the table so the coffee cups rattled and the bottle of mineral water smashed on the ground. He stood up, roaring like a wounded lion.

"You are a sorceress like your mother! What is it you are after? Diamonds, gold, the Tesoro ruby? You stay in my home;

you win the ear of my daughter and fill it with lies! Do you think I would not know if I had another daughter? Do you think I would not feel it here?" He pounded his chest. "I want you to leave my house, I want you out of the country!"

"Hallie's telling the truth," Portia whispered.

"She has brainwashed you!" Pliny roared. "Take the ferry back, I cannot stay and listen to these lies."

Hallie watched helplessly as Pliny stormed across the piazza. He jumped into the Fiat and roared down the road, narrowly missing a boy on a bicycle. Hallie stared at Pliny's crumpled napkin, his unfinished piece of pizza. Her whole body started shaking, and she wrapped her arms around her chest and cried.

"He was just upset," Portia said uneasily. "He'll come back."

Hallie let the tears fall on her plate. "He hates me because I'm his daughter, I remind him of her."

"Pliny has a temper," Portia murmured. "He'll come to his senses."

"And what if he doesn't?" Hallie sobbed. "Where will I live while I finish Villa Luce? What will I do when I'm done? I can't go back to San Francisco."

"Why not?" Portia asked calmly.

"Because I ended it with Peter and because I never want to talk to Francesca again." Hallie cried harder, her shoulders heaving.

"When I was little, I missed having a mother so much I couldn't eat dinner. Marcus would wait till our nanny went downstairs and then he would bring out my favorite chocolate bars. He kept a whole stash of British chocolate under his bed: Violet Crumble, Cadbury Fruit and Nut, Aero and Flake bars. He told me to stop thinking about what I missed and remember what I had: a father, a grandmother, a brother who loved me, a beautiful home, the most beautiful lake in the world as my playground," Portia mused. "I managed to eat one or two chocolate bars, and when I woke in the morning I felt better."

"I should eat a carton of Häagen-Dazs and everything will be all right?" Hallie demanded.

"You should remember what you have: a sister who adores you, Constance, a fabulous career." Portia smiled. "You could get Peter back or use your charms on Angus."

"I don't want a man." Hallie sighed. The tears had stopped and her breathing returned to normal. "But I love you, and I'm happy I'm here."

"Pliny will cool down. In the meantime we will have more chocolate cake."

"I couldn't eat anything." Hallie shook her head.

"Then we will have an aperitif." Portia signaled the waiter. "In Italy, cocktail hour starts right after lunch."

Portia ordered two gin and tonics and Hallie chased the lime around her glass. She listened to Portia chatter about music festivals and open-air markets and the famous villas and gardens she hadn't seen. She didn't want to sightsee; she didn't want to eat gelato and shop for shoes. She wanted to be somewhere she was loved; she wanted to be home.

The sun dropped behind the mountains and the piazza was almost deserted. The waiter brought them their check, pointedly removing their glasses. Hallie felt goose bumps prick her skin and Portia's teeth chattered.

"I'll just see when the next ferry comes." Portia jumped up and headed across the piazza to the ferry terminal.

Hallie waited, hugging her chest to keep warm. She saw a man walk slowly toward her. He kept his hands in his pockets and his head down. He reached the table and pulled out a chair.

"My apologies," Pliny stammered. His eyes were bloodshot and his hands shook. "I was furious, but not at you."

"Oh." Hallie avoided his eyes.

"I never knew she kept diaries," Pliny said, almost to himself. "I loved your mother but I was so young, I didn't know how to be a good husband. I thought I just had to buy her diamonds and make love to her." Pliny's voice trailed off. "We fought but I thought that was normal. Tesoros are very passionate. I never imagined she would leave."

"She was desperate. She thought you loved Sophia more than you loved her."

"I was very angry at Francesca for a long time. But she left me the two things I love most in the world: Marcus and Portia." Pliny's eyes filled with tears. "Now I know she gave me another precious thing: a beautiful daughter."

Hallie couldn't say a word without dissolving into tears. She looked at Pliny's big hands, at the gold rings glittering on his fingers.

"I missed almost thirty years of my daughter's life." Pliny's voice wavered. "I missed teaching her to ride a bicycle, to fish, to avoid a boy's kiss. I missed seeing her grow from an angel into a beautiful woman, and I only have myself to blame."

Hallie watched Portia skip back from the ferry terminal. She let Pliny pull her up and wrap his arms around her. She laid her head on his shoulder and cried like a baby.

They moved to an indoor café and drank hot chocolate spiked with brandy. Hallie told stories about the nuns at St. Ignatius, the boys she met at UCLA, her favorite Italian restaurants in San Francisco. She recounted a funny vignette about one of Francesca's wedding cakes, but Pliny's face clouded over and she didn't mention her mother again.

The piazza filled up with people getting off work, loosening their ties and ordering plates of antipasto. Hallie and Portia and Pliny climbed back in the Fiat, and Pliny drove leisurely to Bellagio. When they arrived at the villa, the dinner bell rang and they rushed upstairs to change. Pliny suggested they didn't tell Sophia yet—she was still in a rage about Portia leaving Riccardo.

Hallie dressed carefully, choosing a black-and-white Dior dress and black Gucci slingbacks. She added an extra layer of mascara and put a diamond clip in her hair. She walked down the staircase and Pliny was waiting at the bottom, freshly shaved in black silk pants and a white cotton shirt. He took Hallie's arm and she floated into the dining room, feeling a new and foreign kind of happiness.

chapter sixteen

Hallie tied a Benetton sweater around her shoulders and slipped on a pair of loafers. It was late September and the weather had cooled. A thick mist shrouded the lake in the mornings and returned in the evening. Many of the tourists had gone home. The locals ate steaming plates of spaghetti in outdoor cafés, pleased to be rid of the impatient French and the loud Americans.

The last few weeks had moved at a dizzying pace. Hallie returned from her buying trip with crystal chandeliers and ornate Persian rugs. The paintings hung on the walls in their new space, and Hallie began adding silk ottomans and Louis XIV chairs. She loved going to work, admiring the Regency sofas she discovered in a castle in Tuscany, the Murano glass so delicate she was afraid it would break in her hands.

Hallie and Pliny carved out time together. He drove into the hills and took her to La Tabla for dinner. The owner had known Pliny since he was six years old. He sat at the table, admiring Hallie's beauty and offering extra glasses of red wine.

On the weekends Pliny drove Hallie and Portia around the lake in his motorboat, stopping at different villages to pick up fresh olives or loaves of garlic bread. He was happiest when he was on the water, bouncing over the waves so Hallie and Portia clutched their seats and screamed with laughter.

The hardest part of the last few weeks had been Hallie's call to Constance. She took the phone out on the balcony, and dialed Constance's number.

"Darling!" Constance beamed. "It's been too long. I was afraid you'd been swept up by Lake Como and forgotten how to speak English."

"My Italian is terrible," Hallie confessed. "Everyone at the villa speaks English."

"How is Portia? Francesca said she and Riccardo were back together."

"They were." Hallie hesitated. "But she's filed for divorce."

"Divorce!" Constance gasped. "What did Sophia say?"

"Sophia is not happy," Hallie murmured. "But Pliny is supporting her. Riccardo wasn't good for Portia."

"No woman enjoys being married to a gigolo," Constance agreed. "Marriage demands fidelity, that's why it's written in the vows. You'll never have that problem with Peter; he only has eyes for you."

Hallie took a deep breath. "Peter visited on his way to Paris. I ended it."

"You did what?" Constance's voice was sharp.

"I broke up with him," Hallie replied in a rush. "I don't know how long I'll be here, or what I'll do after. I can't string him along."

"A career is important, but it is no replacement for love, marriage, and family."

"I don't think I was really in love with Peter," Hallie said lamely.

Constance was silent for so long, Hallie was afraid she had hung up. "You're like your mother, chasing some European fairy tale. You belong in San Francisco with a good man by your side. You're not going to find someone like Peter."

"I'm not looking." Hallie blinked away tears.

"Maybe not now," Constance warned. "But when the glamour and glitz wears off you will be."

Hallie couldn't tell Constance she wasn't looking for glitz and glamour; she was getting to know her father. Hallie imagined Constance absorbing the news and knew her fragile health couldn't stand it. She smiled bravely and hung up, feeling severely chastised.

Hallie avoided Francesca's calls, and texted her back, using the time difference and her long hours at work as excuses for her lack of communication. She still didn't know if or when she could talk to her, so she buried her in the back of her mind, under the many decisions she had to make at work and the daily activity at the villa.

Portia, miraculously, had walked into her old ballet school and emerged a dance teacher. Madame LaFarge finally gave in to her arthritis and turned her classes over to younger instructors. Portia taught two classes a day. She pirouetted around the villa in the evenings, chattering about the seven-year-old girl who would be a prima ballerina, the twelve-year-old who shouldn't be allowed near a pair of pointe shoes.

"Where are you going?" Portia pranced into Hallie's bedroom. She wore her new uniform of black tights and a brightly colored leotard. One of Pliny's fisherman's sweaters hung over the leotard and she wore satin slippers on her feet.

"To the farmers' market," Hallie replied. "Unless it rains."

"It never rains in September," Portia said dismissively. "You smell too good to be going to the market. Is that Obsession?"

"Am I wearing too much?" Hallie sniffed her wrist.

"Depends on who you're trying to impress." Portia sat cross-legged on the bed.

"Angus is taking me, as friends." Hallie checked her hair in the mirror. "I've never been to the markets in Tremezzo."

"You're going on a date?" Portia raised her eyebrows.

Hallie blushed. "Picking out tomatoes and radishes in the afternoon is not a date."

"It doesn't have anything to do with interior design." Portia's eyes narrowed. "And it could easily lead into Saturday night and Sunday morning."

"We're just friends," Hallie insisted. Hallie had told Angus she broke up with Peter and they fell into an easy friendship. Angus created delicious dishes with fresh fish and vegetables grown in Max's greenhouse. He joked about Hallie's addiction to paella and her inability to pass up chocolate.

"Men and women can't be friends." Portia shrugged her slim shoulders. She was still thin, but her body had a new energy.

"Angus seems lonely," Hallie mused. "He doesn't have any friends, and I don't think he has much contact with Max."

"Have you ever seen Max?" Portia leaned forward. She thought Hallie's mysterious employer was even sexier than his estate manager.

"I'm sure I will, when I finish the job. I like making my own decisions."

"Think carefully before you sleep with Angus," Portia warned. "It's not good to mix business with pleasure."

"I'm not going to sleep with him!" Hallie retorted. "We're not even having dinner. We're going to tramp around the market and buy red peppers and radicchio."

"I am going on a date," Portia said proudly. "And I'm not ashamed to admit it."

"With who?" Hallie asked. Portia hadn't had any male visitors at the villa, and she seemed to spend all her time rehearsing dance routines.

"Alfonso," Portia replied, her mouth curling in a smile.

"Alfonso!" Hallie exclaimed. "When did you see him?"

"I ran into him in Como. He's been stopping by the dance studio."

"How often?" Hallie inquired.

"Every day," Portia mumbled. "We grab a quick bite at lunch or a coffee after work."

"You've been seeing Alfonso every day without mentioning it!"

"You didn't tell me you were playing Peter Rabbit with Angus," Portia shot back.

Hallie flinched. She hadn't heard from Peter since he left Bellagio. Sometimes late at night, she searched the Internet for an article he wrote, but when she found one she closed the computer before reading it. She wanted to know Peter was working and happy, but she didn't want any contact with him.

"Where are you going?" Hallie asked.

"He's going to surprise me." Portia hugged her chest. "When Alfonso and Marcus were university students they were so serious. Alfonso wore thick glasses and his hair barely reached his collar. Now he looks like a lion."

"You like him?" Hallie asked.

"Apparently he had a big crush on me." Portia pulled a thread on her sweater. "He still talks about politics and finance. But his eyes are like gems, and he has the smoothest hands."

"You shouldn't judge a man by his hands," Hallie said, smiling.

"When we sit at a café, he doesn't stare at the Swedish au pair at the next table, or make eyes at the waitress," Portia said seriously. "He only looks at me."

Hallie met Angus at the boat dock. He wore khakis and a bulky red sweater. He helped Hallie into the motorboat and they crossed the lake to Tremezzo. Angus tied the boat at the dock and they walked through the narrow alleys.

"In a few months there'll be snow on the ground," Angus said as they approached the market. "I love Lake Como in the winter. It's so peaceful, like watching a silent movie."

"Don't you get lonely?" Hallie asked. Some of the cafés had already moved their tables indoors and the wind nipped Hallie's cheeks. She slipped her sweater over her head, grateful she had worn slacks and loafers.

"I grew up the middle of seven children." Angus stopped at a market stall. He sampled sliced honeydew melon and gave a piece to Hallie. "Everyone at the dinner table talked about the Red Sox and the Knicks. I wanted to discuss Ancient Egypt and Mesopotamia. You can be lonely surrounded by people."

"My mother tried to be my friend," Hallie replied. "She didn't understand I wanted a mother. I had girlfriends at school to paint my nails and listen to music with."

"Have you talked to her?" Angus asked.

"Not yet." Hallie gulped. She had discussed Francesca with Angus over fettuccine Alfredo and warm garlic bread. He listened closely, his long legs spread out in front of him.

"You owe it to yourself to call her." Angus cradled a yellow tomato in his hand. "She may have a good reason for not telling you."

"The last few weeks with Pliny makes me realize how much I've missed." Hallie sighed. "I showed him how to make a tuna fish sandwich. We discovered we both love caramel toffees, we can finish a box in one sitting."

"If you talk to Francesca, you might have two parents at the same time." Angus touched her arm lightly.

Hallie paused, holding a shiny red apple in her hand. She remembered when the other children brought a mother and father to back-to-school night, or had two parents attend a teacher's conference. Francesca was chic and sophisticated with her big brown eyes and close-cropped hair, but Hallie wished she also had a father who wore a suit and carried a leather briefcase.

Hallie grinned. "You always know what to say."

"I was the family negotiator." Angus smiled. "I won the Good Samaritan Award two years in a row in high school, and was voted 'most likely to change the world.'"

"You can still do that." Hallie looked up at Angus. He was examining a box of figs, his expression strangely serious. "There's plenty of time."

"People don't learn from the mistakes of previous cultures." Angus paid for the figs. "Rome burned and it will burn again."

"I thought you said people are good," Hallie mused.

"They are inherently good," Angus agreed. "But there's too much temptation with the Internet and social media. When people are cruel it has a ripple effect like a tsunami."

"Speaking of tsunamis, it looks like rain." Hallie tried to lighten the mood. "We should hurry and finish shopping."

They bought squash and sweet potatoes, bundles of asparagus and heads of lettuce. Angus asked the prices in Italian and nodded *grazie* when the sellers insisted he take an extra basket of strawberries or bag of yams.

"What did he say?" Hallie whispered when an old man insisted Angus accept a box of ripe, purple plums.

"He said I was lucky to have such a beautiful girlfriend, and I must spoil her with the sweetest fruits." Angus carried the plums under one arm.

"Did you tell him I'm not your girlfriend?" Hallie glanced at the man, who bowed and smiled a toothless smile.

"And have him take back the plums?" Angus grinned. "I'll make a pie with fresh whipped cream."

"These scarves are gorgeous." Hallie stopped at a stall where silk scarves blew in the wind like sails. "I must buy one for Portia."

"I'll negotiate," Angus suggested. "They don't respect you unless you demand a good price."

Hallie moved on to a stall selling sketches while Angus chatted with the woman selling scarves. She had thought the market only sold fruits and vegetables, but there were stalls displaying silver jewelry, handmade leather purses, and brightly colored clothing.

"She gave me the second one for free," Angus said proudly, handing Hallie two scarves wrapped in tissue paper. "And she gave me something else."

Angus pressed a warm lump in Hallie's arms. Hallie felt something wet burrow into her elbow. She jumped and discovered a puppy with damp fur, a round body, and a tiny tail beating rapidly against her chest.

"Angus!" Hallie exclaimed. "Are you crazy?"

"She insisted I take him." Angus laughed as the puppy licked Hallie's chin. "I was afraid she might drown him. He really likes you."

"I can't have a puppy!" Hallie protested. "Sophia keeps the villa as pristine as a furniture showroom."

"I'll keep him in my rooms." Angus stroked the puppy's head. "You can play with him in the gardens after work."

"But I don't know my plans." Hallie let the puppy burrow into her shoulder. She remembered standing in the pet store, hugging Miles, whose paws were as big as her hands. She recalled the way he slept snuggled against her feet, his breathing the last thing she heard before she fell asleep. She remembered playing with him in Constance's garden, chasing tennis balls and running races across the lawn.

"There's no hurry, my rooms are as big as most houses." Angus let the puppy lick his hand. "What will you name him?"

"Milo," Hallie said quickly, the name arriving fully formed on her lips.

"Come on, Milo." Angus led them toward the boat dock. "Let's see if we can find a tennis ball."

It started to sprinkle as they reached the edge of the village. Angus grabbed Hallie's hand and they ran, but the drops became heavy steel-colored sheets. They took shelter under a fig tree and Angus took off his sweater and held it over them.

At first when Angus touched her hair she thought it was the rain. She moved closer to the tree trunk, and he rubbed his hands over her shoulders. He put his arms around her, then he tipped her face up to his and kissed her deeply on the lips.

Hallie stood in Angus's embrace, tasting plums and strawberries. She heard the bleat of the ferry and the sound of raindrops falling on leaves. She smelled Milo's wet fur, and kept her mouth pressed against Angus's.

When he finally let her go, her lips engorged and her clothes damp and sticky, the rain had turned to a drizzle. They walked quickly to the boat dock and crossed the lake to Bellagio. Hallie pressed Milo into Angus's lap and jumped out of the boat. She ran up the steps to the villa, her heart beating wildly.

chapter seventeen

I'm too old to be a dancer," Portia groaned. "My body feels like it's been strung up on a torture rack."

Hallie turned and glanced at Portia. "You look like you're fifteen." They lay on lounges beside the pool, their bodies coated with Acqua di Parma sunscreen.

The rain of the previous weekend had given way to a week of brilliant sunshine. Hallie had worn shorts and tank tops to work all week, staying after work to play with Milo on the lawn. They played hide-and-seek between the statues, and chased a balled-up sock through the rose gardens. Milo seemed to grow every day. His stomach was thicker, his paws bigger, his fur was smooth and shiny.

"I love teaching," Portia admitted, turning over on her stomach. "But my jetés travel half as far as they used to, and my arabesque looks like a stork."

"I doubt that." Hallie laughed. "I'm exhausted from chasing after Milo. I forgot how much work having a puppy is."

"It looks like it agrees with you." Portia studied Hallie. "Or maybe it's Angus, but you're definitely glowing."

"Nothing is going on with me and Angus," Hallie replied, realizing that was not quite true. There was a change in their relationship since their kiss, an electricity that Hallie could not ignore.

Monday morning had dawned bright and sunny. The view from the ferry was breathtaking, as if someone had taken a brush and wiped away every imperfection. The lake was emerald green and the flowers on the promenade were vibrant shades of purple and yellow. As the ferry approached the Villa Luce, Hallie felt an uneasy anticipation, as if she was starving, but didn't know what she was hungry for.

Hallie didn't see Angus until lunchtime. She made her own salad and took it out on the balcony, sitting alone at the wrought-iron table. She watched Angus cross the lawn. He wore navy shorts, a white T-shirt, and his thick hair fell smoothly over his forehead. He gripped an old sock in one hand, and Milo firmly in the other.

"He kept me up all night," Angus said grinning, putting the puppy on the tile floor. "And he ate scrambled eggs for breakfast."

"Sounds like a healthy diet." Hallie laughed, avoiding Angus's eyes. Suddenly she could feel his hands on her shoulders, his mouth pressed against hers.

"I'm going to the village to buy dog food." Angus leaned against the railing. "I reread *Tom Sawyer* over the weekend."

"I haven't read it since high school," Hallie mused, pushing a baby tomato around her plate.

"I was wrong about Tom and Becky." Angus hesitated. "They weren't just friends; he kissed her outside the school house."

"Oh." Hallie speared an asparagus tip with her fork.

"After they kissed, she was angry with him, and he spent half the book getting back in her good graces." Angus sat at the table opposite Hallie.

"Why would I be angry?" Hallie put her fork down. "It was raining, we were excited about Milo."

"I don't want to just kiss you on a boat or under an olive tree," Angus said. "I'd like to get to know you, go out to dinner, stroll along the promenade."

Hallie felt her stomach tighten, as if someone pulled a string on a corset. She pictured Peter grabbing his backpack and storming out of the hotel room. She remembered feeling like someone had placed a brick on her chest.

"I liked the kiss," Hallie admitted. "But I'm not ready for dinner and dating."

"Dinner's like lunch but with better silverware." Angus smiled. "We can go to a trattoria in Lenno, skipping the silverware and eating pizza with our hands."

"I'll stick with lunch for now," Hallie replied, offering Milo a piece of ham. "We better feed Milo, he's starving."

"I once spent three weeks sifting through rubble to find a Greek artifact." Angus scooped up Milo. "I'm very patient."

"You're allowed to date." Portia poured sunscreen into her hand. "It's good for the skin."

"I like Angus," Hallie mused. "But I'm still getting used to being Hallie Tesoro. Pliny hasn't even told Sophia about me."

"You can't blame him." Portia sighed. "Sophia makes the sign of the cross every time I walk by. The funny thing is she used to dote on Alfonso when Marcus brought him home from university. He always complimented her on her brunches."

Hallie raised her eyebrows. "It sounds like things are getting serious."

"He's taking me to Il Gatto Nero tomorrow night. It's nearly impossible to get a reservation," Portia replied. "Alfonso bribed the maître d' with yards of his most expensive silk. You and Angus should join us!"

"Tag along to a romantic dinner?" Hallie frowned.

"Sisters are supposed to double date," Portia replied, her eyes sparkling. "I can ask Angus questions about Max. I love a good mystery."

"I don't want to sit across a table and talk about what books Angus likes to read," Hallie explained. "I knew Peter so well for so long, I don't want to know someone new."

"Then skip dinner and go straight to the sex." Portia grinned. "Angus has gorgeous legs."

"I don't want a man," Hallie insisted. "I want to finish the Villa Luce, I want to spend time with Pliny and get to know Lake Como."

"If you really want to be Italian, that means embracing *la dolce vita*." Portia flipped on her stomach. "Eating, drinking, and making love."

"The two most beautiful women in Lake Como," a male voice said behind them. "Posing like models for Michelangelo."

Portia leaped up and kissed Alfonso on the cheek. He wore beige linen slacks and a silk shirt open to the third button. He carried a slim box in one hand and a bunch of lilacs in the other.

"Are you spying on me?" Portia demanded playfully. "I thought you were in Milan till tomorrow."

"I wrapped business up early." Alfonso settled on the chaise lounge. "I brought you a gift for tomorrow night."

"I don't need presents," Portia said, scowling.

"Riccardo bought you gifts because he was a scoundrel." Alfonso handed the box to Portia. "I bring you presents to show off your beauty. You are Aphrodite and Venus rolled into one."

"He's impossible to resist." Portia giggled to Hallie. She tore off the tissue paper and discovered a dove-colored silk dress with a heart-shaped bodice.

"It's Armani," Alfonso said. "Straight off the runway. I practically plucked it off the model."

"I hope she was wearing something underneath." Portia held the dress in front of her.

"It's gorgeous." Hallie nodded. "You look like a china doll."

"Alfonso does have excellent taste." Portia rewarded him with a kiss on the lips. "Convince Hallie she and Angus should join us; I want to show off the new dress."

"Hallie has a new beau?" Alfonso beamed. "Then we will make it a party of four."

"Angus and I are friends," Hallie protested, shooting Portia a look.

"A sexy male friend who gave her a puppy," Portia interjected.

"Angus was afraid Milo would be drowned," Hallie insisted.

"Has he asked you on a date?" Portia asked.

"He wanted to take me to dinner," Hallie admitted. "I said I'm not ready."

"What is this term 'not ready'?" Alfonso frowned. "Americans stay children too long. They spend their whole lives playing in the sandbox."

"It means I just broke up with Peter," Hallie retorted. "I don't want to throw myself in a new relationship."

"We need love like we need to breathe." Angus shrugged. "What are you waiting for? For the wrinkles to start, for your hair to turn gray?"

Hallie glanced from Alfonso to Portia. They both looked young and sleek and sophisticated. Alfonso's eyes were sharp as pebbles and his fingers tapped restlessly on the chair. Portia was like a cat preening in the sun, lapping up Alfonso's praise.

Suddenly Hallie couldn't think of a reason to say no to Angus. Peter, the apartment on Russian Hill, Kendra's design store were all part of another life. If she was going to live in Lake Como, she had to move forward.

Hallie hesitated. "I don't know if Angus could afford it."

"It will be my treat," Alfonso insisted, winking at Portia. "We will teach the Americans how to dine."

Hallie had spent the last hour in her closet, debating what to wear to dinner. She finally chose a pleated skirt and matching angora sweater. Glancing in the mirror, she thought she was dressed for a Junior League fashion show. But she didn't want to flash her breasts or expose her legs. She wanted to take things slowly. She wished she could skip dinner altogether and eat pizza with Pliny.

Lea knocked on her door and announced the arrival of a visitor. Hallie ran the brush through her hair and rubbed lip gloss on her lips. She grabbed her purse and ran down the stairs to the foyer.

Angus stood under the crystal chandelier, his feet shifting nervously. He wore beige slacks and a blazer that didn't reach his wrists. He smiled when he saw Hallie, his eyes crinkling at the corners.

"I'm a little rusty at dating," he admitted. "I couldn't decide whether to bring you flowers or perfume. Milo chewed up the roses, now he has a terrible stomachache."

"I don't need anything," Hallie murmured.

"No you don't." Angus's eyes traveled over Hallie's body. "You're perfect."

"I was afraid you'd think I'm forward . . . asking you to dinner."

"Nothing has made me happier since we caught the Lavarello," Angus replied. "We'll learn some new recipes and I can try them on you later."

"Portia said the food is amazing," Hallie mumbled. She pictured a candlelit table, Alfonso and Portia holding hands, Hallie sitting awkwardly across from Angus. She grabbed the staircase railing and was about to run upstairs, but Angus placed his wide hand on her arm.

"It's only dinner," Angus said quietly. "I won't even make you eat your vegetables."

Hallie glanced at Angus's hazel eyes and relaxed. They had fished together and been stuck in a rainstorm. A delicious dinner, accompanied by Alfonso and Portia's bright chatter, couldn't be so hard.

They drove in Alfonso's black Peugeot. Angus's long legs were jammed into his chest. Hallie pressed her body against the window, watching the lake change colors. The sun dipped behind the mountains, turning the sky into a kaleidoscope.

The restaurant was in the hills, high above Cernobbio. The maître d' led them outside to the balcony and Hallie gasped at the view. Como was lit up like Main Street in Disneyland, and Bellagio shone like a precious jewel. The villages of Varenna and Menaggio shimmered like fireflies swarming around a flame.

"The most magnificent view in Lake Como." Alfonso opened his arms expansively. "The wine selection is unrivaled and the fish is fresh every day."

Hallie listened to Alfonso and Portia chat about the jazz festival in Tremezzo and a new restaurant in Como. Alfonso ate heartily: antipasto, garlic bread, oysters on the half shell. Portia sipped her wine, giggling and flirting. The tense, watchful expression she wore when she was with Riccardo was absent, replaced by an easy smile.

Hallie tried to remember what she and Peter talked about at dinner: the magazine, her clients, a new exhibit at the Asian Art Museum. She glanced at Angus but he seemed content sipping his wine. Every now and then he offered his opinion on art or local cuisine, sending Hallie a small smile across the table.

"I envy the British their great mystery writers." Portia ate a slice of melon wrapped in prosciutto. "Hallie and I used to read her Agatha Christie novels aloud every night."

"We both had terrible nightmares." Hallie smiled.

"To think we have a mystery in our midst," Portia said mischievously. "Alfonso insists he's never met Max Rodale, but he's provided silk for the whole villa."

"Only Angus knows our employer personally," Alfonso concurred.

"You have to tell us about him," Portia purred to Angus.

"I rarely see Max, he travels constantly," Angus explained. "When he's at the villa he sequesters himself on the third floor."

"Was he disfigured in some terrible accident?" Portia's eyes twinkled.

"He's just very shy," Angus replied, dipping a breadstick in olive oil. "He's devoted to art."

"He must have suffered a tragic love affair," Portia continued. "Like Antony and Cleopatra or Tristan and Isolde."

"Not all great loves are tragic," Angus mused. "Some of the greatest partners in history have been husband and wife: Pierre and Marie Curie, Queen Victoria and Prince Albert."

"Love makes one capable of climbing the highest mountains," Alfonso agreed, draping his arm around Portia.

"Alfonso has a list of impossible places he wants to travel together." Portia giggled. "The Himalayas, Machu Picchu, Kilimanjaro."

Alfonso nodded. "I have always wanted to explore the world, like Christopher Columbus."

"I used to think Alfonso was a bookworm who only liked to add up numbers," Portia said. "I'm glad he proved me wrong."

Hallie watched Alfonso kiss Portia softly on the lips. She turned to Angus, wanting to change the conversation to something light: Milo's antics or crazy Italian drivers. But he was studying Hallie intently, his fingers wrapped around his wineglass. Hallie stabbed a tomato with a toothpick and stared at the lights twinkling on the lake.

The waiter brought out another bottle of wine and served entrees on white ceramic plates. Hallie ate fresh salmon, roasted vegetables, and mounds of fluffy white rice. She sipped the red wine and slowly the knot in her stomach unraveled.

Hallie told a story about a castle she visited in Tuscany, where the owner greeted her in a bathrobe. She described the modern design stores in Milan, and the dusty antique shops in Florence. She felt Angus's fingers brush against hers, sending an electric shock through her body.

By the time the waiter cleared the plates, everyone talked at the same time. Angus told stories about Pompeii, Alfonso regaled them with tales of demanding clients, and Portia described her students' flawless arabesques. Angus put his arm around Hallie and left it there, his fingers stroking her back.

Driving back to Bellagio, Hallie sat close to Angus, her knee pressed against his. She hadn't felt the weight of another man's thigh against hers since Peter, and suddenly her body stiffened. She watched the road intently, trying to calm the butterflies in her stomach.

Alfonso and Portia urged them to join them at a disco in Como, but the thought of loud music and thick smoke made Hallie's head ache. Alfonso dropped Hallie and Angus off at the villa, kissing them both on the cheek.

Hallie walked up the gravel path, listening to Angus's footsteps beside her. She wanted him to kiss her, like he did in the rain. But as they approached the front door her steps faltered. It was as if she was stuck on a moving walkway that inexplicably slowed down. She opened her mouth to invite him inside, but no words came out.

"Portia is a whirlwind," Angus said when they reached the twelve-foot front doors. "And Alfonso is like a Roman orator, talking to a huge crowd."

"Portia seems very happy," Hallie said tentatively. "He treats her like a queen."

"It was a wonderful evening." Angus stroked Hallie's cheek.

The touch of his hand on her face was so gentle, her hesitation melted away. Hallie felt his mouth on hers, his hand traveling over her breasts. She remembered how wonderful it felt to be kissed, to smell aftershave and male sweat.

"I should go," Angus stepped back. "Milo has never been left alone this long. He's probably chewed up the rug and some eighteenth-century furniture."

"I'll see you on Monday," Hallie whispered.

"I'll practice my new recipes." Angus grinned. "We'll have a feast."

Hallie walked up to her bedroom and hung her dress in the closet. She climbed into bed, remembering dinner, Angus, their kiss. She lay in the dark and reached for her cell phone. There were no voice mails from Constance, no messages from Francesca. She put the phone on the bedside table and drew the comforter around her shoulders.

chapter eighteen

Hallie knelt in the front pew of the tiny chapel and drew her hands together. She couldn't remember the last time she had been to church. When she was a child she attended Sunday school, but she wasn't allowed in the main sanctuary. She and Peter joined Constance for Christmas services, but St. Dominic's was so full of familiar faces, it felt like a cocktail party.

All night she had stayed awake, tossing in bed. Everything was new: her home, her family, her job, and now Angus. She needed advice and didn't know where to turn. She slipped on a pair of pants and a turtleneck and crossed the lawn to the chapel.

Hallie and Angus had been on a few of dates since dinner with Portia and Alfonso. She enjoyed his stories about his family, the places he'd been in Europe. She loved the way he moved around the kitchen, how he roughhoused with Milo.

But when they sat together on the sofa, she didn't know whether to jump in his lap, or run from the room. Her body wanted him, but her mind couldn't decide. When he kissed her good night she didn't want him to stop, but when his hands probed too deep she pushed them away.

Hallie wished she could call Constance, but Constance would be appalled she'd moved on. Hallie even missed Francesca's input. When Hallie was in high school, Francesca would wait up with a carton of ice cream and two spoons, and critique Hallie's dates.

Hallie had tried to talk to Portia, but between the ballet school and Alfonso, she moved at light speed. In the morning, Portia ran out the door in her leotard and tights, clutching a thermos of coffee. No matter how late Hallie stayed up, Portia came home later. Hallie could hear her singing downstairs but by the time she ran up to bed, Hallie was already asleep.

"Dear God," Hallie intoned, shifting her knees on the stone floor.

"Hallie!" a voice interjected.

Hallie turned and saw Portia crouching in the back pew. She wore black tights and a green leotard. She clutched her thermos of coffee in one hand and a gold cross in the other.

"I thought you were at dance school." Hallie slid into the pew beside her.

"I'm playing hookie." Portia held the cross tightly. "I needed some guidance."

"You could have come to me," Hallie murmured.

"You've been wrapped up with the Villa Luce and Angus."

"You've been busy with Alfonso and the dance school!" Hallie exclaimed. "I didn't think you had time for me."

"We really are sisters." Portia laughed. "Too proud to ask each other for help."

"You go first, before you rub the gold off the cross," Hallie offered.

"Alfonso invited me to his niece's first birthday party," Portia said. "I'm terrified."

"First birthday parties are easy," Hallie replied. "They don't have magicians or scary clowns."

"I'm frightened of Alfonso's mother and sisters." Portia grimaced. "They're going to measure my hips to see if they're suitable for childbearing."

Hallie waved at Portia's spandex tights. "Your hips are perfect for anything."

"I'm serious," Portia said, frowning. "In Italy, when you meet the family it's as good as a proposal."

"Do you love Alfonso?"

"He's gentle and caring and has a heart as big as the lake." Portia turned the cross over in her hand. "I would love to spend my life with him."

"Then what's wrong?"

"Pliny and Francesca loved each other and she deserted us." Portia's eyes were wide. "Maybe Francesca got back to San Francisco and realized she was happier without us. Some women aren't cut out to be mothers. What if I'm just like her?"

"I thought you got over that." Hallie frowned. "In Capri . . ."

"Capri was madness," Portia interrupted, her eyes flashing. "I was under Riccardo's spell."

"Have you talked about it with Alfonso?" Hallie asked.

"He's mentioned he wants a little Portia," Portia mumbled. "A girl with curly black hair he can spoil with rainbow gelato."

"He wants you more." Hallie touched Portia's hand.

"What are you doing here so early in the morning?" Portia demanded. "I thought Americans didn't attend church till noon."

"Angus wants to cook dinner for me tonight," Hallie murmured.

"He's an excellent cook, he makes you lunch all the time."

"In his rooms," Hallie replied. "I've never been up there. Max is in London, the villa is empty."

Portia raised her eyebrows. "You're afraid of having sex?"

"I like Angus." Hallie nodded. "I just don't want to jump into anything."

"Angus is gorgeous and available," Portia replied. "What are you waiting for?"

"It's like diving off a high-dive board." Hallie sighed. "I don't know what will happen when I hit the water."

"You can't know unless you try," Portia said decisively. "I bet it will be sexy and delicious and you'll be pining for more."

"Maybe that's what I'm afraid of," Hallie said, smiling.

"I'm getting claustrophobic." Portia got up, opened the heavy oak doors, and stepped into the sunshine. "Don't you think it's odd that I'm frightened of having children and you're afraid of making love?"

"We're not giving Tesoro a very good name." Hallie followed Portia back to the villa.

"Worse than that"—Portia linked her arm through Hallie's—"we're not enjoying life."

Portia ran upstairs to choose an outfit suitable for a child's birthday party and Hallie went into the kitchen to find something to eat. She took a loaf of bread and a jar of strawberry jam from the pantry and sat at the long oak table. She poured a glass of orange juice and spread the bread thickly with jam.

"That's not breakfast without a cup of espresso," a voice reprimanded her.

"My stomach is jumping around like a grasshopper." Hallie turned and smiled at Pliny. "I don't need any coffee."

"All Italians drink coffee in the morning." Pliny stood at the espresso machine. "Have you been walking in the gardens?"

"I was in the chapel." Hallie blushed. "Having a chat with God."

"I thank him every day for bringing you home to me." Pliny made two strong cups of espresso. "If you need something, I have God's ear."

"Just working a few things out," Hallie said, nibbling the slice of bread.

"Tonight the mayor and his family are joining us for dinner." Pliny sipped his espresso. "The dedication of the statue is in two weeks."

"Sophia must be excited!" Hallie exclaimed.

"It is impossible to tell when Sophia is happy." Pliny shrugged. "You should join us. The mayor's son studied at Oxford. He is a banker in Milan."

"Are you trying to set me up?" Hallie laughed.

"I am a traditional father," Pliny admitted. "I want my daughters to have good husbands. If I had been stricter with Portia, she would not have ended up with Riccardo."

"Trying to stop her would have been like trying to get a bull to avoid a red flag," Hallie said.

"She was a Tasmanian devil," Pliny agreed. "But I still failed."

"She's happy with Alfonso," Hallie replied. "He's good for her."

"Portia needs a strong man." Pliny nodded. He wore black slacks and a white shirt rolled up to the elbows. "Shall I tell Lea to set an extra plate for dinner?"

"I have a date," Hallie confessed, buttering another slice of bread.

"A young man?" Pliny raised his eyebrows. "Where did you meet him?"

"He's the estate manager at the Villa Luce," Hallie replied. "He's American."

"You must introduce me." Pliny finished his espresso. "I have to make sure he deserves you."

"I'm lucky you weren't around when I was a teenager," Hallie teased. "I'd never be able to bring a boy home. They'd be terrified of such a strict father."

Hallie walked to the fridge to get a carton of milk and heard a crash behind her. She turned around and saw Sophia holding a silver tray. A ceramic mug and a crystal pitcher lay in shards on the stone floor.

"What is this?" Sophia's face was white and she gripped the tray as if she was holding on to a life preserver.

"We were having breakfast," Hallie stammered. "I woke up early and I was hungry."

"I heard every word," Sophia hissed. "What is this talk about fathers and daughters?"

Hallie looked wildly at Pliny. He sat rigid at the table, his fingers curled around his espresso cup. Hallie waited for him to say something, but his mouth formed a surprised *O*.

"I'm so grateful to you and Pliny for letting me stay," Hallie began, her legs shaking. "It's like having another family."

"We are family." Pliny stood up. "Hallie found diaries Francesca wrote when we were married. Hallie is my daughter, she is your granddaughter."

"Are you mad?" Sophia whirled around. "She is a sorceress sent by her mother to steal our jewels."

"Francesca wrote that she was barely allowed to see her children," Pliny continued. "She was angry at me for not being a better husband. She discovered she was pregnant, and escaped to San Francisco."

"Francesca caused enough trouble, and now she has sent this girl to stir it up again!" Sophia spat.

"Francesca didn't tell anyone," Hallie said slowly. "She kept her secret to herself."

"Mama, it is not your fault." Pliny touched his mother's quivering shoulders. "You ran the Villa Tesoro the way it has been run for centuries. Francesca was so young; she didn't understand the way things are done. It is my fault, I should have listened to her more closely."

"Francesca married an Italian prince." Sophia's blue eyes

flashed. She wore a beige silk dress with a wide gold belt. Her hair was knotted in a bun and she wore ruby slippers on her feet. "She lived a life of luxury."

"I will bring the diaries." Pliny walked toward the door. "You will read them yourself."

"Stop." Sophia held up her hand. "I don't need to see the diaries."

"Have you read them?" Hallie asked. She wondered if Sophia knew they were hidden in the library the whole time.

"I have not read them." Sophia turned to Hallie. "Lea told me Francesca wrote diaries, but she could not find them."

"Well, I found them," Hallie said defiantly. "What Pliny is saying is true, I can show you."

"I know it is true," Sophia said shortly.

"You know?" Pliny stepped back.

"I suspected it when Hallie visited as a teenager," Sophia replied. "I was certain when she returned for Portia's wedding."

"How did you know?" Pliny demanded. "Why didn't you say something?"

"Follow me." Sophia waved her jeweled hand at Hallie and Pliny.

They climbed the stairs to Sophia's study and waited while she unlocked a cabinet. Hallie's heart beat so quickly she felt like a racecar driver preparing for a race. She glanced at Pliny but he was in a daze. He sat on the leather sofa with his head in his hands, tapping his feet on the wood floor.

"This is how I knew." Sophia took a framed photo from the cabinet and handed it to Hallie.

Hallie glanced at the faded photograph. It was of a woman wearing a cream satin gown, pulled tight at the waist and secured with pearl buttons. The high collar framed her face and she held a parasol in one hand. Her eyes smiled at the camera and she wore a feathered hat on her head.

It was her eyes that made Hallie gasp. They were large and blue and shaped exactly like her own. The woman's nose was a replica of Hallie's. Even her cheeks seemed to have the same planes. The hair that escaped from her hat was a fine honey blond.

"Valentina Bottecci," Sophia said. "My mother. She died of diphtheria when I was twelve."

"I always thought I looked like Constance," Hallie murmured.

"Constance shares the same blond hair and blue eyes," Sophia replied. "Perhaps that's why I thought we could be friends, though her daughter is the devil."

"Her daughter is Hallie's mother," Pliny said sharply, studying the picture. "She is the mother of all my children."

"She would have taken them away if I hadn't stopped her," Sophia said bitterly. "If I had known she was pregnant, I would have put bars on every window in the villa."

"Why didn't you tell me I was your granddaughter?" Hallie interrupted. She felt like she was riding a carousel and couldn't jump off.

"I spent years fixing the Tesoro name after Francesca ran away." Sophia's eyes glittered. "I didn't want a new scandal. You were raised an American, it was best you stayed in America."

Hallie felt a chill run through her body. She wished she could walk through the study door and be in Constance's library, like the children in *The Lion, the Witch and the Wardrobe*. She missed Constance's grace, the way her fingers danced on the piano. She missed the Pacific Heights mansion with its cozy kitchen and intimate garden. She missed the views of the bay and the fragrant cherry blossom trees.

"I can leave." Hallie's voice shook. "I can rent a room until I finish the Villa Luce."

"I will never forgive Francesca for what she did to my family."

Sophia walked around the desk and stopped in front of Hallie. "You may be my granddaughter by blood but you will never be a true Tesoro. I don't want to see you!"

Hallie watched Sophia stride out the door. She felt Pliny put his arms around her and she rested her head on his shoulder. She waited until Sophia's steps receded and then she let the tears roll down her cheeks.

chapter nineteen

Milo met Hallie on the gravel driveway, his tail thumping against the ground. He was a rambunctious puppy with golden fur and a white mark on his nose. He stopped and let Hallie rub his stomach, his tongue lolling happily in his mouth.

Hallie wore pencil-thin pants and a Stella McCartney sweater, and her hair was tied in a low ponytail. She clutched a tin of Lea's lemon cake and a small bottle of amaretto. She heard Alfonso and Portia roar down the driveway, and wanted to stop them and beg them to take her home.

After the scene in Sophia's study, Hallie retreated to her room and curled up on her bed. When she closed her eyes she saw the photo of Valentina Bottecci, another link to the past she never knew existed. She pictured Sophia's venomous eyes, her hateful words.

More than ever, Hallie wanted to call her mother and tell her everything she learned. It was as if she was discovering hidden details in a painting: her father, grandmother, great-grandmother. Francesca had painted over all of it and given Hallie nothing except an imaginary Phillip Elliot.

Portia had found Hallie hugging a pillow to her chest, and insisted she dry her eyes. She had waited while Hallie shrugged on a pair of pants and a sweater and tied her hair with a blue ribbon. She had raided the pantry and insisted Hallie take the cake and a bottle of amaretto. Then she had piled Hallie in the back of Alfonso's Peugeot and dropped her off at the Villa Luce.

"You're beautiful and you have your whole life ahead of you," Portia had said, turning to Hallie in the backseat. "Angus is waiting to cook you dinner and rub your shoulders."

"I just want to go to bed," Hallie had moaned.

"Then go to bed." Portia's eyes had twinkled. "But eat first. Sex on an empty stomach can be dizzying."

"I meant by myself," Hallie had protested. "I don't want to make conversation."

"That's why you're bringing the amaretto. A few sips and the evening will be a pleasant blur. Forget Sophia and Francesca, enjoy yourself."

Alfonso had turned the car around and Portia had waved gaily out the window. Hallie trudged up the path to the villa, listening to the crickets chirp in the dark. She and Milo reached the entry and Angus flung open the doors.

"I'm glad you came." Angus kissed Hallie on the cheek. "I would have picked you up."

"Alfonso and Portia were on their way to a birthday party," Hallie said. "Milo met me at the gate."

"I baked lasagna all afternoon," Angus said, grinning. "He's dying to have someone to play with."

"You didn't have to go to any trouble." Hallie held the cake tin like a shield.

"I'm trying a new recipe," Angus replied. He wore a checkered apron over khaki slacks and a navy T-shirt. "Come upstairs, I'll show you my rooms."

Hallie followed Angus up the circular staircase, then down a long narrow hall. At the end of the hall, the space became open and bright. The floors were mosaic tile, and the walls were painted yellow. Palm trees in terracotta pots lined the room and the French doors opened onto a stone balcony.

"This doesn't look like Versailles." Hallie glanced at the open kitchen, the leather sofas, the glass dining-room table.

"I spent so many years working with ancient treasures, I craved twenty-first-century furniture." Angus opened a bottle of wine. "Max let me decorate the rooms myself."

"You're very talented." Hallie smiled. "I should hire you as my assistant."

"I'm a one-note wonder." Angus poured two glasses of wine. "I like leather and glass, and plants to help a room breathe."

Hallie remembered the cake tin pressed against her chest. "This is for you."

"You didn't have to bring anything." Angus placed it on the counter.

"Portia insisted," Hallie replied. "She made me come. I was curled up on my bed."

"Hallie, I . . ." Angus began.

"Sophia found out I'm her granddaughter," Hallie continued. "Apparently, she'd suspected all along. I look exactly like her mother."

"That's wonderful," Angus replied.

"She was furious, she hasn't spoken to me since." Hallie's voice trembled. "Pliny says she will come around, but I'm terrified she'll throw me out for good."

"Sophia is a very proud woman." Angus frowned, taking a salad bowl from the fridge. "But she'll realize she's missing out on having a beautiful granddaughter."

"I'm so angry at Francesca." Hallie's eyes filled with tears. "She could have told me when I was a teenager, or when I turned twenty-one. I missed everything, my whole history."

"It's all here." Angus put the bowl down and wrapped his arms around Hallie. "Bellagio, your family, me. It's waiting for you."

Hallie rested her head on Angus's shoulder. She felt his fingers press into her spine. She wanted him to unzip her slacks, slip off her panties, make everything disappear. Then she felt something nip at her ankles, and saw Milo nuzzling her shoe.

"Milo is not being a good host." Angus scooped up the puppy.

"He's smarter than he looks." Hallie laughed, admiring the colored rugs thrown over the floor. "This reminds me of lofts in San Francisco."

"The previous owner created it for his mother-in-law." Angus set a loaf of bread on the table. "He built her her own kitchen, and rooms big enough so she wouldn't venture downstairs. Max broke down a few walls and modernized the appliances."

"What are Max's rooms like?" Hallie asked, suddenly curious.

"I don't know." Angus turned back to the fridge. "I never go upstairs."

"Portia's right." Hallie sighed, sitting at the table. "It is mysterious. Maybe we should storm the third floor."

"I'd rather have dinner with you," Angus replied. "The only mystery I want to solve is sitting right here."

Angus cut thick slices of bread. He tossed the salad and placed a pot of butter on the table.

"The butter is from a nearby farm and the vegetables are from the garden." Angus waited for Hallie to take the first bite.

"It's delicious," Hallie murmured, touched by Angus's effort. Suddenly she flashed on Peter's sunny-side up eggs and homemade waffles. She pictured reading the Sunday *New York Times* in bed with a mug of milky coffee.

"If it's so good, why do you look like you're about to cry?" Angus asked.

Hallie blushed. "The room, the food, they remind me of San Francisco."

"Do you miss it?"

Hallie nodded. "I miss little things. The sound of the cable car on the street, the fog horn late at night. And I miss Constance."

"Are you going to go back?" Angus clutched his fork tightly.

"I love Lake Como," Hallie replied. "I love the Italians' sense of beauty, the pace, the joy for living."

"I haven't been back since college." Angus ate his salad. "America is like a sleeping giant. When it wakes up, hell is going to break loose. I don't want to be there."

"America has a lot of great qualities," Hallie protested. She pictured the first time Peter came into the design store, looking like an overgrown Boy Scout. She remembered his heavy backpack, his easy smile and boundless optimism.

"I don't mean to be a wet blanket, America is just not for me," Angus said, sensing her mood. "I love the history of Europe, the knowledge that people have been making mistakes for centuries."

"I shouldn't have come." Hallie put down her fork. "I'm not very good company."

"Hallie." Angus pulled her to her feet and kissed her on the lips. "You were in a serious relationship. We can go slow, I promise."

"How did you know?" Hallie mumbled.

"It's one of the things I love about you." He stroked her hair. "You're transparent. We haven't even eaten the lasagna. If we don't watch it, Milo will devour the whole thing."

"I don't want to be responsible for his stomachache." Hallie laughed, sitting back at the table. She wiped her eyes and waited while Angus replaced the salad bowls with platters of lasagna and grilled vegetables.

Slowly her tension evaporated. Angus told a funny story about Milo wrestling a garden snake. He described a neighbor who played opera music late at night, windows wide open so everyone could hear.

By the time they finished the lasagna, Hallie had relaxed. She stroked Milo while Angus cleared the dishes. Angus put the cake on the table and poured them each a shot of amaretto.

"We used to sit around a campfire for hours on digs." Angus cut two slices of cake. "Drinking bourbon and playing games."

"What kind of games?" Hallie tasted the sweet liqueur.

"Charades, truth or dare. My favorite was the question game. Would you like to play?"

"As long as there's no penalty for losing," Hallie said, smiling.

"I'll go first." Angus stretched his long legs in front of him. "Favorite book?"

"Anna Karenina," Hallie replied quickly.

"Favorite movie?"

"The Great Gatsby."

"Favorite food?"

"Your lasagna." Hallie grinned, taking another sip of amaretto.

"Where do you see yourself in five years?"

Hallie put her shot glass down and petted Milo. "I don't know."

"I'll answer first." Angus looked at her closely. "I'd like to run tours in Lake Como: show tourists the historic sites they can't find in guidebooks. I'd like to live in a villa with my wife and two children. I'd like to have a boy I can teach to fish, and a blond, blue-eyed little girl who plays with Barbies."

"I'm terrible at games." Hallie stood up abruptly. "It's late, I should go."

"You haven't seen the view from the balcony." Angus took her hand. "Bellagio glitters like a tiara."

Hallie followed Angus onto the balcony, feeling the cold air fill her lungs. She saw Bellagio and Varenna and the string of lights that was Como. She felt Angus's hands on her shoulders and his lips on hers. She tasted amaretto and lemon and smelled his mint aftershave. She let his mouth move down her neck and stop at her chest. She felt him reach under her sweater and cup her breast gently in his hand.

Suddenly Hallie wanted him so badly, her body ached. She let his hand move lower, slipping under her pants. She felt his strong hand on her back, massaging her spine.

"Let's go inside," Angus murmured in her ear.

Angus led her down a hall through a high wood door. His bedroom was sparsely furnished, with a king-sized bed low to the floor. There was a wood nightstand and a lamp with a yellow bulb. The sheets were white and fitted neatly on the bed.

Angus slipped her sweater over her head and unzipped her pants. He took off his slacks and shrugged off his T-shirt. Hallie rested her head on his shoulder, feeling the smooth sweat on his skin.

Hallie let him pull her down on the bed. She felt him enter her, the slow push, the deep opening inside her. She grabbed his shoulders, finding his rhythm. When he came they rocked back and forth, like a boat caught in a storm. Hallie waited until his breathing was even and he was asleep to let the tears come.

She didn't know why she was crying: Angus instead of Peter, Sophia instead of Constance, the green of Lake Como instead of the blue of the bay. The silent tears kept falling, until she was exhausted and spent. She closed her eyes and felt something wet lick her face. She opened her eyes and found Milo hunched on the bed. She hugged him tightly and the tears started again.

chapter twenty

Hallie wrapped herself in a silk robe and sat at her desk. She had spent an hour in the bath, soaking in lavender bubbles. Her skin tingled and her hair was wet and clean. She flipped through a magazine and sipped a cup of hibiscus tea.

In the morning she and Angus had made love again. It was better, slower, and afterward she slept. When she woke up, they got dressed and strolled into Lenno.

Angus chose a café that served scrambled eggs and bacon. The owner was an ex-cowboy from Wyoming. He joined them at the table, laughing about the differences between Americans and Italians.

"I married a girl from Como." The cowboy rolled his eyes. "I opened a restaurant because I couldn't get a decent meal at home. Now I can put ketchup on my eggs without anyone making a fuss."

"Hallie's from San Francisco," Angus said, grinning.

"You're smart to choose an American girl." The cowboy winked. "They know how to cook a burger."

After breakfast they browsed the shops of Lenno. Angus insisted on buying Hallie a tin of hibiscus tea, a box of Swiss chocolates, a leather bracelet.

"I haven't bought anything for anyone in years." He filled a bag with dangling earrings, a silk scarf, a small sketch of Lake Como.

Angus drove her home in the motorboat. Hallie sat next to him, her new scarf wrapped around her head. When he dropped her off at the dock, he kissed her slowly. Hallie drifted up to the villa and submerged herself in the bath, feeling lazy and luxurious and decadent.

Hallie's phone buzzed. She glanced at the screen and picked it up.

"Hallie, dear!" Constance exclaimed. "I'm glad I caught you."

"I'm sitting at my window, gazing at the lake." Hallie smiled.

"As I remember Lake Como becomes dreary in the fall," Constance mused. "Maybe it's time to come home."

"It's even more beautiful," Hallie said. "The tourists are gone and the colors are stunning."

"Your mother joined me for Sunday dinner," Constance announced.

Hallie hesitated, suddenly anxious. "That's wonderful."

"Do you know the last time Francesca came to dinner?" Constance demanded. "Christmas, and only because she loves Louisa's bread pudding. She's worried about you."

"Why would she be worried about me?" Hallie asked.

"She's been calling you for weeks with no reply. Francesca may not be the most involved mother, but she cares about you deeply."

Hallie felt something hard lodge in her throat. She stood up and paced around the room. "I've been busy with the design, and Portia."

"How is Portia?" Constance's voice softened.

"She finally found someone who deserves her. Alfonso is perfect."

"That is good news," Constance replied. "Dr. Michaels gave me permission to go to the opera gala."

"I bet you were the belle of the ball," Hallie replied, tying a knot in the belt of her robe.

"I saw Peter at the bar at intermission," Constance continued. "He was on the arm of a ravishing redhead."

"If you are trying to make me jealous it's not working." Hallie pulled the knot tighter. "I'm glad Peter is happy."

"I think you should come home," Constance said. "You belong in San Francisco, you can't just pick up and move to Italy."

"The Villa Luce is going to be gorgeous." Hallie pretended she hadn't heard her. "Pliny is lovely and I'm having a wonderful time exploring the villages."

"Then call Francesca and tell her all about it," Constance insisted, hanging up before Hallie could answer.

Portia walked in as Hallie put down the phone. She wore a white sundress that made her skin look golden brown. Her hair snaked down her back and she wore diamond drop earrings.

"Why are you wearing a robe on such a beautiful day?" Portia threw herself on the bed.

"I took a bath," Hallie mumbled, still flinching from Constance's harsh tone.

"A bath in the afternoon?" Portia asked suspiciously. "Your skin is glowing and you smell of sex."

Hallie sniffed her wrist. "I smell like lavender bath salts."

Portia's eyes narrowed. "Did you spend the night at Villa Luce?"

Hallie blushed. "I might have." She didn't talk about sex with women in San Francisco. Kendra was more interested in

Queen Anne furniture, and her married friends wanted to talk about weekend homes and ski vacations.

"I knew it!" Portia jumped off the bed. "You look like Maggie in *Cat on a Hot Tin Roof.*"

"When do you see old American movies?" Hallie laughed.

"Pliny watches them late at night." Portia perched on the desk. "Did Angus cook you a delicious meal and ply you with alcohol, or did you just fall into his arms?"

"Angus made lasagna," Hallie recalled. "And we drank amaretto and walked out on the balcony."

"And . . ." Portia leaned forward like a sparrow testing its wings.

"I wanted him so much, I almost stripped naked," Hallie replied. "But when we got to his bedroom it felt wrong."

"Is he a bad kisser?"

"Angus is a wonderful kisser." Hallie sighed. "He just wasn't . . ."

"He wasn't Peter," Portia scoffed. "And Alfonso isn't Riccardo. All men are different, that's what's wonderful about being a woman. Sex is like a smorgasbord, you're allowed to sample more than one thing."

"Riccardo's smorgasbord didn't work out well," Hallie reminded her.

"You're single," Portia insisted. "Now is the time to have fun."

"In the morning it was better." Hallie hesitated. "We ate breakfast in Lenno and he bought me tea and chocolates. We strolled along the shore and watched the fishermen."

"That sounds so romantic." Portia hugged her chest.

"I like being with him." Hallie wrapped her robe more tightly around her waist. "I just don't want to move fast."

"Alfonso is already picking out our gravestones." Portia rolled her eyes. "He wants to be buried together in the Diamante family plot."

"Did he propose?" Hallie asked.

"I'm not even divorced," Portia replied. "I did meet his whole family."

"Tell me everything," Hallie insisted, grateful not to talk about Angus.

"His grandmother is ninety-nine. She kept poking her cane at Alfonso's sister and telling her she's fat. His sister is four months pregnant. Alfonso has three sisters and two sisters-in-law and they were all pregnant! It was like sitting in a room of prize cows."

"They couldn't all be expecting." Hallie laughed.

"Maybe a couple of them had babies on their breasts or toddlers tugging at their ankles," Portia conceded. "I counted thirteen children, not including the guests."

"That takes the pressure off you," Hallie said, grinning.

"The first thing his grandmother asked is what age I got my period," Portia said. "Then she wanted to know if I had any childhood diseases. I told her I'd send her my physician's chart."

"She couldn't have been that bad."

"She made Sophia look like a fairy godmother." Portia sighed. "I almost ran away."

"But you didn't," Hallie said seriously.

"We stayed for birthday cake." Portia sat cross-legged on the bed. "Alfonso's niece was afraid of the candles and Alfonso helped her blow them out. After the cake, he took the boys outside to play soccer."

"Sounds like he'd be a great father," Hallie murmured.

"Later we went to Hotel Metropole for a drink," Portia said. "All he talked about was how one nephew had grown six inches, and another would be a star soccer player."

"Did you tell him your fears?"

"We shared a bowl of oysters and a bottle of Dom Pérignon," Portia continued. "I went to the ladies' room and sat in the stall, trying to muster my courage."

"What happened?"

"I couldn't tell him then, not after the birthday party. I tried to sneak out the back door, but he found me," Portia replied. "He made me drink another glass of champagne and tell him what was wrong."

"What did you say?" Hallie prompted.

"I told him everything." Portia's eyes glittered. "That sometimes I am so angry at Francesca, my blood boils. That I try to imagine braiding my daughter's hair or putting a Band-Aid on my son's knee and I get a hard feeling in my chest. I can't do it; I can't risk ruining my children's lives. I'm so afraid I'd be a terrible mother, and run away like Francesca."

"What did Alfonso say?" Hallie asked.

"He said how much he loves being an uncle, walking into a house with presents and having his nieces and nephews attack him. But he's been a bachelor for so long, he doesn't know if he wants children," Portia said slowly. "He wants to travel: go to Peru and India and see the Great Wall of China. He doesn't think we can do those things with a baby."

"But you said he wanted a little girl."

"He thought that's what I wanted," Portia whispered. "He thought all women want babies."

Hallie had never seen Portia cry: not when she found out about Riccardo's mistress, not when she was nine years old and got her ears pierced at a tattoo parlor in Haight-Ashbury. Now Portia sat on the bed and let the tears roll down her cheeks. Her shoulders heaved and her thick eyelashes were wet.

"You should be happy." Hallie walked over to the bed.

Portia flung her arms around Hallie. "Is it wrong to have good fortune when so many people suffer?"

"That doesn't sound Italian," Hallie rebuked her. "God wants you to be happy."

"Will you come to the chapel and pray?" Portia wiped her

eyes furiously. "Then we'll go into Bellagio and eat fettuccine Alfredo."

"Let me change." Hallie dislodged herself from Portia's arms and went into the closet.

"There's a man wearing a straw hat tying a boat to the dock," Portia called from the balcony.

Hallie joined Portia on the balcony. She saw a tall man wearing a checkered shirt and a broad straw hat jump off an old rowboat. He scooped something out of the boat and trudged toward the villa.

"It's Angus and Milo," Hallie murmured.

"Hi!" Angus stood under the window, like Romeo courting Juliet. "Milo and I want to know if you'd like to go fishing."

"I have plans with Portia," Hallie called down, smiling at Angus's suspenders and blue jeans.

"Go," Portia interjected. "Catch a fish for me."

"Are you sure?" Hallie asked.

"Angus just crossed Lake Como in a rowboat!" Portia exclaimed.

"Okay." Hallie squeezed Portia's hand. "I'll see you at dinner."

Hallie changed into a pair of jeans and a wool sweater. She slipped on a pair of tennis shoes and ran down to the lawn. Milo struggled out of Angus's arms and bounded toward her.

"You look like Tom Sawyer," Hallie said, giggling.

"I'm dressed for fishing." Angus grinned. "We haven't explored the west shore. There are some great fishing spots near Varenna."

"You rowed over from Lenno in this?" Hallie climbed into the peeling green boat.

"You said you wanted to take things slow." Angus shrugged. "I brought ham sandwiches and a thermos of hot chocolate. And a copy of *Anna Karenina* and *The Great Gatsby* in case the fish aren't biting."

"I thought you said there were great fishing spots." Hallie sat on the wood bench.

"Great for the fish." Angus sat beside her. "Sometimes frustrating for the fishermen."

"It's lovely." Hallie glanced at the books, the thermos, the bag of dog treats for Milo.

"I don't mind how slow we take it." Angus laced his fingers through Hallie's. "As long as we're together."

Hallie bent down and stroked Milo so Angus wouldn't see the tears in her eyes. She glanced up at Portia waving from the balcony.

"Let's push off." Hallie smiled. "We'll never catch anything tied to the dock."

chapter twenty-one

The day of the statue dedication dawned crisp and sunny. Hallie and Portia wore silk Armani dresses they bought in Milan. Portia's was emerald green and matched the glittering choker she wore around her neck. Hallie's was turquoise and made her eyes gleam like sapphires.

Hallie teetered on the cobblestones in her narrow heels, feeling nervous and overdressed. But she glanced at Pliny wearing a pinstriped suit, at Sophia in red satin with the Tesoro ruby on her finger, and knew she and Portia had chosen wisely. The people of Bellagio expected the Tesoros to dress up for the occasion.

Marcus and Angelica had arrived at the villa the previous evening. Angelica was already five months pregnant, her dark skin stretched tight over her stomach. Lea served a four-course dinner of mozzarella and melon, homemade raviolis, veal parmigiana, and butterscotch tiramisu.

Pliny sat at the head of the table, making sure everyone's champagne glass was full. When the last bite of tiramisu was eaten and the champagne had been replaced by a hundred-year-old brandy, he pushed his chair back and cleared his throat.

"I am fifty-six years old." Pliny ran his hands through his pepper-colored hair. "And I have the good fortune of having my mother and children at the same table. My life has always been rich. Our ancestors gave us the Villa Tesoro and business interests that allow it to run smoothly. But I didn't know how truly rich I am, until Hallie appeared at our door."

Hallie froze. She glanced nervously at Sophia and Marcus. Portia squeezed her hand and Hallie gulped, trying to calm her churning stomach.

"Hallie, I have discovered, is my third child, my second daughter, my baby," Pliny said, almost shyly. "She is beautiful and talented and as poised as a princess. I am blessed she found her way home."

"What's going on?" Marcus asked. He had close-cropped black hair and round owl-like glasses.

"Hallie discovered Francesca's diaries," Portia explained. "Francesca was pregnant with Hallie when she left Lake Como. Hallie is our sister."

"Wow." Marcus blinked. "I'm gone for the summer and miss everything."

"I hope you're not . . ." Hallie stammered.

"Thrilled to have another sister." Marcus got up and walked around the table to Hallie. "I always knew I'd be outnumbered by women in this family." He pulled her to her feet and hugged her. "I'm delighted."

Hallie embraced Marcus and Angelica, and finally Portia joined the circle. Hallie glanced at Sophia, afraid her eyes would be like daggers.

Sophia waited for everyone to return to their seats and then she stood up. "I have known that Hallie was Pliny's daughter for some time. Francesca brought so much grief to this family; I did not want to accept it. But as I look at Hallie across the table I see my mother when she was very young." Sophia paused. "God has instructed me to open my home and my heart."

Sophia took a flat jewelry case from her lap and handed it to Hallie. Hallie opened the clasp and gasped. A diamond-and-ruby bracelet lay on a bed of black velvet.

"It belonged to my grandmother, Valentina Bottecci." Sophia snapped it around Hallie's wrist. "Now it rests on the arm of another great beauty, Hallie Tesoro."

Hallie's legs trembled and she sat down abruptly. She wanted to thank Sophia but her eyes filled with tears. She covered her face with her hands and waited for the sobs to subside.

Marcus stood up and took off his glasses. "I thought I had exciting news, but it seems I've been preempted."

"What news?" Pliny asked.

"Angelica," Marcus announced, turning to his wife, "is carrying twin girls."

The room erupted into applause and laughter. Pliny popped another bottle of champagne and refilled everyone's glasses. Portia and Marcus had a lively discussion about baby names. Angelica smiled like a Cheshire cat, rubbing the huge mound of her stomach.

After Pliny and Marcus went outside to smoke cigars, and Portia and Angelica disappeared upstairs to the nursery, Hallie searched for Sophia. She found her in the salon, laboring over a piece of needlework.

"I am making a pillowcase for the new baby," Sophia said without looking up. "Now I must make two."

"I could help," Hallie offered. "Constance taught me how to do needlework when I was a girl."

"My eyes see clearly far away." Sophia nodded. "But sometimes they miss things right in front of them."

"You didn't have to give me the bracelet," Hallie murmured.

"It is my duty to pass on family heirlooms to the next genera-
tion," Sophia said stiffly.

"Well, I . . ." Hallie stammered. She spun the bracelet around
her wrist, wondering whether she should offer to return it.

"It is a duty I am happy to perform." Sophia put down the
needlework and gazed at Hallie. "Pliny is right. You are an accomplished young woman, and a credit to the Tesoro name."

This time Hallie didn't let her eyes fill with tears. She picked
up the needlework and concentrated on moving the needle
through the tiny holes. When she looked up, she thought she
saw Sophia's eyes glistening.

Hallie sat in the front row for the dedication, between
Portia and Marcus. Sophia and Pliny stood on a small stage
erected for the occasion. Hallie saw Angus and Alfonso mill-
ing in the throng. She waved and Angus grinned, giving her
a thumbs-up.

Hallie had never seen the piazza so full. Local residents
crowded the stage, and tourists stopped to see what was the fuss.
Hallie felt like she was in a foreign movie. She smiled and nodded and tried to answer questions asked in rapid Italian.

After the mayor unveiled the statue, Hallie joined Portia and
Marcus in a receiving line. Hallie stood under the noon sun, letting strangers shake her hand. She gazed at the bright piazza
and thought she had never felt so far from the fog-lined streets
of San Francisco.

"I feel like I was at a movie premiere," Hallie said, sighing,
when she and Portia escaped to an outdoor café.

"Wait till you see the party at the villa." Portia sipped sparkling mineral water. "It will rival any Hollywood affair."

"I thought it was going to be an intimate dinner," Hallie said.

"An intimate dinner for two hundred of Sophia and Pliny's

closest friends." Portia rolled her eyes. "We should go home and take a siesta, it will go on all night."

"I was going to go to work," Hallie mumbled. Angus had kissed her quickly after the unveiling and gone back to the Villa Luce.

"Your work today is being a Tesoro," Portia replied. "We must get our beauty sleep and then make ourselves up like goddesses."

"I didn't know being a Tesoro was so demanding," Hallie said, grinning.

"The masseuse is coming at five o'clock and the makeup artist at six-thirty." Portia stood up. "We have to select our gowns and jewels. Sophia will want to approve our choices."

"I can't wear a Tory Burch dress and Gucci flats?" Hallie followed Portia through the piazza.

"Tonight is your first affair as a Tesoro." Portia took her hand. "You're going to look like Catherine de Medici."

Hallie stood at the top of the stairs, surveying the grand salon. The party was already in full swing. Waiters passed around silver trays of bruschetta and scampi. Flowers had been added to every surface: purple irises, white orchids, and vases of pink and white roses. The smell of women's perfume wafted up the stairs, filling Hallie's lungs with a musky scent.

Hallie descended the staircase slowly. Her hair was knotted in a chignon, secured with a diamond chopstick. Her eyes were lined with gold eye shadow and her eyelashes were thick with mascara.

When Portia had shown her the gown, Hallie thought she couldn't possibly wear it. It was gold chiffon so sheer, it was almost transparent. Hallie had slipped it on, feeling like Venus de Milo rising out of the seashell.

"I'm practically naked." Hallie had frowned, turning in front of the mirror.

"You're gorgeous," Portia had insisted. "We'll dress it up with jewelry."

"Shouldn't I wear something more . . . covered?"

"This is Lake Como, not the San Francisco Ballet." Portia had clipped a sapphire pendant around Hallie's neck. "You're perfect."

Gliding down the staircase, Hallie knew Portia was right. The room was full of sleek, glittering evening gowns. Breasts were covered by wisps of silk; legs were exposed by long slits. Hallie had never seen so many ruby necklaces and diamond bracelets. She descended the last step, feeling sexy and exhilarated.

Hallie remembered the party Sophia had held when Hallie arrived. She had felt out of place, a San Francisco debutante in a sea of glamorous Italians. She remembered how Portia had been so miserable over Riccardo, and she still fretted about Peter and Kendra.

Hallie recalled the black-tie events she and Peter had attended: weddings at the Ritz and the Fairmont, symphony galas, parties at Google and Apple. Suddenly she expected to see Peter move through the crowd, carrying an apple martini. She gazed at the men in black tuxedos, and felt an odd, empty feeling in her stomach.

Then she saw Angus walk toward her. He wore a black tuxedo with an ivory silk shirt. His hair was brushed smoothly to one side and his eyes sparkled. He looked tall and handsome and confident.

"You look like Aphrodite." Angus kissed her cheek.

"I feel naked." Hallie blushed, trying to erase the images of San Francisco and Peter.

"You're even more beautiful naked," Angus murmured. "Let's get some champagne."

They drank Dom Pérignon and nibbled caviar balls and lobster tails. Pliny introduced them to old families who had lived in Lake Como for centuries. Hallie's head spun with long Italian names, meandering family trees, elaborate titles found in nineteenth-century novels.

Portia appeared in a silver gown with a tight bodice. An emerald necklace hung between her breasts and her black hair was coiled around her head. Diamond earrings dangled from her ears and she wore high diamond-encrusted heels.

"The Tesoro women outshine every other female in the room," Alfonso remarked. He wore a perfectly fitted black tuxedo with a silk handkerchief in the pocket. He gazed at Portia proudly, like an artist admiring his creation.

"It takes hours to create this fantasy." Portia waved her hand over her dress.

"You are a princess." Alfonso kissed Portia's hand. "And I am the luckiest commoner to have you on my arm."

Hallie watched Portia and Alfonso drift off to the dance floor, and saw Sophia approach. Sophia wore a red satin gown with a high collar and a full skirt. Hallie made a small curtsey and offered Sophia a glass of champagne.

"Drinking is not good for me." Sophia shook her head. "I don't want to speed my ascent to the angels."

"Constance's doctor won't let her drink, either," Hallie replied.

"Portia tells me you haven't told Constance about your heritage." Sophia looked at Hallie sharply.

"I will," Hallie mumbled. "I just haven't found the right moment."

"It would not be easy to learn your daughter lies," Sophia mused.

"Constance had a series of strokes last year." Hallie twisted the champagne flute in her hand.

"We must not talk about old age and illness at a celebration," Sophia said abruptly. "Dance and enjoy yourself. We will discuss it later."

Hallie and Angus walked outside to the black-and-white dance floor. A ten-piece orchestra played beneath the olive trees, and couples glided under paper lanterns. Angus led Hallie to the middle of the floor and placed his hand on her back. He tipped her face up to his and kissed her softly on the lips.

Hallie buried her face in his shoulder and tried to calm her thoughts. She remembered dinners in Constance's dining room: Louisa's stuffed game hens and scalloped potatoes. Her mind flashed on Francesca standing in her tiny kitchen, adding rosettes to vanilla icing.

"Hallie," Angus whispered gently.

"I . . ." Hallie murmured, blinking back tears.

"You're crying again." Angus took her hand and led her off the dance floor. He found a stone bench, and motioned for Hallie to sit beside him.

"When Sophia asked if I'd told Constance that Pliny is my father," Hallie said, "I realized how much I miss her, and then I thought about Francesca."

"Maybe it's time to call Francesca," Angus suggested.

"I'm still angry at her," Hallie replied. "She lied my whole life, not just to me but to everybody."

"Sometimes people lie with the best intentions," Angus mused. "Give her the chance to explain."

"I don't know if I'm ready," Hallie mumbled.

"I'll stay with you while you're on the phone," Angus offered.

"You're very persuasive." Hallie felt Angus's hand travel down her back. He pulled her close and wrapped his arms around her. They hadn't made love since the first night, but suddenly she wanted him. Her body melted into his, her breasts crushed against his chest.

"Can I persuade you to take a moonlit boat ride across the lake?" Angus whispered into her hair.

Hallie felt electric shocks prick her skin. She wanted to slip off her heels and run down to the boat dock with Angus. She wanted to unzip her dress and make love under the stars.

"I can't leave my own party." Hallie pulled away reluctantly. "Portia said it is my duty to be a Tesoro tonight."

"I guess that's what I get for falling in love with a princess," Angus murmured.

"Angus, I . . ." Hallie started.

Angus's eyes were like fireflies in the dark. "I don't mind if I have to wait one hundred years."

"We'd be pretty old by then." Hallie giggled.

"You're like Sleeping Beauty." Angus pulled Hallie up. "I can wait for the happy ending."

Hallie watched women in high heels navigate the gravel driveway. She heard car doors slam and engines start. She climbed the stairs to her room, her head throbbing from the smoke, the music, the endless glasses of champagne.

Portia had gone to bed, claiming a terrible headache. Hallie sat in the salon with Angus, sharing a plate of profiteroles. She replayed his words in her head and wondered what it would be like to fall in love again. She imagined curling up with Angus in the evenings. She pictured waking up together, taking strolls along the promenade. When he finally kissed her good night, she kissed him back hungrily, wanting more.

Hallie opened the door to her bedroom and found Portia curled up on the bed. She had changed into baby-doll pajamas and fuzzy slippers. Her hair was tied in a ponytail and her face was free of makeup.

"I thought you went to bed," Hallie said, slipping off her heels.

"Alfonso had to catch an early flight to Rome," Portia replied. "I was tired of making conversation."

"I thought the party would never end." Hallie took her hair out if its chignon.

"I saw you sitting outside with Angus," Portia remarked. "It looked serious."

"Angus said he was falling in love with me," Hallie murmured.

"What did you answer?" Portia asked.

"I might be falling in love." Hallie hesitated. "He's so calm and confident."

"And he looks dreamy in a tuxedo," Portia said, giggling. "I saw Alfonso talking to Lorenzo Favio. He owns the finest jewelry store in Milan."

"A wedding!" Hallie's eyes sparkled. "You'll be the most beautiful bride."

"It wouldn't be till next summer," Portia cautioned. "You'd have to promise to be my maid of honor."

"I'm an expert at weddings," Hallie said, smiling. "Let me get out of this dress, we can start making lists."

"You never told me Angus went to Stanford," Portia called as Hallie hung her dress in the closet.

"He went to college in New Hampshire," Hallie called back, slipping into a silk robe. She lathered Chanel Rejuvenate on her cheeks, until her skin felt smooth and silky.

"Here's a picture of him at Stanford." Portia frowned, handing Hallie a book.

Hallie glanced at the cover. It was the copy of *Paul Johns Unplugged* Peter had left in the hotel room. Hallie looked at the photo of seven young men at a bar. They held mugs of beer and gave a thumbs-up to the camera.

"It can't be Angus," Hallie replied.

"It looks exactly like him," Portia insisted. "He doesn't look a day older."

"It can't be him," Hallie repeated, flipping the page. She found another photo of the seven men standing in front of a boat. The caption read "Stanford Crew Team Wins Regatta."

"Angus would have said if he went to Stanford." Hallie handed the book to Portia. "It's one of the most prestigious universities in the world."

"Here's another photo." Portia gazed at the page. Then she looked at Hallie strangely, as if she'd witnessed some terrible accident.

"What is it?" Hallie asked.

"It lists the names of the members of the team," Portia whispered. "Angus's name isn't on here."

"I told you." Hallie's shoulders relaxed.

"It says 'Max Rodale, Class of 2001.' "

"What are you talking about?" Hallie ripped the book from Portia's hands. Her heart hammered in her chest. She stared at the photo of the crew team smiling in their burgundy shirts. Paul Johns kneeled in the front row, and behind him Angus stood tall and proud, a gold medal draped around his neck.

" 'The crew team was led to victory by senior Max Rodale. New members to the team include sophomore Paul Johns and junior Alex Green,' " Hallie read aloud.

"You said Peter was Paul's roommate." Portia frowned. "He would have known Angus."

"Peter didn't meet Paul till junior year," Hallie replied. "Angus would have already graduated."

"It doesn't make any sense." Portia twisted her ponytail around her finger. "Why would Angus lie about his name?"

"I don't know." Hallie's hands trembled. "Max Rodale is a billionaire."

"Did you ever look him up on the Internet?" Portia asked.

"I felt it would be intruding." Hallie walked over to the desk. "Angus said Max's privacy was so important to him."

"Now would be a good time to start," Portia replied. "There must be an explanation."

Hallie searched Max's name and came up with one short paragraph.

"Max Rodale started the Web site Connect while a senior at Stanford. Connect helped adopted children find their birth parents, even in the cases of closed adoption. Rodale sold the site to Yahoo! for an undisclosed amount, reported to be in the high eight figures. Rodale disappeared from Silicon Valley soon after. Rumors flew that he started an ashram in India, but they were never substantiated."

Hallie walked to the balcony. Her teeth chattered and her body shivered. She remembered the stories Angus told her about Max: his trips to Venice and Florence, his passion for art. She recalled the tales of Angus's childhood: the big family in Boston, the small house with not enough bedrooms.

Hallie walked back to the computer. She typed in Angus Barlow and searched for an Angus Barlow from Boston. She looked for an Angus Barlow who had gone to college in New Hampshire, who was an archaeologist. She came up with nothing.

Portia peered over her shoulder. "You need to talk to him."

"Talk to him!" Hallie exploded. "I never want to see him again."

"Maybe Angus is afraid people would only like him for his money," Portia floundered. "Maybe he was about to tell you."

"He said he loved me!" Hallie's eyes flashed as if she was possessed. "But he didn't trust me enough to tell me his name."

"He must have a reason," Portia insisted. "You don't want to throw it all away."

"Don't you think I've heard enough lies!" Hallie snapped the computer shut.

"You said you're falling in love with him," Portia implored.

"I don't want to see anyone." Hallie wrapped the robe tightly around her. "I'm going to bed."

"Hallie . . ." Portia hesitated.

Hallie threw off the covers and climbed into bed. She drew the comforter over her head, trying to stop her body from trembling.

"Please turn the light off when you leave," Hallie whispered.

Hallie waited until she heard the door close and the room was dark. Then she turned on the bedside light and picked up *Paul Johns Unplugged*. She flipped through the pages to the photo of Angus. She flipped back to the beginning and read Peter's dedication. Then she closed the book, turned off the light, and cried.

chapter twenty-two

Hallie stayed in her room for a week. She kept replaying her conversations with Angus: how he met Max on a train to Rome, how Max was so shy. She thought about Max's private rooms on the third floor of the villa, Angus's quarters on the second floor. She pictured the bed she shared with Angus and her whole body screamed.

Portia appeared in the mornings before dance school, insisting she eat a piece of toast or soft-boiled egg. Hallie waited till Portia left, then she put the breakfast tray in the hall for Lea to take away. She got up long enough for Lea to change the sheets and fluff the pillows, then she climbed back into bed.

Hallie lay awake at night, wondering what to do. She couldn't go back to the Villa Luce. With no references, she wouldn't find other work in Lake Como. She could return to San Francisco, but she had left Kendra in the lurch. Kendra wasn't likely to welcome her back, and jobs at design firms were scarce.

Hallie imagined occupying the tiny bedroom in her mother's apartment, or her old room in Constance's mansion. She pictured Constance's disappointment that there would be no wedding, that Hallie had thrown away her golden future. She imagined having to confront Francesca about Pliny.

Hallie remembered their long lunches on the balcony, Angus's delicious polenta and risotto. She pictured Angus showing up in the fishing boat, promising they could take things slowly. She wondered what other women he brought to the villa, who else he lied to, if any part of his history was true.

Portia knocked on the door on Friday afternoon. She was dressed in a sweater and matching skirt instead of her usual leotard and tights. Her hair was held back with a diamond clip and she wore narrow Gucci pumps.

"You look like you're going to a job interview." Hallie smiled weakly. Her cheeks were drawn and her eyes were a pale, washed-out blue.

"Alfonso and I are having dinner with his grandmother," Portia patted her hair. "Then he's taking me to Venice. We're going to spend five nights at the Danieli!"

"Sounds like you'll return with a ring on your finger." Hallie got out of bed and walked to the balcony. In the afternoons she stood there for hours, drinking in the lake. She kept waiting for its beauty, the green of the water, the reds and yellows of the villages, to bring her back to life.

"I don't know." Portia shrugged her slim shoulders. "Hallie, I . . ."

"You don't have to be glum because of me." Hallie turned back to the room. "I'll be thrilled if you and Alfonso get married."

"What are you going to do?" Portia asked.

"I keep going over my options." Hallie sat on the bed. "But I can't get further than this room."

"I'm sure Pliny and Sophia would love for you to stay as long as you like," Portia murmured.

"I need to work," Hallie retorted. "I can't just sit here and stare at the walls."

"You could take a break," Portia suggested.

"Coming to Lake Como was a break!" Hallie jumped up. "I was trying to figure out what to do about Peter. I could travel, see Italy and France, but what would I come back to? I don't belong anywhere."

Hallie heard a knock at the door. It was probably Lea with afternoon tea. Every afternoon she tempted her with jasmine tea, shortbread cookies, and crustless cucumber sandwiches. Hallie spooned honey in the tea, stirred it with a silver spoon, and let it sit until it was cold.

Angus entered as Hallie stepped onto the balcony. He wore corduroys and a bulky black sweater. His hands were jammed in his pockets and he shifted nervously from foot to foot.

"What are you doing here?" Hallie demanded.

"Portia said it was okay," Angus stammered.

"You let him in!" Hallie spluttered.

"He's been prowling the villa for days," Portia explained. "He said he wouldn't leave until he talks to you."

"Both of you get out!" Hallie stormed. "I don't want to see anyone."

"Hallie, give him a chance to explain," Portia pleaded.

"Explain three months of lies!" Hallie's eyes flashed. "Inventing a whole other person, hiring me under false pretenses, doing anything to get in my pants."

"I should have told you the truth," Angus said slowly. "I wanted to tell you, I was trying to find the right time."

"How about the moment you met me?" Hallie roared. "Before you claimed you were an archaeologist from Boston."

Angus ran his hands through his hair. He glanced at Portia as if asking for her help.

"I'm going to go," Portia murmured, closing the door before Hallie could stop her.

Hallie stood across the room from Angus, her body shaking. She remembered standing in his arms when she was upset about Peter and Kendra. She remembered losing herself in his kiss when she found Francesca's diaries. She thought how tall and handsome he looked, like a soldier sent to heal her wounds.

"There's a reason I lied," Angus began.

"I'm sure you were protecting yourself from the hordes of women after your money," Hallie spat. "I wasn't one of them."

"That's not it," Angus said plaintively.

"Was any of it true?" Hallie's voice shook.

"The part where I was falling in love with you," Angus replied, gazing at her steadily.

Hallie thought how she had trusted him, how she had told him everything. She remembered how his shoulders were so strong; his embrace was so comforting.

"Do you think I'd waste my time on someone who can't tell the truth?" Hallie demanded, throwing open the door. "Get out, before I call Pliny and tell him to toss you in the lake."

After Angus left, Hallie walked out to the balcony again. It was late afternoon and the lake was quiet. Indian summer was almost over and the air was frigid. She saw a lone ferry cross the water, and a couple riding bicycles along the promenade.

She gazed at the inlets and coves and thought how she had arrived with such high hopes. Lake Como was a playground and she was going to reap its pleasures. She was going to sit in the piazzas and eat pizza and sip lemonade. She was going to explore the churches and magnificent gardens. She was going to stay up until midnight and sleep until noon. She had done all those things, and had never been so miserable.

Hallie remembered when she was eight years old coming home from school. Alice Ferris had taunted her for not having a father at the May Day performance. All the other dads had been there, watching their daughters dance around the maypole. Hallie had only had Francesca, clapping loud enough for two.

Constance had found Hallie in the kitchen, eating a bowl of cereal. She had still worn her May Day costume: a yellow and white dress and white Mary Janes. Her hair was in two pigtails tied with bright yellow ribbons. Hallie had buried her face in the bowl, wiping away the tears.

"What's wrong?" Constance had asked. She had worn a brown cashmere dress with a matching Chanel bag.

"Alice Ferris said I'm a changeling."

"What do you mean?" Constance had sat at the table.

"She said my parents are fairies, and Francesca is borrowing me. She said soon I'd have to go back to fairyland."

"Why would you have to go back to fairyland?" Constance had smoothed Hallie's pigtail.

"Because I don't have a father. Alice said all little girls have fathers. I can't be real."

"You have a father," Constance had insisted. "He's just not here."

"I've never met him." Hallie had gulped. "I never will meet him, because I don't know who he is."

"That doesn't mean you're a fairy. It means your mother and I get to love you twice as much as other children."

Hallie remembered burying her face in smooth cashmere. She remembered going to bed and praying that she wouldn't be sent back to fairyland; she wanted to live in Constance's mansion with her mother and grandmother. Now she didn't feel like she belonged anywhere. She wished Alice Ferris had been right and she was a fairy, so she could just disappear.

Hallie walked back inside and pulled on a pair of kneesocks. She slipped off the robe and put on a turtleneck and a pair of jeans. She added a wool sweater and a striped scarf.

Suddenly she felt like a lion, trapped in its cage. She wanted to go outside and run along the lake. But she was afraid that Angus was still lurking around the villa, like a phantom in the night.

"Hallie, I . . ." Portia opened the door cautiously.

"What are you doing here?" Hallie said icily. "I thought you left with Alfonso."

"He's waiting downstairs." Portia walked into the room. "I couldn't leave without seeing if you were all right."

"How dare you allow Angus in this house." Hallie tried to keep her voice steady. "I told you I didn't want to see him; even you betrayed me."

"He'd been standing outside for hours," Portia explained. "He brought Milo. I thought he should have the chance to explain."

"Where's Milo?" Hallie murmured.

"Angus left him in the kitchen with Lea," Portia replied.

Hallie wanted to run downstairs and hug the smooth brown puppy. She wanted to feel his leathery tongue against her cheek. "Tell Lea to send Milo back." Hallie swallowed. "I don't want anything from Angus."

"What did Angus say?" Portia asked tentatively.

"What does it matter what he said?" Hallie demanded. "He's lied about everything, I don't want to hear any more lies."

"He told me he loves you," Portia replied.

"I don't need a man like you do!" Hallie exclaimed, feeling the blood pump through her veins. "And I would never be with someone who lied and cheated."

Portia gazed at Hallie with sharp, black eyes. Suddenly she resembled Sophia. Her face was hard, her shoulders were narrow and erect.

"I forgot that Americans are so strong," Portia said slowly. "You don't need anyone. You certainly don't need a sister."

Portia ran out of the room and down the staircase before Hallie could stop her. Hallie raced after her, slipping in her socks.

She reached the entry as Alfonso and Portia drove away, the wheels of the Peugeot spinning on the gravel.

Hallie walked back inside and closed the door. She went into the kitchen and found Milo asleep next to the fireplace. She picked him up and held him close, his small heart beating against her chest.

Hallie spent the next two days running along the lake, chasing tennis balls with Milo, climbing the hills above the villa. While before she couldn't get out of bed, now she couldn't stop moving. She rested only to grab a ham sandwich in the kitchen while Milo ate a bowl of dog food.

Pliny begged her to drive with him to Lecco, to share a pizza and a bottle of red wine. But Hallie had to keep going, like a toy whirring in circles until its battery died. She tried calling Portia, but her cell phone was off. She felt terrible for what she had said, but she was still furious at Portia for promoting Angus's cause. If she kept running, hiking, and walking, she wouldn't have to think. At night she snuck Milo upstairs and crawled into bed, hoping Sophia wouldn't hear the puppy's yelps.

Hallie stood in the garden on Sunday afternoon, throwing Milo a tennis ball. He bounded across the lawn and dropped the ball proudly at her feet. Hallie scooped up the ball and saw a figure walk up from the boat dock. It was a woman in slim black pants and a red jacket. She had close-cropped dark hair and wore sneakers on her feet.

"Francesca?" Hallie dropped the tennis ball and waited while her mother crossed the lawn. She had a nylon bag slung over her shoulder and carried a large pink box.

"I almost didn't get this past security." Francesca handed the box to Hallie. "The security guard said the cake had a liquid filling. Then I let him try a piece and he slipped me through. It's a butter-rum cake."

"What are you doing here?" Hallie demanded. She was so surprised for a moment that she forgot how angry she was. She held the box, smelling the sweet, buttery scent.

"Pliny called me a couple of days ago and said you were ill," Francesca replied.

"Pliny called you?"

"I left him a few messages," Francesca explained. "I called everyone. I didn't hear from you for weeks. He said you came down with a terrible flu and hadn't left your room for a week."

"I'm better now," Hallie mumbled. "You wasted a trip."

"You don't look better." Francesca frowned. "Your skin looks like sandpaper. You should be in bed."

"There's nothing wrong with me, you can go home."

"I've been on a plane for fourteen hours," Francesca continued. "Is that any kind of welcome?"

"Does Pliny know you're here?" Hallie asked suspiciously.

"No. When I hung up with him, I decided I had to come see for myself."

"You haven't been in Lake Como for thirty years," Hallie said stiffly.

Francesca gazed at the lake, at the bare trees and autumn colors. "It's still gorgeous."

"I don't want to talk to anyone right now." Hallie started toward the villa. "I'd like to be alone."

"Pliny told me you found my diaries," Francesca called out.

Hallie turned around and stared at her mother. "He told you?" Her body tensed like an elastic band about to snap.

"I need to explain." Francesca put her hand on Hallie's arm. "Those diaries don't say anything. I was never good at writing. I always felt like Constance or one of the nuns was looking over my shoulder."

"The diaries tell everything." Hallie pulled away. "You deserted your husband, your son, your baby daughter. You didn't tell me for twenty-nine years that I had a father. You deprived me of my family, my history, my country."

"It's not that simple," Francesca pleaded. "Walk with me along the lake."

"I'm going inside." Hallie walked faster toward the villa.

"Please, Hallie." Francesca ran after her. "Give me an hour. If you're still angry, I'll go."

Hallie stood still. That frenetic energy that had consumed her evaporated. She couldn't face her mother and she couldn't turn away. She was too tired to make decisions. She wanted to drop down on the grass and bury her face in Milo's chest.

"Please, Hallie," Francesca begged.

Hallie looked at the woman who had raised her. She glanced at the large dark eyes, the fine lines on her forehead. She saw the hands that made her school lunches, that washed her filthy sports socks, that wrote out checks when she needed them.

"Okay." Hallie nodded. "An hour."

They walked through the gardens to the promenade. The olive trees formed a halo over their heads and Milo bounded along at their side. Hallie walked with her head down and her hands in her pockets. Francesca skipped beside her, breathing in the crisp arctic air.

"I forgot how wonderful the air is," Francesca mused. "So far from a city. It's so quiet, no cars or buses or cable cars ringing their bells."

"If you came to sightsee you should find another partner," Hallie said shortly.

"I started the diary because all the other girls at Madame Lille's kept one," Francesca began. "I kept writing at the villa, because I didn't have any friends. It helped to read and write in English, but I was never good at expressing myself. The only way I can show my feelings is with flour and frosting." Francesca paused, stealing a look at Hallie. "The minute I met Pliny, I fell madly in love with him. He was so handsome, so beautiful, I craved him. When I stood close to him, my body was on fire."

"I don't need to hear this," Hallie murmured.

"You do," Francesca insisted. "I wanted to be a good wife and mother, but living at the Villa Tesoro became intolerable."

"You could have insisted Pliny move to a villa nearby!" Hallie stopped in the middle of the promenade. "You didn't have to take me seven thousand miles away from my father and siblings."

"Pliny would never have moved out from his mother's house," Francesca replied. "I was so young and so alone. Sophia dictated my every move and Pliny did nothing to support me."

"You just picked up and left," Hallie insisted. "How could you desert Marcus and Portia?"

"That's what you don't understand, that's what I couldn't write," Francesca implored. "Those last few weeks, I made myself ill. The thought of leaving my children was intolerable. I loved Marcus and Portia so much, but I was not allowed to be with them."

Hallie stumbled, as if the urgency in Francesca's tone slowed her down. She glanced at her mother and saw her eyes were wide and her arms were wrapped around her chest.

"If Sophia had known I was pregnant with you, she would have kept me under lock and key. You don't know how hard it was to get on that train, on that plane. When I reached San Francisco, I stayed in bed for months. Constance thought I had morning sickness, but really my heart was breaking."

"You lied to her, too," Hallie said quietly. "Constance thought Phillip Elliot was my father."

"I couldn't tell anyone. I was terrified Sophia would appear and take you back to Lake Como."

"Why didn't you tell me when I was older?" Hallie asked,

her tone softening. She glanced at her mother and saw the pain that had been missing in the diary. Francesca's eyes were big as saucers and her body looked shrunken with misery.

"I was afraid you'd go to Italy, and then I'd lose everything." Francesca hung her head. "I know that was selfish, but you loved Constance, St. Ignatius, UCLA. Then you had your career and Peter. You weren't missing anything."

"I missed my father," Hallie retorted.

"We didn't communicate for a long time." Francesca hugged her chest. "When Marcus was four, Pliny started sending me photos of Marcus and Portia. I lived for those photos, I kept them in my bedside drawer."

"I still don't understand why you didn't try to bring Marcus and Portia to America," Hallie said, frowning.

"Constance hired a private detective, the best lawyers. I sent letters to Sophia, begging her to allow them to visit," Francesca replied. "They were returned unopened. Constance finally went to Lake Como. She made Sophia agree to let Marcus and Portia visit every summer."

"How did she accomplish that?"

"Constance never told me." Francesca shook her head. "But Marcus and Portia came once a year. I was happy."

"Why did you come to Lake Como now?" Hallie asked warily.

"I thought you were sick." Francesca gazed at the lake. "If anything happened to you, I'd be devastated."

Hallie remembered the nights during high school when she came home from a date, certain the boy would never call again. Francesca fed her chocolate cake and sat with her by the phone, willing it to ring. When it did, when the boy told her what a good time he had, and nervously asked her out again, Hallie and Francesca would do a little dance around the living room.

"I know I should have told you sooner," Francesca repeated. "I lied with the best intentions, I loved you so much."

Hallie stopped walking, tears filling her eyes. She bent down and petted Milo, trying to stifle her sobs. Her whole body shook, like a tidal wave reaching the shore. Francesca put her arms around her and Hallie cried against her mother's shoulder.

"Somebody else just said the same thing," Hallie said finally, pushing away.

"Is the somebody male?" Francesca asked. "Is he why you look like a walking wax figure?"

"Yes." Hallie nodded, unable to say more. She walked quickly into the village. She saw a couple sitting at an outdoor café, sipping hot chocolate and espresso. She saw tourists in gloves and boots buying souvenirs at the kiosk. She saw two children throwing stones into the fountain.

"Let's have some coffee and cake." Francesca touched Hallie's arm. "I've been longing for Italian coffee and I used to love their chocolate torte."

They entered a café and ordered cappuccinos and thick slices of cake. They sat by the window and Hallie slowly began to relax. She told Francesca how she and Angus met, in the hall of mirrors. She described the Villa Luce: the ornate frescos, the glittering chandeliers, the sweeping views of the lake. She told how excited she was to design the new wing, how she finally had her own project that would lead to other things.

She talked more slowly about their first kiss, Angus's strength when Hallie discovered the diaries. She described how calm Angus was, how he was such a good listener. She told how Peter had shown up unexpected and she gave him back his ring. She said she didn't think she really loved Peter, only Constance and her friends thought he was perfect.

Hallie told how her relationship with Angus changed into something romantic, something that made her feel warm and excited. She told Francesca how Angus said he was falling in love with her, and she thought she might be falling in love with him.

"He sounds like a lovely person," Francesca murmured, eating a forkful of cake.

"He is a lovely person." Hallie nodded. "Until I found out he isn't Angus at all. He's really Max Rodale, the reclusive owner of the villa. Portia found Angus's photo in Peter's biography of Paul Johns. Angus was standing with the crew team and the caption read Max Rodale. Angus made up everything. He wasn't an archaeologist; he didn't go to college in New Hampshire. I don't know where he grew up or who his family was. Angus sold an Internet company and made a fortune. Everything since then has been a lie."

Francesca frowned. "He must have a reason."

"That's what Portia said!" Hallie exclaimed. "But there's no reason to say you love someone and lie at the same time."

"There could be," Francesca said slowly. "You should give him a chance to explain."

"He came to the villa to explain but I wouldn't let him." Hallie slumped in her chair.

"I'm not saying you should take him back." Francesca sipped her coffee. "But you could hear what he has to say."

"What difference would it make?" Hallie demanded. "I never want to see him again."

"I didn't take you to church very often, but I do believe in God." Francesca looked out the window. "One of the greatest gifts human beings have is the power to forgive."

"You think I should forgive him?" Hallie's blue eyes were wide.

"I think you should listen to him, and then decide for yourself."

Hallie sat quietly, stabbing the cake with her fork. She remembered sitting in the middle of the lake, trying to catch the

Lavarello. She remembered how Angus let her talk about the diaries, about her anguish over Francesca. She remembered how his shoulders were strong and his lips were sweet.

"Go see him," Francesca suggested. "Then you can put it behind you."

"Okay." Hallie gulped. "I'll take Milo."

Francesca paid and they walked down to the ferry terminal. Hallie hugged her arms around her chest, trying to keep warm.

"What are you going to do?" Hallie asked when she purchased her ticket.

"I'm going to go tell Pliny I'm here," Francesca murmured.

"Give him the rest of the cake." Hallie grinned. "He loves vanilla frosting."

Hallie found Angus in the kitchen, making a risotto. He wore tan corduroys and a green T-shirt under a white apron. His hands moved quickly, dicing onions, slicing tomatoes, adding oregano and parsley.

"Hi," Hallie said quietly as Milo bounded across the room.

"Hi." Angus put the knife down and walked awkwardly toward her.

"Milo missed the villa," Hallie mumbled, keeping her eyes on the tile floor.

"I missed him." Angus bent down and let Milo lick his cheeks. "I was making a late lunch. Care to join me?"

Hallie shook her head. "I just filled up on cake with Francesca."

"Your mother is here?"

"She showed up this morning, like a spirit appearing out of the lake."

"What is she doing here?" Angus moved closer to Hallie, nervously running his hands through his hair.

"Pliny told her I was sick," Hallie replied. "He also told her I found her diaries."

"What did she say?" Angus asked.

"It's not important." Hallie shrugged. She was too exhausted to repeat her conversation with Francesca. She suddenly thought she was wrong to come. She couldn't ask Angus why he lied, because she didn't know if he'd answer with the truth.

"I should go," Hallie said. "I just wanted to bring Milo. You should keep him. I don't know my plans and Sophia doesn't want a dog at the villa."

"Hallie, wait." Angus blocked her path. "There's a reason you came."

"Francesca said I should give you a chance to explain," Hallie mumbled. "She said sometimes people lie with the best intentions."

"It doesn't make it right, but it's true." Angus took her hand. "Sit down and have a plate of risotto."

Hallie followed Angus to the breakfast room and sat at the round glass table. It was too cold to eat on the balcony, but she could see the rose garden, the view of Bellagio that used to fill her with joy. She let Angus serve a plate of risotto and a glass of mineral water and listened to his story.

"I grew up in Connecticut. My father was head of pediatrics at Greenwich Hospital and my mother was from old New York money. She spent most of her time at the Met and the Guggenheim and started her own modern-art collection. She found out she couldn't have children and would have been quite happy serving on her boards, but my father was desperate for children. He would have adopted the whole pediatric wing. He loved going to baseball games, watching football, playing soccer. When he wasn't working, he always had some kind of ball in his hand. We did everything together, but he died when I was eleven, dropped dead at the operating table." Angus paused, drinking the red wine he had poured for himself.

"I was devastated. My mother didn't know what to do with me. She sent me to boarding school in Massachusetts. Before I went, I found out I was adopted. I discovered the health forms she signed and underneath family diseases she wrote 'unknown.' I'll never forget." Angus gazed at Hallie. "That was the ugliest word in the English language.

"I spent most of my time in high school trying to discover my birth parents," Angus said. "It was a closed adoption and my mother refused to help me. Finally, I gave up. That was pre-Internet, and it was easy to reach dead ends. I concentrated on sports, I hung out with my roommate. He was a scholarship student from Boston with five brothers and sisters. I applied to Stanford, my father's alma mater, but I didn't want to do pre-med. I double-majored in history and computers." Angus gulped down more wine.

"I messed around with search engines and started a site where adoptees could look for their parents. You'd be surprised how walls come down online, and how slim are the degrees of separation. I helped hundreds and then thousands of teenagers and adults find their real parents." Angus's eyes sparkled. "I thought I was doing good, helping people achieve their dreams. I sold the site to Yahoo! six months after graduation. I bought a house in Los Altos Hills, a silver Porsche, a wardrobe of Hugo Boss and Armani. I invested in different things, considered joining a few start-ups. One evening about four months after the sale, a girl showed up at my door. She was about twenty, with bright red hair and pale cheeks dotted with freckles. She looked like a grown-up orphan Annie. I invited her in; lots of people came to my house. I used to have parties and invite all the Silicon Valley big shots. She sat down in my living room and took out a knife. She said she wasn't going to hurt me but she was going to tear up every leather sofa and suede chair." Angus flinched, as if she was in the room.

"I got her to give me the knife and tell me what happened. She said her boyfriend, Harry, just graduated from community college, was going to start USF in the fall. She said he became obsessed with finding his birth parents; he spent every minute on the computer. She told him to quit; it didn't matter where he came from. But he found Connect and stayed on it all night and day until he discovered his birth mother. She was a manicurist in Burlingame, fifteen minutes from their apartment. Harry went to see her. She was in her late thirties, she'd had him when she was fifteen." Angus paused, stabbing the risotto with his fork.

"She told him his birth father was in prison for life. He had raped and molested six teenage girls." Angus glanced at Hallie. "Including her."

Hallie gasped. "Oh."

"Harry went home and told his girlfriend that his father was a rapist. He was so upset, he stormed around their apartment breaking things. She screamed at him that it didn't matter, that it didn't make who he was any different. Harry got so angry he put his arms around her neck, not hard enough to hurt, but enough to frighten both of them. His girlfriend ran to a friend's place. When she came back she found Harry hanging from the ceiling fan with a rope around his neck."

"It wasn't your fault," Hallie insisted. "You didn't even own the company."

"I was sitting in a million-dollar mansion while her boyfriend was hanging from their ceiling," Angus replied. "If it wasn't my fault, whose was it?"

"He could have found his birth mother another way," Hallie tried again.

"But he didn't." Angus threw his fork on the plate. "He found it through my site. No one ever wants to take responsibility, especially on the Internet. It's a big free-for-all. I sold the house and the car; I never wanted to see a computer again. I went to India, but I didn't belong there. I was twenty-five, I couldn't spend my whole life questioning eternity." Angus got up and walked to the glass doors.

"I went to Rome. I'd always been fascinated by the Renaissance. I started collecting Renaissance art. I loved the human anguish Michelangelo and Raphael portrayed on the canvas. I took a day trip from Florence and discovered Lake Como by accident. I loved the beauty of the lake, the timelessness of the villages. I thought I could find peace here, so I bought the villa."

"Why did you make up Angus?" Hallie asked, puzzled.

"I was never Max Rodale to begin with. I didn't know who I was." Angus scowled. "I hated what Max did, I wanted to be someone different."

"You can't just change who you are," Hallie said slowly.

"You can." Angus jammed his hands in his pockets. "If you go somewhere no one knows you. I finally felt like the brick had been lifted from my chest. I could keep living."

"You weren't responsible for that boy's death," Hallie murmured.

"Angus isn't, but Max was," Angus implored her. "That's why I lied. It had nothing to do with money. I don't care about money. I'd be happy living in a tent."

"You have to forgive yourself," Hallie said, remembering her mother's words.

"Will you help me?" Angus walked toward her. He pulled her up and kissed her softly on the mouth. He buried his face in her hair, stroking her thighs. Hallie tasted the wine on his breath, felt her body respond.

"I can't." She pulled away.

"I love you," Angus said. "You can move into the villa, we can travel, collect art. You can redo every room."

"I couldn't be with someone who doesn't love himself," Hallie replied. "I'd never know what's true and what's a lie."

"But I had a reason to lie," Angus protested. "I was trying to erase the past."

"And you may have another reason to lie," Hallie said gently. "But that's not an excuse. I should go, Sophia may have thrown Francesca into the lake."

"Can I take you home?" Angus offered.

Hallie remembered the afternoons spent fishing on the lake, the glorious sunsets watched from his motorboat. She shook her head. "I'll take the ferry."

"You have to come back," Angus insisted. "You have to finish designing the villa."

"There are plenty of talented designers in Como." Hallie walked toward the door. "I don't think we should see each other again."

Hallie ran down the steps to the lake. She heard the door open and saw Milo bounding toward her. She heard Angus call her name, and kept walking.

chapter twenty-three

Hallie slipped a jacket over her cotton shirt and grabbed her purse. She was going to meet her mother for lunch and explore the boutiques in Bellagio. Francesca suddenly had a desire to wear something other than jeans and sneakers, and they had spent the last three days on a shopping spree.

Pliny had been courteous and polite but Sophia would not allow Francesca to stay at the villa. She got a room at the Hotel Metropole and slowly formed a truce with Hallie. They ate breakfast on Francesca's balcony, devouring Swiss muesli and mixed berries. They strolled through the shops where Francesca bought silk dresses, cashmere sweaters, leather bags and shoes. She insisted on buying scarves and gloves for Hallie, and a Moschino purse for Constance.

At first Hallie was hesitant to spend time with her mother, like a horse that refused to take its bit. But gradually she found she enjoyed her company. She liked ambling along the promenade pointing out their favorite villas. She enjoyed laughing at the Italian fashions, the ridiculously high heels and plunging necklines.

"Italian women display more cleavage in October than women in San Francisco show in June." Francesca frowned, trying on a scooped-neck silk blouse.

"It's gorgeous, buy it," Hallie encouraged her. She loved seeing her mother wear a knee-length skirt and two-inch heels, holding a square Prada handbag.

"Only because I'm stuck here till Portia returns." Francesca handed the blouse to the cashier to ring up. "Once I return to San Francisco, it will all get stuffed into my closet."

Portia was still in Venice and Francesca didn't want to leave without seeing her. Hallie still didn't know what she was going to do, but she was relieved that she had put Angus behind her. The more she replayed his story, the more she pitied him. His pain was as raw as if the boy's suicide happened yesterday. But Hallie didn't think she could love someone capable of spinning a web of lies.

Hallie's phone rang. The caller ID showed an unfamiliar number.

"Is this Hallie Elliot?" a female voice inquired.

"It is," Hallie replied.

"This is Jane Finch, personal assistant to Vanessa Getty in San Francisco," the voice continued. "Mrs. Getty would like to speak with you, if you have a minute."

"Hallie Elliot." Vanessa Getty's voice purred down the line. "I was poring through *Architectural Digest* and discovered photos of the Villa Luce in Lake Como. I have never seen anything like it. The furniture, the drapes, the artwork. You have such an eye, it is like an Italian castle."

"Thank you." Hallie frowned, wondering how photos of the Villa Luce had ended up in *Architectural Digest*.

"My assistant did a little research and discovered the designer was from San Francisco!" Vanessa said excitedly. "My mother-in-law is a dear friend of your grandmother. I decided you must design our villa in Napa. I want to fill it with antiques, Venetian glass, sculptures by Michelangelo."

"I hadn't thought about returning to San Francisco," Hallie stammered.

"You must say yes!" Vanessa implored. "I've been searching for a designer for months. When I opened the pages I knew you had the right vision. The rooms are so grand, yet intimate."

"It's very flattering." Hallie paused. "But I need time to think about it. I just finished the Villa Luce."

"Take your time," Vanessa replied. "Say hello to Constance for me. Hallie, I'm so excited to have found you. I can't wait to meet and hear your ideas."

Hallie hung up and stared at the phone. She imagined a glorious villa perched on a hill in Napa. She saw rows of vineyards, the sun setting over the trees, a soft fog blowing in from the ocean.

Hallie picked up the phone and dialed Constance's number.

"Hallie, dear." Constance's voice was faint. "I've been wanting to call you, but I came down with a nasty flu."

"Are you all right?" Hallie asked.

"I'm improving," Constance replied. "Francesca didn't tell me she was going to Italy. She just got on a plane and vanished."

"It's good to see her," Hallie said truthfully. "I think she's enjoying herself."

"I almost fainted when she told me she was in Lake Como," Constance continued. "But she was very worried about you. Pliny said you were ill."

"I'm good as new," Hallie said cheerfully. "Have you spoken to Ann Getty lately?"

"I haven't seen Ann since the Opera Ball," Constance mused. "She was wearing the loveliest Diane von Furstenberg original."

"I just got a call from Vanessa Getty," Hallie said in a rush. "She saw photos of the Villa Luce in *Architectural Digest*. She wants me to design her villa in Napa."

"That's wonderful news!" Constance replied. "Vanessa and Billy are lovely people. I heard their new villa is spectacular."

Hallie hesitated. "I wasn't planning on coming back to San Francisco."

"How is the Villa Luce coming along?" Constance asked.

"My work is done," Hallie said evasively. "I'm not sure what I'm going to do next."

"You said Portia is happy with Alfonso," Constance broke in. "There is no reason for you to stay in Lake Como."

"You think I should take the job?" Hallie wavered.

"Of course you should take it!" Constance replied. "Vanessa's friends will be begging you to design their houses. You'll have your pick of projects."

"It is a golden opportunity," Hallie murmured. "I guess I'll say yes."

"Darling, I'm thrilled." Constance beamed. "You can stay here if you like."

"I should get my own place," she said, smiling. "But maybe I can stay with you until I get settled."

"Let me know when you arrive," Constance said. "I'll send Louisa to pick you up at the airport."

Hallie hung up and hugged the phone to her chest. Her mind flashed on Angus, his reddish-brown hair and almond-shaped hazel eyes. She pictured his long legs and thick fisherman's sweaters. Angus must have submitted the photos to *Architectural Digest*.

Hallie started punching numbers, then put the phone down. She wanted to thank him, but it was better that they didn't talk to each other. She would send him a loaf of Boudin sourdough bread and a box of Ghirardelli chocolates from San Francisco.

Hallie arrived at the Hotel Metropole and saw Pliny getting into his Fiat. He wore black wool pants and a cashmere sweater and his sunglasses were perched on his forehead. He waved to an up-stairs window and maneuvered the car down the steep driveway.

"Why was Pliny here?" Hallie asked Francesca. Hallie stepped into the hotel room, admiring a bouquet of roses in a ceramic vase.

Francesca sat at an antique desk, dressed in cigarette pants and a white silk shirt. She wore leather loafers and had a colored scarf wrapped around her head.

"We had to discuss details of Portia's divorce." Francesca pointed to the stack of papers on the desk. "Portia will be back this afternoon."

"I hope she's not still angry at me," Hallie replied. "I said some terrible things."

"Sisters quarrel and then they make up." Francesca shrugged. "I'm anxious to meet Alfonso."

"I just got off the phone with Constance." Hallie frowned. "You didn't tell her you were coming to Como?"

Francesca hesitated. "She's been ill. I didn't want to alarm her."

"You still haven't told her Pliny is my father?"

Francesca stood up and poured a cup of coffee from the silver pot standing on the sideboard.

"Constance is quite frail." She handed Hallie a cup of coffee. "I don't think it would be good for her."

"I guess you're right," Hallie agreed. "I'm going back to San Francisco."

"You're what?" Francesca's eyes were wide.

"Vanessa Getty called." Hallie sat on a velvet chair. "She saw pictures of the Villa Luce in *Architectural Digest*. She thinks I have a wonderful eye; she begged me to design her villa in Napa."

"Vanessa Getty!" Francesca beamed. "That's wonderful, I'm so proud of you."

"I'll miss Lake Como." Hallie sipped her coffee. "But it's a great opportunity."

"I'm sure Constance is thrilled." Francesca nodded. "She's missed you dreadfully."

"We can fly home together," Hallie suggested.

"I'm actually going to stay." Francesca turned to the window so Hallie couldn't see her face.

"Stay?" Hallie repeated.

"I've got nothing to do in San Francisco till next wedding season," Francesca continued. "I can help Marcus and Angelica get ready for the baby."

"Where are you going to stay?" Hallie demanded, suddenly flustered. She had never imagined her mother would stay in Lake Como.

"Pliny asked me to stay at the villa." Francesca glanced nervously at Hallie. "We've been having dinner together."

"Pliny asked you to stay!" Hallie jumped up, her eyes blazing. "You haven't seen each other in thirty years."

"It's crazy, but I'm still in love with him," Francesca admitted. "It's like when we met in Gstaad, I can't think of anything else. I'm consumed by him. Only now, I'm too old to have children."

"I don't believe this," Hallie mumbled. For some reason, she was furious. She thought of all the years Francesca and Pliny had been apart. She remembered how Francesca had deprived her of her father.

"I didn't come here expecting anything to happen," Francesca explained. "But it did, and Pliny feels the same. We have both matured, we are finally right for each other."

Hallie glanced at Francesca's chic clothes, her new French

nails and pale pink lipstick. She saw the spidery lines around her eyes and the papery skin on her neck.

"I'm happy for you," Hallie said finally.

"I feel like a teenager with her first crush." Francesca sighed. "I can't believe Pliny still loves me. Will you be all right in San Francisco by yourself?"

"I'll be fine. Constance will keep me company."

"Let's buy some presents for Constance." Francesca stuffed her wallet into her Prada bag. "And we need to get you a leather jacket and boots."

Hallie followed Francesca into the hallway, admiring her mother's slim, elegant frame. She felt her anger dissolve and be replaced by a warmth in her chest.

"What did Sophia say about you moving into the villa?" Hallie said suddenly.

Francesca pressed the elevator button and smiled at Hallie. "Pliny didn't ask her."

Portia poked her head in the door as Hallie bought her plane ticket. Hallie closed her computer and jumped up to hug her sister.

"Your hair!" Hallie exclaimed.

"Do you like it?" Portia ran her hands through her new short hair. It framed her face in thick black waves and made her eyes look like saucers.

"I love it." Hallie stepped back. "You look like Halle Berry."

"We stopped in Milan on business, and I waited for hours for Alfonso in a café." Portia perched herself on Hallie's bed. "I kept staring at the salon across the street. It was one of those impossibly chic salons where everyone looks androgynous. Suddenly, I put my coffee cup down and marched across the road. I told the stylist to do whatever he wanted."

"It's perfect." Hallie admired the way Portia's hair hugged her neck, making her look vulnerable and sexy at the same time.

"Alfonso loves it." Portia looked at Hallie. "I'm sorry for bringing Angus here."

"I apologize for the terrible things I said. I didn't mean them."

"I deserved it." Portia shrugged. "I've seen Francesca; she told me what happened with Angus."

"I feel terrible for Angus." Hallie sat on the bed. "But I couldn't love someone who lies. I want to hear about Venice. Did you sit at Harry's Bar and drink dry martinis?"

"It was so romantic." Portia smiled. She wore slim black pants and a red cashmere sweater. "We fed the pigeons in the Piazza San Marco, we ate in the dining room of the Gritti. On the last night, Alfonso took me to dinner at Terrazza Danieli. He ordered caviar and lobster and then he got down on one knee and gave me this." Portia stuck out her finger and displayed a huge, glittering diamond.

"Oh!" Hallie gasped. "It's gorgeous."

"It's not very subtle." Portia laughed. "But Alfonso likes to make big gestures. After dinner we went back to our room and the whole carpet was covered in rose petals."

"I'm so happy for you." Hallie hugged her. "I'll have to come back for the wedding."

"Francesca told me you're going back to San Francisco," Portia said stiffly, sitting cross-legged on the bed.

"You'll be so busy with wedding plans and Alfonso, you won't miss me," Hallie replied, flinching at the thought of being without Portia.

"I'll be miserable without you," Portia insisted. "Is this what you want?"

"You mean am I running away from Angus?" Hallie shook her head. "It's an amazing opportunity. The Gettys are the closest thing San Francisco has to royalty."

"I thought you loved Lake Como," Portia retorted.

"I do, and I promise I'll be the best maid of honor. I'll come back a month before the wedding."

"There's actually not going to be a wedding," Portia said slowly. "As soon as my divorce is final, we're going to elope."

"A Tesoro can't elope." Hallie frowned. "Sophia will be furious."

"It would be worse if a Tesoro was a pregnant bride." Portia glanced at Hallie with large, liquid eyes.

"You're pregnant?"

"I was throwing up the whole time we were in Venice." Portia sighed. "The doctor confirmed it."

"I thought Alfonso didn't want children."

"It was an accident," Portia said. "But Alfonso is thrilled, he's already stocking up on cigars. He was looking online for baby carriers and researching which airlines permit newborns. We're going to have a very well-traveled baby."

"What about you?" Hallie faltered. "Are you nervous?"

"It's the craziest thing. From the minute I discovered I was pregnant, I've been obsessed with babies. I spent hours picking out blankets and booties; I want to hug mothers in the playground. I feel like I've joined a secret society." Portia's eyes sparkled. "When I go to bed all I think about is names: Allesandra, Gia, Petra."

Hallie grinned. "It could be a boy."

"Then it will be Pliny Alfonso," Portia said firmly. "I'm going to spend the next eighteen years proving that I am the best mother. I have never felt this kind of love, I could spend all day with my hands on my belly."

"The maternal instinct is a powerful thing." Hallie smiled.

"I may feel differently after sleepless nights, childhood tantrums." Portia hesitated. "But Alfonso will be there to help. He will be a wonderful father, I won't be doing it alone."

"I'm going to be an aunt." Hallie grinned.

"I'll be home changing diapers while you become a famous designer." Portia rubbed her stomach. "You'll meet an international businessman and design his homes in Singapore and Sydney."

"I'll leave romance to you and Francesca." Hallie laughed.

"Francesca told me about her and Pliny." Portia rolled her eyes.

"They're like Romeo and Juilet. They're going to give Sophia a heart attack."

"Sophia might start letting people lead their own lives," Portia said grimly.

"Pliny and Francesca will be so thrilled to have another grandchild. And Marcus's baby will have a cousin."

"I asked God to help me forgive Francesca." Portia's eyes clouded over and she hugged her chest. "If I ever feel like running away, can I call you?"

"Night or day." Hallie put her arms around Portia's thin shoulders. "But you'll do great. You're a natural mother."

"I hope it's a girl," Portia said darkly. "I've spent thirty years trying to figure men out."

chapter twenty-four

Hallie's suitcases were lined up next to her bed. She had left
Francesca's diaries and *Paul Johns Unplugged* on the bedside table. She needed room for the Gucci pumps, Armani dress,
and fur-lined suede boots her mother had dropped off in the
morning.

"No one wears fur-lined boots in San Francisco," Hallie protested when Francesca showed up, laden with boxes.

"I want you to look gorgeous," Francesca said, piling the bed
with cashmere sweaters and thick leather belts.

"You don't have to feel guilty that you're not coming back."
Hallie stroked a Pucci blouse. "I'm happy for you and Pliny."

"I thought Sophia was going to come after me with a kitchen
knife. We agreed to have separate bedrooms." Francesca grinned.
"With connecting doors."

"Maybe you and Portia can have a double wedding," Hallie
joked. Portia had sworn her to secrecy about the baby and the
elopement.

"Marriage is for young people." Francesca folded a Valentino
silk blouse. "Promise me you won't devote yourself completely to
your career. You don't want to miss out on having a family."

"I have a huge family." Hallie grinned. "I'll meet someone eventually. Maybe it'll be love at first sight; we'll have a whirlwind romance and get married in a week."

"I was very young when I met Pliny," Francesca said, smiling. "But look at everything I got; I wouldn't change a thing."

Francesca left to move her things out of the Hotel Metropole, and Hallie spent the day packing. Her flight left Milan at ten at night and arrived in San Francisco in the morning. Constance was still confined to her bed and was sending Louisa to meet her at the airport.

"I'd pick you up myself, but Dr. Michaels has spies everywhere." Constance sighed when Hallie called to confirm her flight.

"I could take a taxi," Hallie said, imagining her grandmother in dark glasses and a trench coat.

"I'm happy to get Louisa out of the house," Constance replied. "I can have a nip of brandy and a few macadamia nuts."

There was a knock on the door and Pliny entered, holding a small box wrapped in silver tissue paper.

"You don't have to drive me to the airport," Hallie said. "I'm happy to take the train."

"I don't want to miss a minute I can spend with you." Pliny handed her the box. "This is for you."

Hallie carefully undid the tissue paper. She opened the box and took out a gold locket. She snapped it open and saw a picture of Pliny with his arm around Hallie.

"I don't expect you to wear it all the time," Pliny said shyly.

"It's gorgeous." Hallie fastened the clasp around her neck. She put her arms around Pliny and kissed him on the cheek.

"*Ti amo,*" he said. "My beautiful daughter."

Hallie slipped on her new leather jacket. She followed Pliny downstairs, taking in the marble floors, the frescoed ceilings, the glittering chandeliers.

"I'm going to run down to the dock." Hallie turned to Pliny. "I want to take a last look at the lake."

Hallie stood on the boat dock, remembering the first time she saw Sophia in her black silk dress. She saw Portia, fragile as a bird, and the Villa Tesoro rising grandly above the lake.

Her mind flashed on fishing with Angus, being caught in the rain at the outdoor markets. She remembered their first kiss in the middle of the lake, Angus's strong arms encircling her.

Hallie felt something nuzzle her legs. She turned and found Milo burying his nose in her shoes.

"I'm sorry." Angus approached her. He wore brown corduroys and a thick green sweater. He was freshly shaven and his hair lay in waves across his forehead. "He's not well trained, he couldn't wait to see you."

"What are you doing here?" Hallie asked, turning back to the lake.

"Alfonso told me you were leaving for San Francisco." Angus stood beside her.

"Vanessa Getty saw photos of Villa Luce in *Architectural Digest*," Hallie said slowly. "You submitted them, didn't you?"

Angus nodded. "I wanted other people to see your work. You deserve the recognition."

"Remember when you thought I was paparazzi and threatened to toss me into the lake?" Hallie grinned, stroking Milo's fur.

"You made me realize it's wrong to hide from the world." Angus's eyes were bright. "When I fell in love with you, I wanted to shout it from the balcony."

"Angus, stop." Hallie moved away. "I appreciate what you did, but I'm leaving."

"Just listen." Angus touched her shoulder. "I understand that I'm not responsible for what happened to Harry, or if I am, I'm not going to make it better by hiding in Lenno. You made me want to be a better person, a real person with a name and a purpose."

"I'm happy for you." Hallie walked toward the villa. "I have to go, I'll miss my flight."

"I'm going to open a venture capital firm in San Francisco," Angus called. "I'm going to help other people realize their dreams. I'm going to use part of the profits to start a foundation for the partners of suicide victims."

Hallie turned around and looked at Angus. His eyes gleamed and his whole body trembled.

"I was wrong to lie to you, I'll never do it again. I love you, Hallie. We can take it slow, but I need you beside me."

"I don't think I . . ." Hallie started, but Angus pulled her close. He reached down and gathered her mouth under his. He kissed her deeply, running his hands through her hair.

"I've been like an overgrown puppy, hiding under the rug and licking my wounds," Angus pleaded. "I want to start fresh; I want to make the world a better place."

Hallie gazed at Angus and it was as if a lock in her heart clicked open. She knew, like Francesca and Pliny, like Portia and Alfonso, that they belonged together. She didn't care if they were married or living together; she wanted to spend her life with him.

Hallie hesitated. "I'm leaving for San Francisco tonight."

"So am I." Angus produced a bright red plane ticket from his pocket. "American Airlines Rome to San Francisco."

"What will you do with Milo?" Hallie murmured, tears rolling down her cheeks.

"Alfonso said they'd take care of Milo." Angus put his mouth on hers. "He said they need the practice."

Hallie and Angus approached the house together. Portia, Alfonso, Francesca, Marcus, and Angelica were lined up in the driveway like a scene from *Downton Abbey*. Sophia stood on the top step, wearing an emerald satin dress and gold slippers.

"You didn't all have to be here." Hallie laughed, her fingers entwined with Angus's. "Angus has decided to return to San Francisco. We're going to travel together."

"I'm going to miss you." Portia hugged Hallie tightly.

"You're going to be very busy." Hallie winked, squeezing her arm.

"I have something for you." Alfonso stood beside Portia. He wore wool pants and a cream silk shirt and carried a long flat box.

"I don't need any more silk scarves," Hallie said, accepting his gift.

"Give one to Constance and all your clients." Alfonso's black eyes sparkled. "Perhaps I will start exporting silk scarves to America."

Hallie approached Sophia and took a deep breath. "Thank you for your hospitality."

Sophia's pale blue eyes glistened. "Perhaps you will bring Constance when you return for Portia's wedding."

"I'll get you on the phone with Dr. Michaels," Hallie replied. "If anyone can convince him to let her travel, you can."

"We better go." Francesca consulted her watch. "You don't want to miss your plane."

"You're coming?" Hallie asked her mother.

"Someone has to make sure Pliny doesn't drive like a madman." Francesca smiled, jumping into the passenger seat of the small black car.

Hallie sat silently on the drive to Milan, drinking in the beauty of Lake Como. She watched the lake recede, saw the clusters of villages disappear. She gripped Angus's hand tightly, his knee pressed against hers.

They arrived at the Milan airport and Angus carried Hallie's suitcase onto the sidewalk. Pliny and Francesca climbed out of the car, and they were surrounded by families, hugging and kissing good-bye.

"Give my love to Constance." Francesca hugged Hallie tightly. "Tell her to obey Dr. Michaels's orders."

"Perhaps we will come to San Francisco at Christmas," Pliny suggested. "I have always wanted to try American traditions."

"Louisa will make stuffed Cornish hens and roasted potatoes." Hallie gave Pliny and Francesca a final hug. She blinked furiously, trying to hold back the tears.

Pliny kissed Hallie's cheek. He turned to Angus and held out his hand. "Take care of my little girl."

Angus gazed at Hallie's pale blond hair and sparkling blue eyes. He shook Pliny's hand firmly and nodded. "I will."

acknowledgments

Thank you to my terrific agent, Melissa Flashman, for being such a pleasure to work with. A huge thanks to the amazing team at St. Martin's Press. Hilary Teeman, my brilliant editor, and Sarah Jae-Jones, her wonderful assistant, took my story and made it so much richer. I am grateful to Audrey Campbell and Eileen Rothschild for making sure my books go to all the right places, and to Elsie Lyons for her breathtaking cover designs. Thank you to Jennifer Weis and Mollie Traver for welcoming me into the St. Martin's family.

A big thank-you to all the new friends who have supported me: Jane Porter, Kaira Rouda, Christine Schwab, and Beatriz Chantall Williams. I have found many of you on Facebook and you have made being an author so much fun. And as always, the biggest thanks to my family. My husband, Thomas; my children, Alex, Andrew, Heather, Madeleine, and Thomas—and Lisa—you bring me so much joy.

1. Hallie seems to want to marry Peter to please her grandmother and keep up with all her friends more than because she is deeply in love with him. Do you think Hallie should know better, or is it easy to get swept along into doing what is expected of you?

2. Portia doesn't tell Riccardo she doesn't want children because she is afraid he will leave her. Do you think she should take some responsibility for the failure of their marriage, or would admitting her fears make no difference in Riccardo's behavior?

3. Hallie and her mother are more like sisters, and Constance is the main maternal figure in Hallie's life. How do you think this has influenced Hallie's choices about her career and men?

4. Hallie finds Francesca's diaries and is horrified at what she reads, yet ultimately Hallie forgives her mother. Do you agree with Hallie, or do you think what Francesca did was unforgivable?

5. How do you see Angus? Do you think he is a good person who ended up in a tragic situation, or do you think his character is flawed?

6. Do you think Hallie was right to give Angus a second chance? Have you ever given someone a second chance and were you glad you did?

7. Hallie and Portia live in different countries but their bond is very strong. Describe your own relationships with your siblings. What keeps you connected?

8. Why does Portia have a much harder time forgiving Francesca than Hallie does? Do you think Portia will ever forgive her mother?

Discussion Questions

St. Martin's Griffin

9. Lake Como is described as one of the most beautiful locations in the world. Name a place that you long to visit—would you consider living there, or would you only like to go there on vacation?

10. *Lake Como* is about many different kinds of love—the love between sisters, between fathers and daughters, men and women, mothers and daughters. Name the important relationships in your life. How have they changed over time?

For more reading group suggestions,
visit www.readinggroupgold.com.

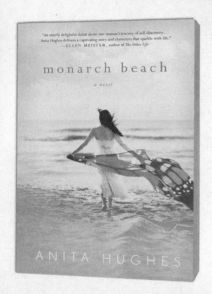

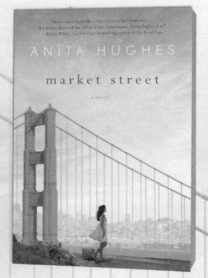

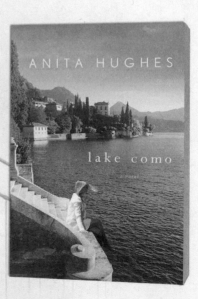

"If Candace Bushnell has a West Coast counterpart, Anita Hughes is it!"

—Karen White, *New York Times* bestselling author of *Sea Change*